A driving Cuban beat pounded through Joe's body and into her....

Cari gasped as his hand on the small of her back pressed her close to him. He lifted her against him as he spun around the room, her feet barely skimming the floor.

"Dizzy?" he murmured into her ear, his breath a hot caress against her neck.

"Yes. No. Not from dancing," she managed to get out. He laughed and his thigh rubbed against her intimately, igniting fireworks low in her belly.

Not fair.

Cari ran her fingernails across the back of his neck, and abruptly Joe's eyes blazed and sexual vibes poured off him, hot and thick and possessive. Now that was more like it! All but purring, she leaned into him until his silk shirt caressed her breasts through the flimsy fabric of her dress.

"Good thing I'm already planning to marry you," he growled.

Her Enemy Protector

CINDY DEES

INTIMATE MOMENTS™

Published by Silhouette Books

America's Publisher of Contemporary Romance

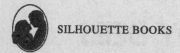 **SILHOUETTE BOOKS**

ISBN 0-373-27487-4

HER ENEMY PROTECTOR

Visit Silhouette Books at www.eHarlequin.com

Printed in U.S.A.

CINDY DEES

started flying airplanes while sitting on her dad's lap at the age of three and got a pilot's license before she got a driver's license. At age fifteen, she dropped out of high school and left the horse farm in Michigan where she grew up to attend the University of Michigan.

After earning a degree in Russian and East European Studies, she joined the U.S. Air Force and became the youngest female pilot in its history. She flew supersonic jets, VIP airlift and the C-5 Galaxy, the world's largest airplane. She also worked part-time gathering intelligence. During her military career, she traveled to forty countries on five continents, was detained by the KGB and East German secret police, got shot at, flew in the first Gulf War, met her husband and amassed a lifetime's worth of war stories.

Her hobbies include professional Middle Eastern dancing, Japanese gardening and medieval reenacting. She started writing on a one-dollar bet with her mother and was thrilled to win that bet with the publication of her first book in 2001. She loves to hear from readers and can be contacted at www.cindydees.com.

Chapter 1

The mansion's white stucco walls gleamed in the moonlight with false purity as one of two burly men operated an elaborate keypad and handprint recognition system. Carina stood silently between the two men, her eyes flashing silent contempt. Although they tried to pass themselves off as protectors, they were, in fact, her prison guards. Alfredo and Neville were their names, but she called daddy's pet gorillas Freddie and Neddie, to their everlasting disgust.

A knock on the door of her apartment in Gavarone's capital city, St. George, in the wee hours of the morning two weeks ago had turned out to be Neddie, telling her to get dressed and come. Now. Eduardo, her father, had ordered her home to his estate outside the city, and Daddy always got his way.

As Freddie and Neddie stood back now to let her enter, she glanced up and noticed that the mansion's adobe-tiled roof was the color of blood tonight. How appropriate was that? She shuddered and took a deep breath. She could do this. *Just go*

inside and play the obedient daughter for one more night.
Man, she hated this house and her forced presence in it. Her
escape plan *had* to work. She'd go stark raving mad if it
didn't. And Daddy would never guess that Tony, her openly
gay clubbing buddy, had the *cajones* to help her escape.

Her rendezvous with him tonight on the dance floor of a
nightclub in St. George had gone well. Freddie and Neddie
had lurked by the bar like trolls the whole time, never suspect-
ing that she and Tony had put the last touches on their scheme
while they gyrated under the strobe lights.

She'd passed off a wad of her jewelry to Tony. He'd pawn
it and buy her a plane ticket from this sleepy little corner of
South America to an even sleepier corner of New England.
Her older sister, Julia, was there already, hiding from their
father. Eduardo would never dream that she'd sentence herself
to such a quiet existence. Little did he know that she desperately craved the peace such a place could offer.

But in Eduardo's house, it was all about playing the game.
Giving him exactly what he expected to see. Truth be told,
she'd gotten sick of the party scene years ago. But right now,
her constant outings to nightclubs were the only bright spot
in her existence. *And how lame was that?* Thankfully, she'd
convinced daddy dearest that if she didn't make occasional
appearances in her regular Gavronese haunts rumors would
get started about her. Rumors that would draw media attention to *him* that he couldn't afford.

It was the one chink she'd found in her father's formidable armor over the years. An international criminal feared
on four continents didn't have too many exploitable weaknesses. But he didn't like to draw unnecessary attention from
the press. Of course, that meant she'd spent the last few years
doing everything in her power to draw media attention to
herself and, indirectly, to him.

And then, of course, there was the money. She did her
level best to relieve her father of as much of it as possible, to

put it back lavishly into the hands of the working people he'd stolen it from. Sometimes she just gave it away. Fistfuls to any random person in need whom she happened to run across. It was a huge bone of contention between them. But until Eduardo actually pulled the financial plug—and oh, the media stink she'd make if he ever did—she planned to spend it as fast and furiously as she could think up ways to do so. It wasn't much, but it was one small act to make amends to society for her father.

Carina paused in the dim cavern of the foyer and kicked off her strappy high heels. Dangling the skimpy shoes from her fingers, she climbed the long, curving staircase toward her room. The mansion's ornate walls pressed in on her heavily. One more night in this wretched house of horrors and then she'd be free. Forever.

"Good evening, Miss Cari."

She looked up at the gravelly voice. Gunter, her father's gray-haired German chief of security, had worked for her father for as long as she could remember. "Hi," she replied.

"Out late, I see," he commented with a hint of disapproval in his voice.

"Good band," she mumbled.

"I'm glad you're back safely, at any rate."

Sheesh. What did it say when the hired help paid more attention to her than her own father? She flashed a genuine smile at the older man. "Thanks."

Her father had been grouchy and distracted ever since the trouble with her older sister a month ago. Quiet, boring, responsible Julia had up and taken off for the United States with copies of all her father's financial records and a whole bunch of his money. *Who'd have guessed sweet Julia had it in her?*

Although Eduardo hadn't said so, he'd undoubtedly dragged her back home to the estate to put pressure on Julia. It wasn't a new trick in his retinue of control tactics over Julia—just an extremely annoying one. Cari was *really* sick and tired of being their pawn. She was an adult trying to have a life of her own. And what was so damned wrong with that?

This situation between Eduardo and Julia was getting worrisome. The maids were whispering that Julia had made off with millions and that her father was threatening to kill Julia when he found her. Surely, that was an exaggeration. *But just maybe, it wasn't.* Both of them had upped the stakes to the point where neither one could afford to back down. And Cari was trapped in the middle. She had to get out before their confrontation blew sky-high, with her caught square in the blast.

Four o'clock tomorrow morning was zero hour for her escape. Twenty-five hours and ten minutes to go. She could make it that long.

She walked down the long hallway toward her bedroom at the back of the house. The half moon high overhead sent cold, blue-white light through the gauze curtains into her bedroom. She didn't turn on the lights as she stepped over the threshold. Rather, she made her way to the French doors leading to the balcony and threw them open. She stepped outside into cool air that raised goose bumps on her arms. Leaning on the wide stone balustrade that surrounded the balcony, she listened to the rhythmic pounding of the surf visible below until the cold soaked her completely through.

Too jittery to sleep, she delayed going back inside despite the shivers coursing through her. Freezing felt better than the dull numbness that so often came over her from living under her father's iron fist.

The ocean was turbulent tonight, with white breakers rolling into the sand, pounding it in a relentless, mesmerizing rhythm. She watched its impersonal grandeur for a long time, feeling smaller and smaller in the face of its power.

She was lonely. Was it too much to wish for someone who would simply love her? No strings attached, no scheming, no danger? Just a little old-fashioned tender loving care? A tear escaped the corner of her eye and ran slowly down her cheek, cold against her skin. *It was the chilly breeze.* She would *not* descend to crying for herself.

Finally, reluctantly, she turned to go back inside. One more night in her gilded prison. One more night in her white lace bed. *One more night as Eduardo Ferrare's daughter.* God, she couldn't wait to disappear, to shed her skin and her past, and to begin a new life.

She padded across the expanse of white carpet to her bed. Lost in her thoughts, she pulled off her silk blouse, leaving on the white cotton tank top underneath. She shimmied out of her short leather skirt and let it fall to the floor as well. Abruptly exhausted, she pulled back the covers in the dark and crawled into bed.

That was odd. Her bed didn't feel right. The mattress moved heavily. She rolled over and plumped the pair of eiderdown pillows she favored and noticed, out of the corner of her eye, a strangely shaped shadow enveloping the bed. Big and dark, it encompassed most of the other side of her bed.

And then two more things struck her simultaneously: a sensation of wetness on her skin and a metallic smell.

What in the world...

She sat up and took a good look at the other side of her bed. And jumped violently. *There was someone lying there!*

The house's ventilation system kicked on just then, its fan billowing her curtains just enough to cast a thin shaft of moonlight across her bed. She caught a glimpse of a silver crucifix earring in her unexpected companion's left ear.

"Jeez Louise, Tony," she whispered. "You scared the daylights out of me! How in the world did you get up here without my father's men seeing you?" She reached over and nudged his shoulder. She whispered, "Hey, you. Wake up. Don't snooze through my great escape on me, will you?"

Nothing. A feeling of dread rose from her stomach.

"Tony. Wake up." She shook him harder.

He was out like a light.

She reached over and turned on the small lamp on the nightstand beside her bed. It cast a circle of yellow light on the room. She turned back to Tony.

Her scream split the night air like the fall of a guillotine.

There was blood *everywhere*. Her white lace bedspread was soaked in red. The sheets, the pillows and now even her clothing were bathed in it. Congealed blood defined a dark gash across Tony's neck. Frantically, she crouched over him, pressing her hand against the long wound.

"Tony!" she cried. "Oh, God, Tony!"

And then she noticed his eyes, glassy and blank, staring off into space. His mouth was open, pulled back into a rictus of terror. She glanced down at the bed and saw his hand clenched around the sheets. A single thought exploded in her brain.

Her father had slit a man's throat in his own daughter's bed.

The horror of it hit her first, sending bile up into her throat. And then the guilt struck. If she hadn't asked Tony to help her, he wouldn't be lying here, dead. She felt violently sick to her stomach.

On top of everything else, a wave of utter hopelessness slammed into her. She'd never escape her father. *Never.* And with that thought, despair closed in on her.

She knew her father was a criminal. A cruel, ruthless man. But never, ever, had he turned that violence directly on her. That had been the one constant in her life. Her father loved her in a distant sort of way, and for all his flaws, he'd always protected her from the world he lived in.

But tonight, he'd smashed that silent covenant to smithereens in a pool of blood.

And that was what broke her. Something cracked inside her heart. It was too much to bear. She couldn't go on any longer. She wasn't strong enough to keep fighting who and what her father was.

A great black pit of despair yawned before her and, numbly, she stepped into it. She scrambled awkwardly off the bed, backing away, nauseated, from her last hope for freedom. She noticed vaguely that she was leaving bloody footprints on the white carpet.

Clumsy with creeping terror, she pulled out the fire escape ladder stored in the trunk by the French doors and fumbled to hook it onto the balcony ledge. Desperately fleeing the horror behind her, she flung herself over the side of the stone railing.

Joe Rodriguez floated just below the surface of the shallow ocean, gently buffeted by the waves gathering to race ashore. His neoprene scuba suit protected him from the worst of the cold, but even at this equatorial latitude, a night dive in the Atlantic Ocean was vicious.

He peered through his night-vision goggles at his diving watch. He had about two hours of oxygen left. He put the periscope's eyepiece back to his face mask. Nothing much was happening at the Ferrare estate in front of him.

His target, Carina Ferrare, the younger daughter of international crime lord Eduardo Ferrare, had just come home. Since it was a Friday night and she'd left wearing a tight skirt and a blouse unbuttoned practically to her waist, Joe guessed she'd been out dancing again. She'd done a *lot* of that in the two weeks he'd been watching her. Apparently, it was the only activity her father let her out of the house to engage in.

It almost made a guy sympathize with her. Except he'd spent too many years scraping bodies off the ground or patching back together the victims of her family's violence to have much sympathy for Carina Ferrare. She lived a life of pampered, luxurious excess paid for in other people's blood and suffering. And surely, she knew it. Anyone with a shred of conscience would be too embarrassed to show her face in public. But the younger Ferrare flaunted her family's ill-gotten wealth. She wore outrageously expensive clothing and jewelry, and from what he'd seen, she tossed money around like candy. No matter the horror of its origin.

The only good news for his mission was that, despite her extravagant lifestyle, he got the distinct impression she was unhappy. The poor little rich girl couldn't buy love, could she? The corner of his mouth twitched in a momentary sneer.

But he had faith she'd jump at any opportunity to get away from her father. Frankly, she struck him as the type to leap at any new adventure—the wilder, the better.

Such a contrast to the older sister. Julia Ferrare was responsible and thoughtful, a gentle soul who had risked her life to do the right thing and stop her father. Julia was the banker who handled all of Eduardo Ferrare's finances, and she'd agreed to testify against her crime lord father just as soon as her younger sister was freed from his clutches.

So here Joe was, preparing to rescue Carina Ferrare, whether she liked it or not. He was the advance man, doing tedious, around-the-clock surveillance to nail down the younger Ferrare daughter's routines and habits. It was his job to figure out the best mode of snatching her, whether to approach her and enlist her cooperation or just throw a bag over her head and grab her. The four other reasonably healthy members of Charlie Squad, a highly classified Air Force Special Forces team, would join him in another week or so to help him run the actual rescue operation.

Charlie Squad had been chasing Eduardo Ferrare for nearly a decade, and they almost had him now. It had been a huge breakthrough when Julia Ferrare had agreed to go before a grand jury and reveal everything she knew about her father's crime empire. Given that she kept the books for the whole operation, she knew more than enough to put her old man behind bars for the rest of his life. But she'd been adamant. Charlie Squad *had* to pull out her sister before she'd say a word.

He wasn't all that worried about gaining Carina's freedom. What charm couldn't accomplish, coercion could. Surely any daughter of Eduardo's understood all about force and its myriad applications.

The hard part was going to be keeping her under wraps once the squad had her. A girl with looks like hers wouldn't be easy to hide until they got her out of Gavarone. Especially since the tiny country was firmly in Eduardo's back pocket, compliments of the millions of dollars in crime money he injected into Gavarone's economy while laundering his fortune.

Plus, Carina was a celebrity in her own right. She turned heads everywhere she went with her wavy brunette hair, light green eyes and exotic features. Not to mention she had legs that didn't quit.

She was a heartbreaker if he'd ever seen one. The kind of self-centered, high-maintenance princess who'd run roughshod over anyone dumb enough to actually love her.

Something brushed against his leg and Joe glanced down. A grouper fish. Smallish but definitely edible. Had he not been on a mission, he'd have speared the thing and had a tasty supper tomorrow. Thankfully, it wasn't one of the plentiful sharks that roamed these waters. He plastered his eye to the lens of the periscope, put the shivering cold out of his mind and resumed the thrilling task of underwater night surveillance.

He counted off the minute or so it would take Cari, as he'd overheard her clubbing friends call her, to reach her bedroom from the front door. Any second now, the lights in her room should go on. He watched the appropriate window. No light, but the French doors opened and she stepped out onto her balcony. Right on schedule. She went out there often to gaze out at the ocean. Damn, she was beautiful—and wistful—as she stared out toward the ocean.

Whether he wished her ill or not, he couldn't help but react to her sad expression. He was a healer, after all. A medic normally in the business of easing pain and suffering. Her melancholy called to him as irresistibly as a siren song. *Aw, hell.* He was a sucker for hard-luck cases, and it didn't hurt when they came in wrappings like hers.

Good thing the very name Ferrare made him clench his teeth in rage and disgust. It lent him a measure of immunity to her charms. Still, he allowed himself to savor the sight of her breathtaking features as she leaned on the balcony, staring out to sea.

After a while, she rubbed her arms and went back inside.

He was probably done for the night. He'd give it a few more minutes until she was safely asleep, then swim the half mile down the beach to the surveillance post he'd set up for this op.

Normally, all of his teammates on Charlie Squad would be at the base camp, providing backup. But they were tied up in Virginia right now. Julia had fingered an informant inside the squad's support team and the rest of the guys were still tracking him down.

If they didn't catch the informant soon, the squad would have to sneak away under other pretexts and make their way down to Gavarone without tipping off the informant—and Eduardo. Colonel Folly, the team's commander, would be coming as well to supplement their depleted ranks.

It had been a rough winter on the team, with several serious injuries among them, but the result had been worth it—their number one enemy was dead center in their sights. Eduardo Ferrare was going down. Soon. The only hitch was that all their hard work and sacrifices weren't going to be worth a hill of beans if Joe didn't figure out a way to get at Carina.

He stowed his periscope and surfaced for the swim back to a hot shower. Suddenly, surprisingly, a light snapped on in Cari's room. That was odd. She ought to be in bed by now.

A high-pitched scream drifted faintly across the water.

His senses jolted to full alert. *Something was wrong.* Cari was in trouble. He swam for shore and the mansion. He didn't have the slightest idea what he was going to do when he got there, but every nerve in his body shrieked for him to get to her. Now.

The tide was going out and he fought against the currents dragging him back out to sea. A hefty little riptide had set itself up. Dammit. He didn't have time to mess around with drifting down the beach and then coming ashore. He kicked harder.

And then he saw her. Out on her balcony. *What in the hell was she doing?* He lifted his head, treading water while he watched her toss a rope ladder over the edge of her balcony and shimmy down it awkwardly. She wore only a skimpy tank top and a pair of bikini panties that were dark-colored and plastered wetly to her skin.

She ran barefoot as fast as her long legs would take her toward the high fence that separated the beach from the grounds of the estate. She paused only long enough to punch in a number on a keypad by the gate and then she was tearing down the beach toward the water. She looked completely out of her mind with fear.

Joe's adrenaline roared and, abruptly, he wasn't the slightest bit cold. Stunned, he watched as she kept right on running, straight into the cold surf. *What was she doing?* She wasn't dressed for this kind of water!

She was headed straight at him. Had her older sister told Cari he'd be out here? Couldn't be. Julia Ferrare didn't know the details of the plan to rescue her sister. She was still recovering from her own injuries, suffered while escaping her father.

But here came Cari, splashing right at him. She was a strong swimmer, and her slender arms pulled her rapidly toward deep water. He knew the exact spot where the beach shelf gave way to a steep drop-off. She was almost there. And then the riptide would snag her and push her out to sea. No matter how good a swimmer she was, she'd be in serious trouble then.

He put his mouthpiece back in and submerged. He'd reach her faster that way than if he tried to fight the currents on the surface. With powerful kicks of his rubber fins, he propelled himself toward her.

The visibility stunk this close to shore. The waves stirred

up sand and sediment, and he could hardly see his hand in front of his face. Only the slightest hint of moonlight penetrated the water. Were it not for his night-vision goggles, he'd be as blind as a bat. He surfaced long enough to get another fix on Cari's position. Slightly to his left. He corrected course, ducked under water again and kicked like crazy.

She had to be getting damned cold. Hypothermia was going to do her in faster than exhaustion or the riptide. He surfaced again to look for her. Just ahead of him. Maybe thirty feet away. Her stroke was faltering. Damn! *She was in trouble.*

He put on a last burst of speed. He couldn't see a blessed thing under the water. She had to be right in front of him. He looked around for any sign of her.

And then he caught a glimpse of her pale body off to his right. Her arms were barely moving. As he watched, her limbs went still. She kicked spasmodically for a second or two and then stopped moving again. He watched in horror as she sank slowly beneath the surface of the water.

What in the hell was she doing? *Don't give up, Cari,* he begged as he surged upward beneath her. *Hang on, just a few more seconds!*

She spiraled downward toward him, a pale, lissome shape, her hair swirling gently around her head. She looked like a mermaid descending into the ocean's black depths.

Except Carina Ferrare was no mermaid. She was a flesh-and-blood woman who needed to *breathe*.

Joe kicked with all his strength and shot up beside her. He yanked the mouthpiece out of his own mouth and shoved it into hers. She started violently as it touched her. He remembered belatedly that she wasn't wearing night-vision goggles and couldn't see him in the water's blackness.

She shook her head and backed away from the mouthpiece. *What was she trying to do? Kill herself?*

He closed in on her, wrapping an arm around her slender

waist and shoving the mouthpiece back into her mouth. He kicked for the surface, dragging her up with him by force.

She fought, but she didn't stand a chance against a trained commando like him. He just wrapped her up so tightly she couldn't move. Their faces burst through to the cold air and he took a great sucking breath.

She spit out his mouthpiece, coughing. "Let me go!"

"Not a chance," he growled. "I'm not going to let you die out here."

"Dammit, does my father always have to win? Can't you just leave me alone? Let me go. *Please.* No one will miss me. Just this once?" she pleaded, her voice laced with hysteria.

She was trying to die? She'd have succeeded if he hadn't been there. What a piece of luck. Hell, this rescue mission was going to be a piece of cake. He'd just swim her down the beach to his staging area and Eduardo Ferrare would think his daughter had drowned. It was perfect.

"Carina, quit fighting and listen to me for a minute. I'm here to rescue you."

She continued to sob hysterically and breathe in great gasping breaths of true panic.

He spoke forcefully. "Your sister, Julia, sent me to get you. You're safe now. I won't let anyone hurt you."

The slippery, struggling woman gradually stilled in his arms. The surf rocked them gently as they floated together, their bodies plastered against each other.

Better.

"Y-you d-don't work for m-my f-father?"

Her teeth were chattering like castanets. Hypothermia was setting in. He had to get her out of this water, and soon. Not to mention that he thought he smelled blood on her. And if *he* could smell it, the sharks roaming these waters damn well could, too.

"No, I don't work for your father. I'm here to get you away from him."

"Did Tony send you?" Her voice broke on another sob.

He frowned. *Who the hell was Tony?* "No," he began. "Your sister, Julia, sent me," he repeated. Her mental processes were slowed, another sign of encroaching hypothermia.

Keeping one arm wrapped securely around her, he lifted his night-vision goggles to look at her directly. Her lips looked black in the moonlight. He swore under his breath. She was starting to shiver violently against him. Part cold, part shock, if he had to guess. Either way, he had to warm her up, pronto. He pulled her even tighter against him. Her body trembled violently against his. She'd never make it back to the op site in this state.

"Wh-what's y-your n-n-name?" she got out between her rattling teeth.

"Joe." Man, she was cold. She felt like an ice cube, even through his rubber suit. He treaded water with easy kicks of his legs, keeping them both afloat while he shared his body heat with her.

Abruptly, a half-dozen powerful spotlights exploded on the beach, flooding the sand with light and spilling their harsh glare over the surface of the ocean.

Cari lurched convulsively in his arms. "Oh, God," she cried in terror. "They're coming for me!"

Joe looked toward the shore. Sure enough, four men in full scuba gear were wading out into the water from the direction of the Ferrare estate. Wow, Eduardo's people had responded fast to her flight.

The men were carrying underwater spotlights and motorized diving-propulsion devices that would pull them through the water at twice the speed he could swim on his own. Hauling Cari, who had no fins and was too cold to move, Joe would never manage to outdistance the men. He cursed foully to himself. There went his perfect getaway. He should've known it wouldn't be that easy.

Joe thought fast for a public place he'd seen Cari frequent that would suit his purposes. He asked her urgently, "Can you get to a club called The Last Tango sometime in the next few days?"

She frowned like she knew the place. "M-maybe. Although I d-doubt my father will l-let me out of the h-house after…" Her voice broke.

What in the *hell* had happened that had sent her out into the ocean in a complete panic? He cut off his curiosity. No time for that, now. He'd damn well find out later, though.

He talked fast as the spotlights drew closer. "I'll be there every night between ten p.m. and two a.m. until you can come. I'll sit at the bar upstairs. Ask around for a guy called Joe. Got it?"

"Joe," she repeated.

"Your father's divers are getting close and it's about time for me to skedaddle. Don't forget. The Last Tango. Joe. I'll be waiting for you."

He gave her a quick smile, then shoved his mouthpiece in, yanked down his goggles and disappeared beneath the surface of the waves.

Chapter 2

The morning after Tony's murder, every trace of the bloody event was gone. There wasn't the slightest hint of a stain left in Carina's bedroom when she returned to it, let alone a corpse for her to go to the police with. But the memory of it overpowered her every time she set foot in her obscenely white bedroom.

It took her a long time to convince her father that she was cowed enough not to try any more stunts. It had been a real feat of acting to suppress her rage and grief over Tony's death, not to mention her terror at what his murder meant for her own safety. But desperation gave her strength.

And then there was the mysterious man who'd saved her life. Joe. Just thinking his name gave her a spark of hope. Enough to keep going. Enough to pretend to be a meek, obedient daughter for as long as it took to keep that date with him.

Finally, on a Saturday morning two weeks after the murder, her father agreed to let her out of the house under heavy guard for a night of dancing. Apparently, people were starting to ask questions. The maids smuggled the occasional Gavronese tabloid to her and rumors were circulating that her father was keeping her prisoner in his house. For once, she was truly grateful for her high-profile party-girl image. It might just save her life this time.

She couldn't wait to get out of the house for a few hours. And, good Lord willing, there'd be more than dancing waiting for her at The Last Tango.

She had no idea who this Joe guy was. Whether or not she could believe his story and trust him was another unknown. But it wasn't like she had any choice. Eduardo had *murdered* her only trustworthy friend in Gavarone.

She prayed a dozen times that day that Joe had waited for her. She didn't know if she could take another big disappointment right now.

He had to be here. He *had* to.

Curbing her impatience as the limousine pulled to a stop in front of the upscale tango club, she waited while Freddie and Neddie went inside to scope out the place. She knew the routine. They would check for exits and put a man on each one so she couldn't make an escape, and they would make sure the customers didn't include any known enemies of her father's.

By the time they finally came back to let her out of the car, she was a jangling bundle of nerves. "Gentlemen," she asked the pair as politely as she could muster around the tightness in her throat, "may I *please* have a little privacy tonight to enjoy myself in peace?"

The two men exchanged a glance. Freddie growled grudgingly, "You can go upstairs. There's a bar and a small dance floor up there and only the one staircase for access. We'll stay downstairs."

"Thank you, Alfredo," she murmured gratefully. *Please be here, please be here, please be here…*

A gaping Neddie lurched into motion as she practically ran past him. She stopped just inside the door. The place gave the impression of an old-fashioned ballroom, with abundant gilding, mirrors and crystal chandeliers. Thankfully, a high-tech lighting system, the modern bar and a stage for a band kept it from being an old-fogey joint. She looked around frantically and didn't see anyone remotely resembling that shadowed face from the ocean. Her heart leaped into her throat. He *had* to be here!

She'd been to this club a few times, but she certainly wouldn't call it one of her regular haunts. It was more mature—classier—than the places she usually chose. She gravitated toward clubs that were wild, easy and, truth be told, a little raunchy. They aggravated the living heck out of her father.

Freddie nodded toward the stairs and she flew up them like there were rockets on her feet. The bar was located at the far end of a wide mezzanine, on the far side of a long, narrow dance floor that ran the length of the balcony. True to the club's name, about once an hour a set of tangos played, and one was in progress now. She dodged promenading couples and made her way over to the gleaming mahogany bar. She bellied up to it and leaned forward to talk to the bartender under cover of the tango playing behind her.

"I'm here to meet a guy named Joe. Have you seen him, by any chance?" She prayed the bartender didn't ask her for more details because she hadn't registered much about Joe that crazy night.

She needn't have worried. The second she uttered his name, the bartender's eyebrows shot up to somewhere in the vicinity of his hairline. He stared at her with open curiosity. "Over there," he nodded with his chin and added, "I thought for sure you stood him up after all this time, but he kept saying you'd show."

Joe was here. He'd waited for her. Abject gratitude at this stranger's perseverance flooded her, and she blinked away tears of relief.

A new set of jitters attacked her as she turned in the direction the bartender had indicated. Over there. In a booth tucked into the darkest corner of the room. What would he look like, her mysterious savior? She'd been pretty freaked out that night, but she did recall that he was incredibly strong, and his eyes had looked black in the moonlight. His voice had been gravelly, but that might've been from the cold water and the dry oxygen in his scuba tank.

Julia had sent him, he'd said. How had he known she would come racing out into the ocean like she had? Was he some sort of mind reader?

She approached Joe from an oblique angle, taking a moment to study him before he did the same to her. The first thing she noticed was his thick, dark hair. Its silky, sable waves begged a girl to run her fingers through them. And he had a face worthy of Michelangelo. A plastic surgeon would kill to create a nose that straight or a jaw that firm. His age was hard to peg. Maybe in his mid-thirties. But his tanned skin was so smooth and taut that she could easily be wrong by five years in either direction.

He glanced over toward her just then, his eyes not showing the faintest recognition. Startled, she watched as his gaze slid past her cautiously, and only when he saw she was alone did his eyes return to her. He smiled. *Oh, Lord, he was so gorgeous it almost hurt to look at him.*

He slipped smoothly out of the booth and stood up, waiting for her. Tall. Six foot two, maybe. Lean. But muscular. Fit. Really fit. Wow. Just wow.

She walked toward him, hyper-aware of her body, of how she tingled everywhere his gaze touched her. His smoky gaze slid downward slowly and thoroughly, approval registering as he lifted his eyes once more. She was completely mesmerized by the way his dark eyes looked straight into her soul. He all but consumed her with that intense look. *Get a grip, girlfriend! He's only a guy.* The little voice at the back of her head whispered, *Yeah, but what a guy.*

He wore competence like a cloak enfolding him, but it did nothing to hide the sex appeal rolling off him in waves. She could seriously see herself devouring him whole, which was completely unlike her. Although she was a flirt and openly generous with her affections when she was out, she cultivated an image among the party crowd of being the unattainable prize and, as such, pretty much never threw herself at any man, or let any man actually get too close to her.

But this guy was to die for!

The thought jolted her. She wasn't about to die for him, and she darn well had no intention of letting him die for her.

One of his hands came up to grasp her elbow and guide her to a seat in the booth. He slid in across from her and smiled again. *Handsome* didn't even come close to describing him. *Hypnotic* was more like it.

"Miss Ferrare, my name's Joe Smith." His voice was like melted chocolate, rich and dark and warm.

Somehow, she managed to refrain from fanning herself with the nearest thing at hand. "Uh, nice to meet you. I'm Carina Ferrare. But you already know that, don't you? My friends call me Cari, but I bet you know that, too…" She cut off her babbling abruptly. Good grief, she sounded like some teenaged airhead.

"Like I said before," he continued easily, "your sister sent me to rescue you from your father."

Alarm shot through her. The very fact that he'd just uttered those words made him a target of her father's wrath. She couldn't help but glance nervously over her shoulder at the stairs. No sign of Freddie and Neddie. "How do you know my sister?" she asked cautiously.

"She's engaged to a friend of mine. And she's very worried about your safety."

"Julia's engaged? To whom? When did that happen? Why didn't she tell me?" It was so implausible to imagine her sister meeting some guy and falling for him in a few weeks' time that she almost laughed. If this guy was lying, he'd have to come up with something a whole lot more believable than that.

The man called Joe smiled again. "Julia's going to marry a guy named Jim. He's a friend of mine. A good man. As for when, I don't think they've set a date yet. Things happened pretty fast between them."

"How did she do it?"

Joe frowned. "How did she fall in love? Who knows? These things just happen."

Carina laughed. "No, no. How did Julia get away?"

Chagrin flashed across Joe's features, lowering his guard for a moment and drawing her to him even more potently than his physical beauty.

"Ah. As I understand it, she contacted some people in the U.S. government who helped her hide from your father."

She narrowly eyed the man across from her. He was built like a soldier, as disciplined in his reactions as a soldier, and he'd been floating around in the ocean, wearing the high-tech diving gear a soldier would have. She took a chance. "Don't you mean she contacted Charlie Squad? You're one of them, aren't you?"

Joe leaned back, staring at her evenly. "I have no idea what you're talking about," he said flatly.

Yeah, right. The denial clinched it. This guy was definitely a soldier from the Special Forces team, which was her father's nemesis. She couldn't count the number of times she'd listened to Eduardo rant and rave about Charlie Squad and what a pain in the ass they were. Hope flared in her chest. If Joe was part of Charlie Squad, she might just stand a chance of getting away, after all.

He interrupted her thoughts. "The important thing is that your sister's safe and happy. She's worried about you, though. She thinks it's imperative that you get away from your father immediately."

Relief and joy reverberated in Carina's breast, along with a hint of envy. Julia had gotten away. Out from under their father's oppressive control. No more acting as his banker, no more house arrest, no more gorillas following her everywhere she went.

No worries about friends turning up dead in her bed.

Cari replied wryly, "I think it's imperative that I get away from my father, too."

"What's the rush?" Joe asked lightly.

A shudder of lingering horror whisked down Cari's spine. She still couldn't sleep with the lights turned off. For the first week after Tony's death, she couldn't even walk into her room. And now she had to have a light on to even step inside what had become a ghost chamber to her. Her father refused to let her move out of the room and had called her a coward for being frightened of her own bedroom, so she'd been sleeping awkwardly on the loveseat in the corner.

A pair of warm hands gripped her icy fingers. "Hey. Are you okay? You look a little pale."

She took a tremulous breath. "Sorry. It was rude of me to get distracted like that."

A melting smile. "Not at all. I'm just glad you're here. I was beginning to worry you wouldn't come."

She sighed. "It took me this long to get out of the house. As it is, a whole carload of my dad's thugs are with me. Freddie and Neddie, my usual bodyguards, are downstairs, and three more are outside in the limo."

Joe frowned slightly. "Then I guess we won't be making our escape from here tonight."

Cari blinked. "You're serious? You were really expecting to take me away tonight?"

He shrugged. "It would've been nice if it were that easy. A guy can always hope, can't he?"

She was silent while a waitress approached and set a glass of mineral water in front of her. She fiddled with the wedge of lemon perched on the lip of the glass, bemused by Joe's choice of drinks for her. Most men plied her with booze to help along the cause of getting into the rack with a famous party girl.

The waitress retreated and Cari said, "My father's a really powerful man. Dangerous." She added for emphasis, "Deadly dangerous."

"I know."

Joe's quietly uttered words made her look up at him sharply. His gaze was sympathetic, but it was something else, too. Intelligent. Razor-sharp. This guy knew exactly who and what her father was.

"I have to warn you, Joe. Anyone who crosses my father ends up dead. As in six feet under."

Another calm nod.

"And you still want to try to rescue me?" she asked incredulously. This guy was *definitely* in Charlie Squad! Either that or he was nuts.

"Yup. Except I'm not just going to try. I'm going to succeed."

"How?" she asked in escalating disbelief. Even if he was in Charlie Squad, her father's security measures were legendary. She was guarded around the clock, and if Joe tangled with her father's men, he and possibly a whole lot of innocent bystanders would end up dead.

"I have a plan," he said mildly. "Would you like something stronger to drink?" He looked across the room, trying to get the attention of a waitress.

Nobody plotted against her father this casually. "Which is it?"

He looked back at her in surprise. "I beg your pardon?"

"Which is it? Are you insane or brain dead to cross my father on his home turf?"

Joe draped an arm across the back of the booth. The tanned limb was wreathed in muscles that made her gulp. He asked lightly, "Have you considered the possibility that I'm actually capable of taking on a man like your father and winning?"

She snorted. "Nobody's *that* good." Even if he was in Charlie Squad.

"I am."

Again, he spoke with a quiet certainty in his voice that stopped her cold. *Was* he that good? Could it be? Had her despairing pleas to a heretofore deaf God finally been answered? In a daze, she ordered an iced tea while he asked for another glass of water.

After the waitress left, she asked him bluntly, "Who are you?"

He completely ignored the question, saying instead, "So, Cari. Tell me about a typical day for you at your father's house."

Over the next half hour, she answered his every question, and there were dozens of them. Even though they were pleasantly delivered, they amounted to nothing less than an all-out interrogation.

Finally, he pushed back his empty glass and stared at the bad Van Gogh reproduction on the wall above their booth. Joe sat that way for a long time, and she didn't break his intense concentration. What would it be like to have all that attention focused on her? A tingling started low in her belly that made her squirm against the vinyl seat.

His gaze shifted to her, pinning her in place. "Well, Cari, I don't see any feasible way for you to get out of your father's house and come to *me* without tipping off Eduardo's goons…and hence blocking all our escape routes. I've been watching you for weeks and your father's security is downright impregnable. Worse, we're in Gavarone, on his turf, like you said. His informants are everywhere."

Disappointment slammed into her, flattening her fleeting hopes. For a minute there, she'd thought she might actually have a chance. Why, oh why, had Joe stopped her from drowning if he couldn't come through for her now?

"So," he continued casually, "I guess we're just going to have to go with my original plan. I'm going to come inside the walls and get you with your father's blessing, more or less."

"What?" She stared at him in shock. "You're going to do what?" she repeated blankly.

"I'm going to go into your father's house and get you out myself," he said with quiet finality.

"You're going to break into my father's house? Didn't you hear what I said? The place is an armed fortress."

"I'm not going to *break* in. I'm going to infiltrate the place. I'll come in with a cover story and get inside that way."

She frowned. "My father doesn't hire just anybody. Nobody gets close to him personally unless they've worked for his organization for years and proven their loyalty a hundred times over."

Joe nodded. "True, but he doesn't completely control who gets close to you."

She frowned. "I don't understand."

A slow smile curved his mouth and the thought of kissing it all but made her swoon. "How do you feel about getting married?" he asked.

"Married?" she echoed, clearly one step behind in this conversation. "To whom?"

"Me."

The room swirled around her and she grabbed the edge of the table as dizziness practically knocked her over. "We hardly know each other," she choked out.

"I've been giving this a lot of thought and I think it could work. You have a reputation for being—" he paused delicately "—adventurous."

Now there was an understatement.

Joe was talking again. "I'm betting your father isn't too crazy about your rep. Am I right?"

She snorted. "He hates the way I act. Have you seen the way my bodyguards are plastered to me these days, chasing off any guy who gets near me? Trust me. Daddy dearest despises my…lifestyle choices. And he's doing everything he can to change them."

Joe nodded. "Perfect. I'm proposing that I sweep you off your feet and single-handedly mend your wild ways."

Whoa. Now there was a thought. Tempting, actually.

"It'll all be an act," he added.

Her stomach plummeted to her feet. Damn.

He continued, "You and I will elope. After we've had a whirlwind romance, of course."

Of course.

Joe continued. "I'm betting your father will let me into his house in profound gratitude that someone else will finally be responsible for curbing your wild impulses. In effect, he'll transfer responsibility for keeping you on the straight and narrow from his pet gorillas to me."

She blinked, startled at the depth of insight into her father that his idea showed. It might just work. But a *husband?*

As much as she'd love to play along with that particular little fantasy, she replied reluctantly, "He'd never buy it. He'd see right through a story like that, not to mention he'd check it out thoroughly. And then he'd slit your throat…." She gagged as bile leaped into her throat at the idea of another man, this man, lying dead in her bed, bleeding from a horrible gash in his neck.

Joe's dark eyebrows slammed together abruptly. "My God," he breathed. "Is that what happened?"

She frowned at him, unsure what he was asking.

He leaned forward and reached for her hands, gripping her fingers tightly. "Is that why you ran out into the ocean? Whose throat did your father slit?"

Wow, this guy was sharp. He'd made that leap of logic look easy. "My friend Tony. He was going to help me escape."

She clutched Joe's big, surprisingly callused palms desperately. "And that's why I can't agree to your plan. I don't want you to end up dead in my bed, either."

Joe's eyes went black. Hard and flat. Gone was the warm, sympathetic man she'd been talking with. "Your father killed this guy in your bed?" he bit out.

She nodded, suddenly afraid of the cold man seated across from her, radiating violence.

He cursed viciously under his breath, so low she barely caught the muttered oath. And then he leaned forward, staring at her intensely. "This changes everything. If your father has turned violence on you, you're in more danger than you can imagine. You are going to agree to marry me. As soon as it can be arranged. And I *am* going to get you out of there. Got it?"

She blinked at the icy authority in his tone. He wore it easily. Like a man who'd given orders before and expected them to be followed. Where had the quiet, kind man disappeared to all of a sudden? Who *was* Joe Smith? And *what* was he?

She answered her own questions. Did it really matter who or what Joe was as long as he could do what he'd promised? Aloud, she said, "I need to talk to Julia. To confirm who you are."

Joe blinked, but to his credit, he answered evenly, "All right."

He reached into his shirt pocket and pulled out a new-model cell phone and dialed a phone number. He spoke into the mouthpiece. "Hey, Dutch, it's Joe."

What kind of name was Dutch? Some kind of military nickname, maybe?

"Yeah, I'm sitting with her right now. She wants to talk to her sister."

He waited in silence and she watched him cautiously. Not real conversational, these Charlie Squad guys. And then he held the phone out to her.

Eagerly, she put it to her ear. "Julia?"

She all but cried in relief at the sound of her sister's voice in her ear, sobbing, "Cari? Is that you? Are you all right?"

"So far. Are *you* all right?"

Julia laughed and then made a little sound of pain as if laughing hurt. "Oh, yes. I'm fine. More than fine. But you need to leave Gavarone, honey. Get away from Eduardo."

"I was thinking the same thing," Cari retorted quickly. Then she asked seriously, "Did you send Joe to help me?"

"I sure did. He's a hunk, isn't he? I thought he might be your type."

Cari grinned. "You got that right, Sis."

"He'll take care of you. Trust me. Trust him."

Cari looked up as Joe leaned forward and murmured, "That's long enough. I don't want the call traced."

She said into the phone, "Apparently, we can't talk anymore or this call might get traced. I love you, J.J. And thanks."

A laugh. "You're welcome. And I love you, too. Take care, and get out of there—" The line went dead.

Cari handed the cell phone back to Joe, who tucked it back into his shirt pocket.

"Satisfied?" he asked.

How could she not be? Her sister had sent this gorgeous stranger to save her life. If Julia trusted him, why in the world shouldn't she?

"So," Joe asked lightly, "are you going to marry me?"

Joe waited tensely for Cari's response to his question, *his marriage proposal*. His gut tied itself in a thousand knots at the very thought.

The other guys on the squad hadn't liked the idea, either. It was fraught with risks. But he'd been doing 'round-the-clock surveillance on Ferrare and his daughter for over a month now and not once—not *once*—had he found a weak spot in the bastard's security measures. If Cari refused to go for the fake marriage thing, he and the rest of Charlie Squad had no idea what to try next. And after that little bombshell she'd just dropped about her father killing Tony—whoever the hell he was—the squad had no choice but to move fast.

The squad had pondered and tossed out dozens of plans. And it always came back to this one: the only way to get Cari out without putting her life in serious jeopardy was for someone to infiltrate the Ferrare fortress and sneak her out by cunning. And even then, it was going to be one hell of a trick to pull off. The only positive was that Eduardo's security was set up to keep bad guys out, not good guys in. It ought to be possible to move Cari out from under her father's nose if Joe was careful and fast when the time came.

A few days ago, Colonel Folly had run this marriage idea past Charlie Squad's psychiatrist, and she'd assured him that Ferrare would be desperate to hand over control of his uncontrollable daughter to someone else. She was certain Ferrare would leap at the idea of a son-in-law to rein in Carina.

Still, Colonel Folly had resisted the eloping scheme—that is, until the psychiatrist had dropped the other shoe. She predicted that Eduardo Ferrare would *kill his daughter* rather than let anyone *take* her away from him. The only possible exception might be if Eduardo *gave* his daughter away to someone of his own free will—as in approving a marriage. Reluctantly, the colonel had green-lighted the op. Now, Joe just had to get Carina to go for it.

"Okay," she breathed.

"Okay what?" he asked cautiously. He needed to hear her say the words.

"I'll marry you, Joe. But there's one thing…"

Jeez, his pulse had just shot up like a rocket. "What's that?" he asked, much more calmly than he felt.

"It has to be a real wedding. My father will demand proof, and he'll verify it himself. We won't be able to pull off faking it. We'll have to actually exchange vows and get a marriage license—the whole nine yards."

An instant panic speared into him, followed by an involuntary surge of exultation at possessing this beauty for himself. And then his brain kicked back into gear. *Get a grip, old man. This is just a mission.* They'd get an annulment as soon as she was clear of her father. And she *was* a Ferrare.

Although, now that he'd met her face-to-face, she wasn't what he'd expected. She seemed more…human. More real. He'd expected a phony, shallow girl. But the young woman before him was intelligent. Self-possessed. Genuinely worried about her sister. And her eyes looked much older than he knew her years to be.

He gathered his thoughts and replied belatedly, "No problem. We'll do a real wedding." Now, why did his throat go tight when he said that? "Anything else?" he choked out.

She frowned, chewing softly on her full, pink lower lip. An urge to kiss that luscious mouth nearly sent Joe around to her side of the booth. God, she was beautiful. And young. Way too damned young for him. Thirteen years too young, to be precise. He was thirty-seven and she was twenty-four.

Her sultry purr interrupted his train of thought. "We need to be seen together around town, so we can claim to have met and fallen in love. You can bet my father's going to want independent confirmation that you're for real."

For real. Now there was a thought. No way was he about to reveal his true identity. Not to Eduardo, who'd kill him for it, and certainly not to Cari. He had no way of knowing if she could keep quiet or not, and he dared not stake his life on it. Her guess that he was part of Charlie Squad was impressive, but he damn well wasn't about to confirm it. To his knowledge, Julia hadn't identified him as a squad member to Cari. Listening to her end of the call, it hadn't come up in the brief conversation. But he would need to confirm that with Dutch. He made a mental note to do it tomorrow.

Joe frowned. "A whirlwind romance could be a little difficult to stage since your father never lets you off your leash."

She shrugged. "Then we'll have to figure out something else. I'm not going to do this unless I'm sure you won't be in danger."

Joe snorted mentally. Not in any danger? Infiltrating the inner sanctum of the most dangerous criminal Charlie Squad had ever run up against? *Dangerous* wasn't quite the word for it.

Now that he was physically sitting in front of the target, the reality of what he'd proposed hit him full force. This could easily turn out to be the most horrendous assignment of his career. Not only could the father kill him, but the maverick daughter was a complete wild card in the equation.

He'd already made one huge tactical mistake with her: he'd told her his real name. At least she didn't know his real last name, but it was bad enough that she knew him as Joe. When they'd been out in the ocean and she was so panicked, so *lost,* and had asked who he was, his real name had just popped out. He'd felt a driving compulsion to connect with her, one human being to another, with no subterfuge between them.

But now that he'd met her again, his misgivings deepened. She was too damned sexy for her own good. The pull of attraction he felt toward her was unmistakable and alarming. He'd already looked deep into her eyes and done something stupid once. Could he trust himself to keep a level head around her? Could he really masquerade as her husband—her *husband*—and not end up in serious trouble?

Did he have any choice? If Charlie Squad wanted to nail Eduardo Ferrare, they needed Julia's testimony, and the only way to get it was for someone to rescue this girl.

Maybe the colonel's idea that they lure Cari and Eduardo's goons to an isolated location and just shoot it out with the bastards was a better idea. Except Cari could end up getting caught in the crossfire, and she was a one-hundred-percent nonexpendable asset. She had to be kept alive at all costs. He shuddered at the idea of bullets ripping through her satin skin, ruining her luscious flesh....

Jeez, he was already in trouble. He'd been with her for less than an hour and his imagination was running away with him. And there wasn't a damn thing he could do about it. A fake marriage was the only thing he could think of to place himself close enough to ensure her safety and get her out alive.

He asked briskly, "Do you have access to e-mail? A cell phone?"

"Limited—and definitely spied upon. E-mail, yes. Cell phone, no. My father took my phone away after..."

He nodded in understanding, his jaw tight. The e-mail was a little help, at any rate. They could strike up an Internet acquaintance. "If I can come up with ways to bump into you and be seen with you in public, maybe go dancing with you a few times, then you'll go through with it?"

She nodded, her gaze wary. She didn't like the risk involved with his plan. Not that he could blame her. Neither did he, although probably for completely different reasons. In the final analysis, he was possibly more afraid of her than of her father.

He returned her nod and said lightly, "Then it's a deal."

He had no damned idea how he was going to pull off courting Cari Ferrare. She was a prisoner in her father's home. But he'd make it happen. He had to. The bastard had slit her boyfriend's throat in her own bed, for God's sake. He shoved back the rage that bubbled up in his gut at the thought. He knew better than to let his natural empathy get the best of him. He might be medic and healer for Charlie Squad. But on this op, he was the prime operator. And he had a stinking suspicion he was in for some bloodshed before it was all said and done.

Joe pulled the paper napkin out from under his water glass, scribbled on it and shoved the paper across the table. "This is my cell phone number and e-mail address. You and I met tonight. You were accidentally seated at the table I'd reserved and we ended up sharing it. Make sure you mention me casually to your father over breakfast, or whenever it is you have cozy family conversations with him."

Cari's lovely mouth twitched at that one. "Cozy, huh?" A giggle escaped her and, for just a second, she looked like the dazzlingly beautiful, carefree young woman she ought to be. Of course, with the sights she'd probably seen in her father's home and the hard living she'd already done, it was no wonder she acted older than her years.

An errant urge to protect her from any more hurt washed over him. *Well, buddy, that's exactly what you get to do,* he told himself. There was just the small matter of keeping his own throat from being slit in the process.

"Call me tomorrow if you can get access to a phone," he instructed her. "Thank me for tonight. There's no need to be secretive about it."

She laughed lightly. "I'm glad you said that because every phone in the house is monitored."

"Perfect. I'll ask if we can go dancing again some time and I'll set up a date. Okay?"

"I don't know if my father will let me keep the date, but I'll try."

"Just try to keep the tone of the call casual. Nothing that might arouse his suspicion. If your father objects, tell him you should go out with somebody now and then, for appearances' sake. People will start talking if you never show your face in public anymore. It'll draw too much attention to him."

Cari looked startled at the tactic he suggested, so similar to her own. Her gaze lit with admiration, and she looked like she was wondering whether he was psychic or just really smart.

She took a deep breath and nodded gamely. "Okay."

He had to admit it. She was a brave lady. They slid out of the booth and stood up simultaneously, abruptly coming chest to chest. She stared up at him like he was some sort of conquering god and, damn if he didn't feel like one for a second.

He cleared his throat awkwardly. "Everything's going to be fine. I promise."

He could swear her eyes filled with tears as she turned away, but she spun around so quickly he couldn't be sure. He watched her slender back retreat with quiet dignity down the sweeping staircase and out of sight.

He gave her enough of a head start to collect her goons and leave before he made his way out to the delivery van parked behind the club. With a careful look around to make sure nobody had followed him, he slipped into the passenger seat.

After the white van pulled out into traffic, he pushed aside a curtain and crawled into the high-tech surveillance setup in the back. As he pulled the microphone and battery pack out from under his shirt, he asked his boss, "Did you get all that?"

Colonel Tom Folly scowled. "Yeah. I got it. And I still think you're nuts."

Chapter 3

The dance floor was hot and crowded, but Cari barely noticed the sweaty bodies bumping into her or the choking haze of smoke filling the air.

He was here.

She hadn't seen him yet, but she could feel Joe's presence the moment he stepped into the club. Over the course of their previous meetings—a handful of dates to go dancing under the watchful eyes of Freddie and Neddie—she'd grown extraordinarily attuned to his nearness.

Her father would, no doubt, get a full report from Freddie and Neddie that the American had shown up again and the two of them had danced the night away together. At first, her father had been highly suspicious of Joe and grilled her mercilessly about the new man in her life. But as she limited her attentions exclusively to Joe and all the reports from the guards said he steadfastly treated her with gentlemanly restraint, Eduardo seemed to relax.

The night Joe had sent her home to put on a more modest dress had gone a long way toward softening Eduardo's attitude about the American—just like Joe'd said it would.

If anything, she thought she'd caught a glimpse of relief in her father's expression when she'd told him over dinner tonight that she was going out dancing with Joe again.

Who'd have thought that, in just a few weeks, her would-be rescuer would worm his way into her father's good graces without ever meeting the man? She had to admit it. Joe was good. He'd pegged her father cold. But cold enough to buy the idea of a quickie marriage between them? That part still worried her. A lot.

She and Joe had struck up a lively Internet conversation, but it was hard to do more than trade heavily edited essentials of their life histories with Eduardo's security men monitoring every post. Joe had fed her a rather sordid tale about being an ex-firefighter who'd been wrongly accused of arson. Having met the man, she didn't have the slightest doubt that it was all a load of bull. And she still didn't know any more about the real Joe than she had when she'd first met him.

She'd wanted to spend more time with him. Do more regular dating stuff. But Eduardo wouldn't cut her loose for anything except dancing. Fortunately, she could work with dancing as a form of seduction.

She'd been glad when Joe suggested they meet at this particular nightclub. It played the hottest dance music this side of the equator and was the sort of place where she could ratchet up their relationship to the next level—to an attraction that would justify their elopement later.

Yeah, that was it. She wanted to go to a sexy dance club and drape herself all over Joe, purely in the interest of promoting his safety. Right.

Whether she wanted to admit it or not, she was wildly attracted to her future husband. *Future husband.* At first, that phrase had felt strange and foreign to her, but over the last few days, the sound of it had been getting more and more comfortable.

She was also getting more and more comfortable with the idea of being infatuated with Joe. Hey, why not go with the feeling? It would make their marriage act that much more believable to her father when the time came. So she mooned around the house all day, dreaming about him, and happily let her father rib her about it. She spent hours trying on dresses until she found the perfect one, and she let the housekeeper rib her about that, too.

The other reason Cari was glad they were going somewhere steamy tonight was that Joe's impeccable restraint was starting to get on her nerves. She liked to think of herself as reasonably attractive, but he seemed completely impervious to that fact. It was all well and good to be hot and bothered over him, but it would be nice if he returned a smidgen of the same attraction for her.

The song blaring around her ended. She thanked her partner—the son of a business associate of Eduardo's—for the dance and headed off the big dance floor. The club was packed tonight and it was slow dodging the gyrating bodies around her.

Where was Joe? She couldn't see him over the press of people around her. But he was near. She could *feel* it. She got short of breath just thinking about touching that gorgeous body of his again. He was such a contrast to the beefy brutishness of her bodyguards. Joe's was the toned fitness of an athlete. He was muscular but lean, powerful yet graceful.

She smoothed her palms down the red Marilyn Monroe-style halter dress she'd agonized over choosing all day. She hoped it would shake Joe up a bit tonight. Okay, shake him up a lot. If it didn't, she gave up. The guy would officially be priest material.

In their meetings so far, he'd been a total gentleman with her. Not once had she caught him checking her out on the sly, and he'd been unfailingly polite with her. Her father might be eating it up, but she'd about had it with the squeaky-clean routine.

Sure, he'd leaned close and thrown her the occasional heated look, but those were purely for the benefit of her body-guards and the whole cover story of their falling madly in love. He always apologized under his breath after the fact. *Apologized,* for goodness' sake!

No more apologies tonight, buster.

They were supposed to be having a steamy whirlwind romance, for crying out loud. The idea was for people to witness them hanging all over each other so her father would buy the story when they told him they'd eloped.

Besides, her gut said Joe was capable of more real passion than he was showing. Much more. Right now, she needed more than nice from him. She needed fire. *Sizzle.* Enough to convince her father not to kill him out of hand. Enough to reassure her that she hadn't completely lost her feminine allure. And most of all, enough to satisfy the desire rolling restlessly in her stomach.

It was *definitely* time to shake up Mr. Joe Smith.

Freddie and Neddie had split up as they always did when she came to this particular disco. One covered the front entrance, and the other took the back door so she couldn't sneak out on them. Which was perfect for her purposes tonight. It put both men clearly in sight of the dance floor but not close enough to interfere when she went after Joe.

The song changed. A slow ballad that paired up the sweaty bodies hemming her in. Finally, an escape path opened up for her. She'd almost reached the edge of the dance floor when a warm hand touched her bare shoulder. Pleasure raced through her. Ah, she knew that touch. Craved it.

She smiled and turned around to greet Joe. As usual, her breath stuck in her throat at the sight of him. Tonight, he wore a casual navy silk shirt and crisply pressed, white linen trousers. He blended in perfectly with the Gavronese playboy set that frequented this exclusive club.

With a smile that would melt rock into quivering lava, he

drew her politely into his arms and swayed to the music of the ballad blasting around them.

Enough already with the careful dance-class distance between them! Carina plastered herself against him from shoulder to knee. And sucked in a sharp breath. *Oh, my.* His body was flexible steel against hers, and his shirt clung to muscular shoulders and a set of pecs her father's goons would kill for.

He stared down at her in surprise, and she stared back in challenge. Then a slow smile came across his features and he relaxed into the dance with her. Why did she get the distinct feeling she'd just unlocked a door with something dangerous behind it?

The song changed tempo and a driving Cuban beat pounded through Joe's body into hers. But instead of letting her go, he pulled her even closer against him. It was a good thing his powerful arm circled her waist or she'd have been in real danger of her legs failing as delicious sensations shot through her entire body. She gasped as he spun her around in a fast jive step. Now where in the world did he learn to dance like that? In their previous meetings, he'd never given any hint of knowing how to do this. A man of many talents. She'd *definitely* lay odds some of those talents extended to the bedroom.

He whirled her around, spinning her out to the end of his fingertips and then flicking her back in like a yo-yo on a string. As quickly as his body heat had disappeared, it was back. His hand on the small of her back pressed her so close against him that she practically rode his rock-hard thigh. He lifted her against him as he spun around the room, her feet barely skimming the floor.

"Dizzy?" he murmured into her ear, his breath a hot caress against her neck.

"Yes. No. Not from the dancing," she managed to get out.

He laughed and twirled her away from him again, then gathered her close once more. His thigh rubbed against her intimately, igniting fireworks low in her belly. Flames of desire licked at her, threatening to consume her completely.

Not fair. He looked completely in control, totally unaffected by their spicy dance.

She ran her fingernails across the back of his neck and she might as well have ruffled a tiger's fur. Abruptly, his eyes blazed and sexual vibes poured off of him, hot and thick and possessive. Now *that* was more like it! Women around them on the dance floor ogled him even more blatantly. All but purring herself, she leaned into him until his silk shirt caressed her breasts through the flimsy fabric of her dress.

The music blared and the rhythm pounded through her in time with her body's sudden pulsing need. The drums beat low in her belly, while the Cuban horns blared across her skin and the singer's voice shivered down her spine. Faster and faster the music played, driving her higher and higher with a need to be naked and sweaty with this man.

The music finally ended and Joe's arm loosened enough for her to slide down his muscular leg to the floor once more. He led her to the bar on the far side of the dance floor, away from both her bodyguards. She wobbled alongside him, hardly able to walk. *Oh. My. God.* What had just happened to her? She'd never experienced anything remotely like that— in public or private—with any man.

"Good thing I'm already planning to marry you," he growled as he handed her one of two glasses of ice water he snagged from a bartender. "After a dance like that, I'd feel obligated as a gentleman to marry you."

Her face heated abruptly. Busted. She'd set out to get his attention and, apparently, she'd succeeded.

"In case I forgot to mention it, you look spectacular tonight," he murmured to her under the din.

"Thank you," she answered, strangely shy of the compliment from him. "You look pretty good yourself."

He reached out to tuck a strand of her hair back from her face. "I got our marriage license today," he said casually. "There's a judge standing by day or night to hear our vows."

Wow. He had a *judge* on call? How did he pull that off in this town? She thought her father owned all the judges in St. George. In all of Gavarone, for that matter.

He continued, interrupting her speculation. "So whenever you're ready, we can get married."

She blinked. The words were a bizarre and wonderful fantasy coming out of this gorgeous man's mouth. He was the kind of guy she might like hearing those words from for real. "Uh, when did you have in mind?" she asked.

His answer was brisk. "The sooner the better. I don't like you being in that house all alone with your father. The faster I can get in there to protect you, the better."

"I'm hardly alone in the house," she replied. "My father has a half-dozen full-time house servants, and wads of his...employees hang around all the time."

"His armed, dangerous and not-too-bright henchmen, you mean?"

She laughed at the description. "Exactly."

"Like I said, the sooner the better," he ground out. His jaw rippled as he stared down into his glass of water.

Warmth bubbled up inside her. Joe sounded genuinely worried about her. That was so sweet. If only the idea of walking into her father's office and saying, "Guess what, Daddy? I got married today" didn't scare her half to death, she'd be feeling a lot better about this whole scheme.

"What's got you frowning, princess?" Joe murmured. "You look worried."

She sighed. "I was just thinking about how my father will react to all this."

Joe shrugged. "He'll be pissed off and suspicious as hell. But I'm telling you, I think he'll secretly be relieved. We just have to watch our step. One slipup is all it'll take."

Yeah, to land them both in her bed with slit throats.

She put her hand on his forearm, which rested on the bar beside her. She leaned forward, speaking urgently. "That's what worries me, Joe. You have no idea how violent my father is."

His dark eyes blazed, pinning her against the bar. "Yes, I do. I know exactly how violent Eduardo Ferrare is."

His sudden intensity startled her. Usually Joe was so calm and unruffled. Where had all that abrupt anger come from? A frisson of doubt raced through her. There was more going on here than Joe simply wanting to rescue her. If he was, in fact, with Charlie Squad, then there was some serious bad blood between him and her father. Eduardo had killed a member of Charlie Squad years ago and they'd never forgiven him for it.

What was Joe's hidden agenda? Did he mean to physically hurt her father in some way? Kill him, even? Did she dare go ahead with this whole eloping thing and put Eduardo at risk? He might be a criminal, but he was her father, after all. The only parent she'd ever known. She didn't want to see him *die* just so she could live her own life in peace.

She sighed. How could she not go ahead with the plan? No matter what risk Joe posed to her or her father, she had to pay the price and jump at the chance he had offered her. She'd act as his cover inside her father's house while he accomplished his secret goal and, in turn, he'd help her accomplish hers— to escape. She wanted out. And he… What *did* he want?

Her intuition again screamed that it involved hurting her father in some way. But could she live with setting him up to be harmed? Was her freedom worth that guilt?

As her thoughts whirled, Joe's arm slid around her waist once more. "Can I interest you in another dance?"

Like he had to ask that twice! Her lips curved into a smile. "Let's go, Mr. Astaire."

Joe grinned. "After you, Ginger."

She felt him watching her hips as she sashayed toward the floor in front of him. *Finally.* At last, the guy was showing normal male interest in her!

As Joe steered her back out onto the dance floor, Cari

noticed people all over the room staring at them. Including her bodyguards. Abject relief flooded over her, to the point that she actually felt tears burn at the back of her eyes. Was she really that worried about Joe's safety?

She blinked away the weepy sensation that didn't go at all with her devil-may-care, little-rich-girl act. Her mask firmly in place once more, she looked around the club to gauge the crowd's reaction to the hot vignette playing out between her and Joe. *Ah, all the world's a stage.* At least, in her world it was.

Gavarone's superrich social set was actually quite small. *Inbred,* she snorted derisively. Everybody knew everyone else. So when a new face—especially one as spectacularly handsome as Joe's—showed up on the scene and staked out a woman as notorious as her for himself, it got noticed in a big way.

And then, of course, there were Freddie and Neddie. Hopefully, as long as Joe's attention stayed firmly glued to her, he'd be safe from the loving attention of their fists. She seriously didn't want to find out what her father's orders to the thugs were if Joe happened to show interest in some other woman after showing such intense and public interest in her.

Joe's fingers trailed up her arm, and then he looked at her with sharp concern. "You okay?"

"Why do you ask?" she replied.

"You have goose bumps. You can't possibly be cold in this gaudy sweat pit."

She grinned at the description of the posh club. She'd always thought the place's neon decor was a little garish, too. "It's nothing," she assured him.

He gave her a speculative look. And then dropped her jaw with his next words. "Let's get married tonight."

"Tonight?" she squeaked.

"Sure. Why not?"

Her mind went completely blank. Fear crowded forward in her head until it all but choked her. It was one thing to toy around with her father, but the reality of it was another thing entirely.

Was she truly prepared to go through with Joe's scheme? To face down her father's wrath? To make the break for real?

It hit her like a sledgehammer that she'd known all along on some level that the plan with Tony wouldn't work. Somehow, she'd *known* her father would find out and foil it. She hadn't anticipated how violently he'd do it, but she'd known subliminally that Eduardo would stop her.

Joe, on the other hand…

This guy might actually be able to deliver on his promises. He could get her out once and for all. For the first time *ever,* she truly faced the prospect of making the break with her father.

But as violent and cruel a man as he was, he was still the man who'd raised her. She frowned.

Joe swore quietly beside her. She looked up, surprised. "What?" she asked.

"I know that look. It's cold feet if I ever saw it. Don't lose your nerve on me now, princess. We're in too deep to back out."

"No, we're not," she argued. "You can just walk away and you'll be safe. My father will never know a thing."

"Oh, yeah?" Joe growled. He turned her around, his hands encircling her waist, and nodded toward the front door.

Cari looked in the direction he indicated. And gulped. Freddie and Neddie had their heads together and were staring straight at her and Joe. Both men's faces were thunderous. As she looked on, Freddie pulled out a cell phone and pressed it to his ear.

Oh, God.

He said quietly, "That last dance of ours crossed the line. We have no choice but to go forward now."

"Joe, get out of here right now. They're calling my father. If you're lucky, they'll just put you in the hospital for a few weeks, but if you're not…"

Joe chuckled.

She stopped midsentence. And stared at him in shock.

"You're laughing about this?" she demanded incredulously. "They're telling my father right now that we've been pawing all over each other in public. He's going to tell them to kick your teeth into last month. This is serious!"

Joe smiled down at her gently. "Thanks for worrying about me, sweetheart, but those two jerks couldn't lay a hand on me if they tried. I'd put them flat on their backs in ten, maybe twenty, seconds."

Cari rolled her eyes. "Don't you go all macho on me, Joe Smith. Those guys are both street fighters."

He laid a finger on her lips, stopping any further protests from her. "Trust me. They don't pose a threat."

She frowned.

His grin widened. "Wanna really give them something to stew over?"

Her eyebrows raised in question, but that was all the response she had time for before he leaned down swiftly and captured her mouth with his.

Wow. Heat and man surrounded her completely, invading the darkest corners of her mouth and her mind. His lips and tongue were warm and wet, biting and licking and sucking like she was the best ice-cream cone he'd ever tasted, all sweet and drippy and melting, and he was determined to capture every last drop of her.

Her knees went wobbly without warning and she leaned into him, suddenly hot all over. She devoured him right back, and Lord, if her insides didn't actually start to quiver with desire. She needed him like water in the desert. She hadn't even known it, but her soul had been dried up, shriveled and parched until he breathed life back into her. She all but inhaled him, right there on the spot. Her leg started to creep up, to wrap around him, to press her core against the hard bulge at her belly. But then a sound that was more a groan than a chuckle came from his throat. No. No, no, no! She had to have more of him right now! All of him!

Gently, his fingers wrapped around the back of her knee,

disentangling it from around his thigh. His thumb gave a single caress to the sensitive skin behind the joint, sending white heat shooting up her thigh and straight to her core. Her breath hitched and his gaze snapped to hers, his black eyes blazing.

Oh, yes. They definitely had a spark between them. *More like chain lightning.*

He lifted his mouth away from hers. Cleared his throat.

She clung to his shoulders, not because she was needy and trying to seduce him but because her legs were so weak she wasn't sure they'd bear her weight.

"Uh, well then," he mumbled, "I think that pretty much seals the deal."

"How's that?" she managed to mumble back through the buzz of lust filling her ears.

"When Frick and Frack report to your old man that I just examined your tonsils with my tongue, and in public, I'm betting daddy dearest will stick a shotgun in my face and make me marry you if I don't beat him to the punch."

And abruptly, she became aware of several hundred people staring at her as avidly as if she'd just grown horns and a third eye. Why was her skin crawling all of a sudden at the idea of all those gazes locked on her and Joe? She'd made a spectacle of herself plenty of times. She'd even laid hot kisses on guys in public before, back when Eduardo didn't watch her every move, back before Julia disappeared. But tonight, the party-girl mask just wouldn't stay on. It kept slipping away, leaving her raw emotions unprotected, her heart on display. Her *heart.* Not an act. Not the public image that everyone always saw. But her. Carina. For real.

She never, ever, showed her true self to anyone. Not to her father. Not to rooms full of cynical, voyeuristic jet-setters, and certainly not to Joe. He was practically a stranger, for God's sake! She barely knew him at all. And what she did know of him didn't inspire a girl to think of happily ever after, kids and rocking chairs.

She vaguely realized that she was still bent half-backward over his arm, his strength supporting most of her weight. His body, hard and hot, pressed into her, branding itself on her memory, marking her as his.

And then with a quick bunching of his muscles, she was upright once more, whirling off into a kaleidoscope of light and color. Music throbbed in time with the pulsing desire between her thighs. Her breasts ached for his hard chest against hers once more.

With a snap of his strong wrist, he spun her away from him and pulled her back again. And then his other hand landed in the middle of her back, anchoring her sinfully against him.

She sighed in delight as he swayed back and forth. She might die right here, on the spot, from wanting this man so bad she could hardly stand it. She still tasted their kiss in her mouth and savored the spicy, clean flavor of him. It made a girl want more of him. Much, much more.

For all of her wild ways, she really had very little experience at seducing men. They had always come on to her, the rich, spoiled brat they were sure would spread her legs for the right man with the cash or the cool to earn the privilege. God, she was jaded. How had she gotten that way at twenty-four? She felt a hundred years old.

For a change, she went with her instincts and went on the offensive with Joe. She wanted more of what they'd just done. A lot more. She ran her fingers up the back of his powerful neck into his silky hair and undulated her body against his.

Her feminine intuition was right on target. Joe half growled, half laughed and pulled her even closer. He maneuvered her into the thick of the crowd of dancers, out of sight of her bodyguards. His mouth descended, capturing hers again. He kissed her with his entire body this time, surrounding her in his strength and grace as they danced, locked together in a sizzling embrace.

She was so dizzy she could hardly stand by the time the

song ended. Another tune cranked up and the people around them gyrated as Joe tore his mouth away from hers and stared down at her. He looked as thunderstruck as she felt.

In the din, she barely heard him say, "We definitely have to get married right now."

He sounded like he was talking about a whole lot more than their plan to escape her father. Her heart stuttered in shock. Was he really as attracted to her as she was to him? The thought sent her head reeling even worse than it already was.

"C'mon," Joe shouted over the music.

She followed along as he tugged her hand. He led her quickly off the dance floor and toward the back exit of the club.

They cleared the dance floor and the direct blast of the speakers. "What are you doing?" she asked him.

"Getting out of here," he replied as he hustled her toward the door.

"But Neddie…"

"Is still wading across the dance floor with Freddie. C'mon, hurry!" he urged her.

"But the others… They're in the limo…."

"Exactly. They're still in the limo. Out front."

"How do you know that?" she demanded. "They could be in the alley out back right now."

"Only one way to find out. C'mon!"

The wildness he'd set loose in her still prowled in her veins, hungry. Insistent. She wanted this man. No matter what the cost. No matter what the consequences.

This was really dumb. Dangerous at best, suicidal at worst. But damned if she hadn't let him lead her off the dance floor quickly, and was making haste beside him for the exit.

They burst out into the muggy warmth of the night. The sultry air stoked the lust zinging across her skin.

"This way," he murmured.

She broke into a run beside him as he raced toward a side street. They ducked around the corner, out of sight of the club.

She didn't have any illusions about being safe, though. Freddie and Neddie were bulldogs who'd never let go of their bone.

But when Joe yanked open the door of a dark Cadillac with tinted windows parked at the curb and urged her inside, that did surprise her. The vehicle's driver pulled away quickly. She looked out the tinted glass of the back window in time to see Freddie careen into sight, huffing. But then their car turned a corner and her bodyguard disappeared from view.

She turned around to face front. Joe lounged casually beside her. He lifted an armrest and pulled a soft drink out of a concealed mini-cooler. "Thirsty?" he asked.

Joe had this escape planned before he came inside the club! Otherwise, he wouldn't have had this car waiting for them. She ignored the soda, outraged. "You knew all along you were going to pull me out of there tonight, didn't you?"

He frowned. "I wasn't sure. I had a car waiting, just in case. An opportunity presented itself, so I seized it. Your father's men are too careful to give us many chances to get away from them." He peered at her in the dim interior. "Are you angry at me, Carina? I thought this was what you wanted."

Joe's hand captured hers gently, stilling it against his chest. She was arrested by the slow, steady thud of his heart under her palm. Not the heartbeat of a frightened man.

He said soothingly, "This plan isn't only about getting you away from your father. It's also about getting him to let you live your own life once and for all."

Cari's outrage subsided. "Where are we going?"

Joe looked her directly in the eye. His dark gaze was warm and compassionate. "You're so beautiful," he murmured, "and so damned young."

Young? She hadn't felt young in a long time. Living with her father aged a soul. Joe's smooth voice caressed her, raising the fine hair on her forearms. She tingled all over. And then his next words registered.

"We've got an appointment with a judge, princess. We're getting married, remember?"

She took a deep breath and let it out slowly. She looked up at him uncertainly. "Are you sure about this?"

His smile would have lit the whole night sky if they were standing outside. "Yeah, I'm sure. How 'bout you?"

She stared back at him, losing herself in the midnight depths of his eyes. He'd take care of her. Keep her safe. Give her freedom. All those promises swam in his gaze. But she saw something more in his eyes, too. Something male and possessive that made her hands shake and her breath come in unsteady jerks. Something that made her pause a long time before she answered.

Finally, she took a deep breath and replied in a shaky voice, "Yes. I'm sure, too."

Chapter 4

Breathe, Cari, breathe. Lord, bolting from that club had been a risky thing to do. She was supposed to be a wild child. Adventurous. The kind of girl who'd take eloping in stride or, at least, take it as a big joke. Drawing what shred of courage she could around herself, she turned to peer at Joe in the car's dark interior.

"Since we've got wheels and have already ditched my watchdogs, why don't we just head for the airport? We can hop the first flight to anywhere."

Beside her, one of Joe's silhouetted shoulders shrugged. "We'd never make it far enough out of the city to reach the airport. There are police checkpoints everywhere, and military patrols are crawling all over St. George. Plus, as soon as your pet thugs report to daddy, you'd better believe Eduardo's men will be racing all over this city looking for you, too."

"But—" she started.

Joe interrupted. "Any extraction plane or helicopter stands a good chance of being shot down. There is a civil war going on in Gavarone, after all. I could haul you out into the jungle, but it's crawling with rebels right now and would put you at grave risk. Especially if you were caught with me."

"Why's that?"

Joe grimaced. "Let's just say I'm not well loved by the rebels these days. I was involved in a little run-in with them a while back that took a whole lot of their people out of action."

Her eyebrows shot up. He must be referring to that fiasco last year where the high-tech rifle Eduardo had stolen from Charlie Squad was mysteriously stolen back from the rebels he had hired to take it. Her father had been furious when the rifle slipped through his fingers. He'd also been livid that nobody seemed to want to tell him exactly how it had happened. Maybe someday she'd manage to pry the story out of Joe.

"Look," she argued, "I'm no wilting lily. I can stand tromping around in the jungle for a while if it wins me my freedom."

Of all people, the driver replied, "Joe's right. It's too dangerous to try to move you out of the city right now. Believe me, he's examined every option. And the war severely limits his options."

She frowned. "But there isn't any fighting in St. George. The government regained control of the capital months ago."

Joe retorted, "Then why are there *nightly* bombings, kidnappings and assassinations in the city? Why does everyone who owns anything more than the shirt on his back hide behind locked doors after dark and sleep with a gun under his pillow? This town's a real slice of paradise thanks to your father and the revolution he's funding."

"What? My father—"

Joe cut her off. "Forget it. Forget I said anything."

Not bloody likely. Her father funded the rebels? Actually, it made a certain kind of sense. It was exactly the sort of thing Eduardo would do. His ambitions certainly extended to buying an army and controlling a small country. Nausea rumbled in her gut. She didn't want to think about the hundreds or thousands of people he was responsible for killing with this newest little venture.

And as for Joe…wow. That was quite a speech out of him. Until now, he'd been pretty laid back about life. It was almost as if his act had slipped for a minute there. Like a mask of casual reserve had fallen away to reveal the passionate man beneath.

But then he commented lightly, "If I didn't know better, I'd say you were trying to avoid marrying me, princess. What's the matter? Aren't I your type?"

"Oh, you're my type, all right," she blurted out before she realized what she was saying. Her gaze snapped to his. Sure enough, he was staring a hole through her, his eyebrows quirked.

Oh, God. Here came the taunting, the exploitation of the weakness she'd just shown him. She braced herself for his sarcastic comeback. But he said nothing. He didn't make fun of her crush on him or laugh at her or even smile. In fact, the only thing he did was reach out in the dark and take her hand in his. Maybe he wasn't the only one whose nerves were causing the act to slip a little too much tonight.

The interior of the car went silent. They drove for a while toward an affluent residential section of St. George. Large homes nestled behind tall fences and iron gates and thick landscaping that hid most of them from view.

"Where are we going?" she finally asked again, breaking the thick silence.

The driver answered from up front, "To pay a little visit to a man named Miguel Cabot."

She gasped as the name of one of her father's most loyal supporters congealed in a knot of horror in her throat. "Judge Cabot?" she managed to choke out.

The driver glanced at her in the rearview mirror. "You know something about him that we don't?" he asked.

"Yeah," she replied. "He's got his hand so deep in my father's pockets he could scratch Eduardo's kneecaps."

Joe *smiled* beside her.

"This isn't a joke," she hissed at him. "He'll run straight to my father."

Joe nodded. "That's the idea."

Huh? The skepticism rumbling in her gut must have shown on her face because Joe explained, "Who better to marry us? Someone your father will believe out of hand when the judge tells Eduardo we're legally and properly married."

"But what if he calls my father before he does the ceremony and asks if it's all right?"

The driver answered casually, "He won't."

"I'll bet you a hundred dollars U.S. he talks to Eduardo first," she retorted.

"I'll bet you a thousand he doesn't," the driver shot back.

Carina blinked. For the hired help, the guy was pretty hostile toward her. She was generally well liked by the working classes in Gavarone because she tipped lavishly and was forever giving away ridiculous sums of money to the poorest among them. If this driver was Gavronese, he ought to be delighted to drive her in anticipation of a hefty reward.

A suspicion that he was another member of Charlie Squad hit her and, just as quickly, froze into certainty. The driver had good reason to hate anyone with the name Ferrare. *As did Joe.*

Her horrified gaze swiveled to him. Why hadn't she seen this before? She'd guessed he was Charlie Squad, but she'd let her attraction to him blind her to the reality of who he was. Joe *said* he was here to help her. To rescue her. But was he really? Was it possible that Joe had been setting her up as bait this whole time so he and his buddies could draw out her father and kill him? From what her father said about these American soldiers, they were fully capable of harming a non-combatant like her to get at her father.

Nah. No matter how little she knew Joe, there was no way he'd hurt her. She'd bet her life on it.

Joe interrupted her distressing thoughts, saying mildly,

"Don't take that bet, Carina. You are right—Judge Cabot will absolutely make a phone call to your father first. The thing is, I've arranged for a little intervention in the phone lines at the good judge's house."

She searched the darkness, trying to see his eyes. "What sort of intervention?"

"An actress I've hired for the occasion will take the call, which will be conveniently diverted from the regular phone lines. She'll pose as a housekeeper in your father's home and will tell the judge that *Señor* Ferrare is not available at the moment. There's some sort of uproar over the fact that Carina has disappeared with her fiancé and nobody knows where they've gone. *Señor* Ferrare is threatening to make them get married tonight if Mr. Joe does not bring Miss Carina home soon."

She stared at Joe. Blinked a couple of times. And then burst out laughing. "That's brilliant!"

He flashed that devilishly charming smile of his and, for the first time since they'd gotten into the car, her panic abated a little. They might just pull this off after all. But then something else struck her. If Joe had hired an actress and already spliced into the judge's home telephone line, he'd definitely been planning to do this tonight. He hadn't exactly lied to her outright about having planned this little excursion in advance, but he hadn't been completely square with her about it, either.

But then, it wasn't like either one of them was being blindingly honest with each other here. She'd been careful to keep up her spoiled-little-rich-girl act, and who the heck knew who Joe Smith really was beneath that easygoing, *I'm-just-a-friend-of-your-sister's* act?

They made a good pair.

The car slowed down, turned into a driveway and stopped at an electronically controlled gate.

The driver leaned out the window and announced, in flawless Spanish, "Miss Ferrare to see Judge Cabot."

The security man on the other end of the intercom sounded

startled as he answered, "Come up to the house right away, of course."

Amazing the reaction the Ferrare name garnered in this town. God, she hated being her father's daughter. But, as always, she schooled her facial expression to one of casual acceptance of the guard's reaction.

The driver closed his window and the car rolled forward smoothly again. She noticed him staring at her in the rearview mirror. "They always jump like that when they hear your name?" he asked.

She shrugged. But keeping the move nonchalant took some effort. She replied, "Pretty much."

As they came into view of the floodlights illuminating the front of Judge Cabot's house, Joe muttered, "Stay in the car. I want to have a look around before you get out."

She was used to the procedure. The only surprise this time was how quick Joe was about it. By the time he'd slowly walked around from his side of the car to hers and opened the door for her, she heard him mutter to the driver, "All clear, Tom."

Tom? Her gaze snapped to the back of the driver's head. Was *that* the legendary Colonel Tom Folly? Heck, her father had supposedly crippled the guy's leg just last year. Ruined his field career for good, by all accounts. It would certainly explain his hostility toward her and her family.

Joe's hand appeared in front of her face and she reached out to take it. His fingers were warm and deceptively strong as they wrapped around hers. But then all of Joe was deceptively strong. She'd been surprised a couple of times when they'd been dancing just how easily he picked her up and swung her around, as if he hardly noticed her weight.

Panic jumped and kicked like a scared colt in her stomach again. "Are you sure about this?" she asked him one last time.

His gaze met hers. For a moment, his black eyes were as hard as nails. But the expression in them melted so quickly into a warm smile that she almost wasn't sure she'd seen the former.

"I'm sure, princess."

She noted the fact that he didn't ask her the same question. Not interested in giving her any opportunity to back out, was he? Smart man. Because right about now, the long driveway stretching into the night behind her was looking really good.

The sprawling house's front door opened and a gray-haired man wearing neatly pressed chino slacks and a block polo shirt stepped out onto the covered porch.

"Carina, *mi querida!* You're looking as lovely as ever. Come in, come in."

She wasn't his dear, thank you very much. He was as corrupt as they came, using his courtroom as a weapon to promote crime and suffering among the people of Gavarone. Given her druthers, she'd spit in his face. "Judge Cabot," she said warmly. "I'm so sorry to interrupt your evening at this late hour, but I need your help."

The judge gave a worried look around at the night, as if ears were growing on the gardenia bushes by the front door. "Let us speak inside of how I may help you."

Joe's hand slipped under her elbow as they walked up the front steps, ostensibly to help her, but she'd lay odds he was worried about her bolting. She walked past the heavy, sweet scent of the gardenias and inside to dim lamplight. The hand-distressed hardwood floors and broad hallway running straight back into the house, with its plantation shutters and mahogany furniture, gave it a tropical, colonial feel. Under other circumstances, she'd have liked this place.

She was surprised to see that Colonel Folly—if that's who he really was—had followed her and Joe inside. Normally, a chauffeur would stay with his car. She should probably pass him off as her bodyguard so Judge Cabot wouldn't get suspicious.

She looked over her shoulder at the American colonel. "I'm perfectly safe inside the judge's house. But if my father's orders are to stick with me at all times, do stay out of the way, all right?"

Folly's eyes registered surprise for the slightest instant, but then it was replaced by approval. "Yes, ma'am," he replied gruffly.

The judge led them to a combination library/office lined with law books and sporting a giant cluttered desk. It was an insult to the law to have this man purport to actually care what was inside those leather-bound volumes. Aloud, Cari simpered, "What a lovely room! Look at all those pretty books!"

Judge Cabot smiled, his gaze sharp but his voice obsequious. "What can I do for you at this unusual hour, my dear?"

"I want you to marry me."

Cabot gaped. "I beg your pardon?"

She laughed gaily. "I don't mean I want *you* to be my husband. I mean I want you to perform a marriage ceremony for me and my boyfriend...my fiancé." She dragged Joe forward by the arm to stand beside her.

Cabot paused, obviously thinking fast. She could see the wheels turning, assessing how her father would react if he went through with her request. Doubt and fear trickled across his features before he finally said heavily, "Ah. Well, my dear, there are certain legalities that must be observed. I'm afraid it will be impossible for me to marry you two lovebirds this evening...."

Joe reached into his back pant pocket and pulled out a folded piece of paper. "If it's the marriage license you're worried about, I've got it right here."

Cabot's eyebrows shot up in surprise. He looked more than a little annoyed. But, interestingly enough, he continued to address himself solely to her and ignored Joe. "Actually, I'm more worried about what your father will think of this, Carina. You don't want to deprive him of the pleasure of seeing his baby girl become a bride, do you? It would break his heart."

She waved an airy hand. "Oh, he's been telling Joe to make an honest woman out of me for weeks now. He'll be thrilled."

Cabot looked skeptical. "Well," he drawled, "if you've already got the license and you have your father's blessing..."

He took a step toward the door. "Wait here. There are several things I'll need to get if we're going to do this wedding tonight. I'll be back in a moment."

Joe and Folly exchanged significant looks as the judge left the room.

She muttered under her breath, "There goes the bet."

Folly flashed her a brief smile. But then Joe startled her by taking her hand in his. "How are you holding up?" he murmured.

"So far, so good," she mumbled back, as aware as he apparently was that there could be microphones hidden in this room. She plucked at her red dress. "I can't believe I'm going to get married in this outfit. I always imagined I'd wear some outrageously expensive designer gown—white, of course, and covered in lace and pearls."

Joe glanced down at her attire and fire blazed in his eyes. "I dunno. You may start a fashion trend. A sexy red dress seems just right for the occasion if you ask me."

She laughed. "And that's why the groom doesn't pick the dress. If men had their way, brides would wear lace teddies down the aisle."

He grinned widely. "Now you're talking."

She heard a noise in the hall and quickly leaned into Joe, plastering herself blatantly to him from chest to ankle. She purred, "That's why I'm marrying you, darling. You always know what to say to make me feel better."

The judge walked in just then, and when she drew away from Joe, his arm came up, trapping her against him. Good point. It probably was a good idea for the judge to see them crawling all over each other like cats in heat. All the more reason for him to get them safely married as soon as possible.

Cabot cleared his throat. "My wife will be down in just a minute. We'll need two witnesses for the ceremony, and if your driver will consent to be one of them, Josefina will stand in as the second."

Carina answered carelessly, not even bothering to glance

over at Folly. "Of course he'll do it." Servants in this country, particularly her father's, were expected to do what they were told and not ask any questions about it.

An attractive woman of middle years came into the room, patting her hair in place. A giant diamond glittered on her hand, impossible to miss. Cari's gaze narrowed. Josefina Cabot was an extremely well-turned-out woman, compliments of Eduardo's bribes to her husband. She supposed she shouldn't blame Josefina for being married to a crook, but she still didn't like seeing the woman wearing thousand-dollar sweaters and hundred-thousand-dollar rings paid for in other people's blood.

Cari exchanged air kisses with Cabot's wife, who gushed, "How exciting this is! So romantic. To elope with a handsome young man. Ah, to be your age again, Carina."

The most exciting part for the woman was going to be all the attention she got when she called everyone she knew to gossip about this secret ceremony two minutes after it was over.

"Are we ready, then?" Judge Cabot asked. "Come stand over here in front of me, you two."

A rush of heat swept over Cari and she actually felt lightheaded. Great. That was all she needed to fuel Josefina's rumor mill. Fainting at her own wedding. But then Joe's magical hands were there again, one in the small of her back and the other at her elbow, steadying her and guiding her forward to stand beside him in front of the judge.

Her body didn't feel like it belonged to her. She listened in mild disbelief as the judge droned through the wedding ceremony, lecturing them about the sanctity of marriage, how it was a sacred oath unto death.

Unto death. She prayed fervently that this harebrained scheme wouldn't end up with Joe—or even her—dying at her father's hands. She ought to call this off. Tell Joe to save himself and forget about helping her.

But as surely as she was standing here, going through with

this insanity, so would he. She might not have the slightest idea who Joe Smith was beneath the mask he always wore, but she knew one thing about him for sure. He'd never walk away from her. Not after he'd promised to rescue her from her father.

She gulped as Judge Cabot turned to her and said, "Repeat after me. I, Carina Inez di Ortolo Ferrare, do take thee—" a pause while Cabot glanced down at the marriage license in his hand "—Joseph Chavez Smith, to be my lawfully wedded husband."

Emotion was so thick in her throat that she could hardly breathe. What was it? Fear? Sentimental sappiness? This wasn't a real wedding, after all. It was just pretend. But darned if her throat didn't clench up around the familiar phrases "to have and to hold" and "in sickness and in health."

In minor shock, she listened to herself promise to love, honor and cherish Joe until death did they part. Lord, that felt *really* real!

And then it was Joe's turn. She looked up at him, not sure if she was more stunned or frightened. And then, of course, there was the whole question of whether she ought to be more afraid of God's or her father's reaction to this farce.

But then Joe's hand tightened on hers and his gaze captured hers with mesmerizing intensity.

"I, Joseph Chavez Smith, do take thee, Carina…"

His voice rolled over her and through her, compelling in its quiet certainty. Conveying reassurance. A promise that he would not let her come to any harm. And then he did something odd.

The judge intoned, "I vow to love, honor and cherish thee all the days of our lives…."

But Joe repeated, "I vow to love, honor and protect thee all the days of our lives…."

And darned if her eyes didn't start to burn. Tears filled her eyes until Joe was little more than a dark blur before her. And then the tears spilled over, streaming down her cheeks in hot tracks. She couldn't reach up to brush them away since Joe had a death grip on her hands. But just as well. Josefina Cabot could tell all her friends that the bride had cried with happiness.

Surprisingly, it was Joe who reached up with his fingertips to catch her tears and press them to his lips. How romantic. If she'd truly been in love with this man, the gesture would have melted her heart. She glanced up at Joe in gratitude and was riveted by the passion shining in his gaze. Lord, he was looking at her like he was completely enthralled. Her heart flip-flopped.

And then she remembered. It was all an act. But, Lord, what an act it was. If he'd felt that way about her for real, she'd be blown away. Behind them, Josefina gave a sappy sigh. And the tabloids would report that the groom adored his bride, who worshiped him in return.

She blinked as she realized Judge Cabot was asking for the rings. Oh, God. Rings. Rings hadn't even crossed her mind. But Joe calmly reached into his pocket and pulled out two gold wedding bands. His, an unadorned ring of plain yellow gold. But hers was the surprise. It looked like an antique. It was definitely not new, for it bore the dings and scratches of many years spent on someone's finger. She didn't have time to examine it closely, but at a glimpse, it looked carved in an intricate pattern of vines, leaves and flowers in different colors of white, rose and yellow gold. "It's lovely," she breathed.

"My grandmother's," he murmured back.

As she looked down at Joe slipping the ring onto her finger, Cari realized her hands were trembling. And shockingly, she felt a faint tremor pass through Joe's hand as she took it to slip on his ring. So he wasn't completely unaffected by this whole wedding thing, either, was he? At least they were in it together. And that thought comforted her more than she'd expected.

Judge Cabot droned through the closing lines of the ceremony, talking about what God had joined together no man tearing asunder. Maybe he should be saying, let Eduardo Ferrare not tear them asunder. She realized she was gripping

Joe's hands fiercely, as if by hanging on tightly enough, she could keep Eduardo from coming between them. She tried to loosen her grip on the poor guy, but for some reason, couldn't bring herself to do it. She needed the solid comfort of his strength, needed the way he absorbed her tension, needed the physical contact with him to remind her that he was real while the rest of this was not.

And then it was over. Judge Cabot declared them husband and wife. And announced that Joe could kiss his bride. Oh, God. Another kiss.

Husband and wife. Damn. Words Joe had never expected to hear in conjunction with him. And certainly not in this place or time or with this woman.

You may kiss your bride.

Now why did his heart skip a beat like that? He'd kissed her before. And it had nearly devolved into a public spectacle. He'd hung on to control by a thread. A *hell* of a kiss it had been. Not the sort of lip-lock appropriate to this occasion, in front of his boss, not to mention Judge Cabot, who was one of Eduardo Ferrare's closet cronies.

Joe looked down at Carina and she gazed back at him in trepidation. Lord, she was beautiful. Beyond beautiful. Supermodel-stunning. And she was his wife. For an instant, he allowed himself the fantasy that it was real. And in that moment, his heart swelled with pride—and with something else he damn well didn't care to identify.

He bent his head and kissed his bride. Their lips touched and fireworks ignited in his skull, all but blasting his eyes out of their sockets. Her mouth was soft and warm and so sweet it made his knees weak. His hand crept behind her neck, drawing her closer, and damn if she didn't flow into him like water. Her lips clung to his while her hands looped over his shoulders, leaving her body beneath that naughty little red dress open to the explorations of his roaming hands, which seemed to have taken on a mind of their own. His fingertips slid over her bare back, warm and satin-smooth like the rest of her. He could drown in this woman—

"Ahem." Someone cleared his throat in the distance. "Ahem."

Damn. Cabot. Joe lifted his head but was close enough to hear the little moan of protest in the back of Cari's throat.

"We have some paperwork to fill out. The license to sign."

Relieved to have something to do to take his mind off that kiss, Joe tucked Cari's hand under his arm and followed the judge over to the desk. He signed his name to the documents below Cari's surprisingly neat, almost spare signature. He'd have pegged her as the sort who embellished her name with curlicues and dotted her I's with hearts. He stepped back so Josefina Cabot and Colonel Folly could sign and witness the marriage license—Folly using a false name, of course.

As the judge started to put the freshly signed marriage license in a drawer, Joe asked him, "May I please have a photocopy of that?"

Cabot looked up. "The official copy will be mailed to you in a few weeks."

Joe grinned lopsidedly. "I'm afraid that isn't soon enough. I'm expecting to need a copy of it in about an hour. I'd hate for my wife to be a widow by morning." The words *my wife* felt exceedingly strange on his tongue. But all in all, they didn't taste too bad.

Cabot grunted in rich understanding. He was probably scared spitless that he was a dead man, too. The judge ran the license through his copying machine and handed Joe the warm sheet of paper. "Good luck," Cabot said quietly.

Joe grinned back at him. "Here's hoping luck has nothing to do with it."

"Better you than me," the judge mumbled under his breath.

Josefina Cabot spoke up. "Can I get you newlyweds something to drink? A glass of champagne, perhaps, to toast the occasion?"

"Thank you, ma'am, but I think not," Joe answered politely. "It's late, and we've imposed on you and your husband far too much already. We need to be getting back before Mr. Ferrare worries unnecessarily about where I've taken his daughter."

As he'd anticipated, neither of the Cabots had the slightest interest in causing Eduardo any unnecessary worry. His comment ended all argument about them sticking around to celebrate.

Joe reached for Cari and placed a proprietary hand on her back. Damn, that gentle inward curve felt right under his palm. He guided her from the room and left Colonel Folly to tag along behind them. But as they approached the front door, the colonel stepped around them and hurried down the porch steps to open the car doors.

In a matter of seconds, Joe ushered Cari into the Cadillac sedan, closing the door behind her. With a last wave of thanks to the Cabots, he climbed into his side of the car. The house retreated into the night.

It was done. *He'd married Carina Ferrare.* And now all he had to do was live through the next hour. Thankfully, Folly managed to avoid all the patrols in the area. The man had a sixth sense for that sort of thing.

The closer they got to Ferrare's oceanfront estate, the quieter Carina got. She seemed to shrink into her seat as she pulled inward more and more. Lord knew, Joe wasn't looking forward to facing her father. Eduardo had a legendary temper and was known for killing people first and asking questions later. It would be the toughest moment of this whole op.

It was possible that Cari was just faking the silent desperation rolling off of her, but Joe doubted it. Although, her big sister was an Academy Award-caliber actress when the need arose. He supposed growing up around their father made that a necessary survival skill.

Long before he was ready, Joe saw the massive outline of

Eduardo Ferrare's mansion ahead. The whole place was lit up like a Christmas tree. Crap. His abrupt departure with Carina from the disco had kicked the hornet's nest but good.

Time to face the music.

"Ready?" his boss asked, looking through the rearview mirror at Joe.

Like he was ever going to be ready to face the most vicious bastard in the western hemisphere with nothing but his wits and a marriage license to protect him. Aloud, Joe answered, "As ready as I'm ever gonna be. Let's do it."

Chapter 5

Joe leaned back in the seat as the car turned into the driveway of the Ferrare estate. Time to put on his game face. Charlie Squad's staff psychologist had said Joe needed to appear capable of controlling his new wife's behavior while still being caring and considerate of Cari. However, he also needed to come across as being not bright enough to pose any kind of threat to Ferrare's organization.

He could still hear the wry note in Doc Porter's voice as she suggested he appear to get the job done with mind-blowing sex. The shrink had gone on to comment dryly that being a superb lover by no means translated into being clever at anything else.

Colonel Folly's window slid down and a burly man leaned down to stare in aggressively. "Whaddya want?" the guy snapped.

Folly answered evenly, "Miss Ferrare and her guest would like to go inside."

The furor that erupted was impressive. Cell phones rang, radios crackled and a dozen men converged on the car.

Joe readied himself to fight when the first guard all but came through the window in reaction to Folly's casual announcement, snarling, "Where the hell has she been?"

Folly threw up his hands. "Don't ask me. I'm only the driver."

Cari leaned forward and spoke to the thug hanging in Folly's window. "Rico, I'm tired. Let us in."

Thankfully, the guard waved them through. Four men toting machine guns jogged beside their car as they drove slowly to the house. Joe eyed the escort cautiously. Wow. Eduardo must be apoplectic for these guys to be jumping like this. One of the thugs opened his car door and Joe stepped outside. No surprise, the guy called Rico slammed him against the side of the car and frisked him thoroughly and roughly. Asshole.

Carina was ushered out of the car much more politely, but Joe noticed her guard had a bruising grip on her arm. He caught Cari's wince before she masked it. "Get your hands off my wife," he growled at the guard over the trunk of the car.

That froze them all in their tracks. The looks on the guards' faces would have been hilarious if Joe hadn't been so busy being shocked over how genuinely mad he was that the guy was manhandling Cari. As it was, he had to take a couple of deep breaths and forcibly tell himself to cool it.

He stepped around the car and put a protective arm around her shoulders. "Get my suitcase out of the trunk," Joe snapped to the guard who'd frisked him. "And don't break anything when you search it."

He led Cari toward the house and made a point of not bothering to check over his shoulder to see if the guard had done as he ordered. He was aware, though, that Folly had prudently stayed inside the car.

Freddie and Neddie came charging outside just as he and Cari reached the front steps. The two giants screeched to ungainly halts, scowling ferociously at him. They were dying to get their hands on him, but with his arm securely around Cari, they'd have to wait. Frustration danced on their hamlike features.

"You in big trouble, boy," Freddie growled in broken English.

Joe shrugged. "I brought her home, didn't I?" He might have added that it was more than Freddie had managed to do tonight, except there was no need to antagonize Ferrare's people more than he had to. He was going to have to get along with these goons if he planned to stay alive here for any length of time.

Behind them, Joe heard the car start and then pull away. Thank God the colonel was out of there safely. Oh, and there went his last escape route. He was committed now.

Cari piped up, "Relax, you two. We just wanted to get married in peace, for goodness' sake."

Freddie and Neddie's jaws sagged.

"C'mon," Cari continued brightly, "you can help us break the news to Daddy."

Not surprisingly, the two men declined to follow them into the house. Joe threw Cari a speculative glance. She'd pushed exactly the right button to get rid of her watchdogs. He revised his estimate yet again of just how smart a cookie she was. At a glance, she came across as more concerned with the latest fashions and having a good time than anything serious. Except she kept showing these subtle flashes of calculated brilliance that called her airheaded-party-girl act into serious doubt. Now, if only she could handle her father as smoothly as she'd just played her bodyguards.

"Do you know the layout of the place?" Cari murmured under her breath.

"Most of it," he replied under his breath. They were headed for what he believed was Ferrare's office now, in fact. For years, Charlie Squad had been trying to penetrate that inner sanctum of Ferrare's crime empire. And to think, he was about to stroll into the place itself. Well, maybe walk in gingerly. It was still hard to grasp.

They were stopped at the door to Eduardo's office by a gray-haired man with the roving gaze of a trained security expert. This guy was no beefy flunky. He looked hard and fit. Carried himself as if he were ready for anything to come his way. A legitimate warrior. Probably one of Eduardo's personal bodyguards. Someone to reckon with. *Don't react physically! Shoulders down. Hands relaxed. Don't show recognition of this guy as a threat. Stay loose.* It took concentration, but Joe managed not to fall into a defensive fighting stance in front of the guy.

"Hi, Gunter," Cari said cheerfully. "I…we…need to see my father when he has a moment."

"Given that you are the reason he is busy, I expect that will not be a problem," the man said with a German accent.

Eastern German, if Joe didn't miss his guess. The inflection sounded like it came out of the region toward the Polish border. If this guy had been Stasi trained, he was one tough hombre. The East German secret police had been one of the scariest bunches out there in their day. And Gunter looked old enough to have been one of them.

Gunter put a finger to his ear and spoke quietly into a microphone clipped to his shirt collar. He reached for the door handle but paused with his hand on the knob. In an undertone, he said to Cari in English, "I haven't seen him this worked up in a long time. Not even after Julia—"

Joe completed Gunter's sentence in his own head. Not even after Julia, Eduardo's elder daughter, stole Ferrare's entire cash fortune and handed it over to Charlie Squad. She'd wiped out every liquid asset her father owned. And Eduardo was madder now than he'd been over that? *Whoa.*

Joe might have been in threat mode before, but now his body kicked into imminent threat-of-death mode. Adrenaline ripped through him, and he kept wanting to settle into a fighting stance. *Safe, dammit. Think safe and unassuming!*

The door swung open before them. Through his private

battle, Joe was vaguely aware of Cari reaching out to grab hold of his hand. He gave her fingers a reassuring squeeze and they stepped inside.

The ceiling soared three stories overhead, and floor-to-ceiling glass windows—bulletproof, no doubt—lined the far wall, letting in what would be a spectacular view of the ocean during the day. The room was ultramodern, clean-lined, decorated in pale woods and shades of white.

He caught sight of the large glass-and-steel desk across the room, or rather the man seated at it. Eduardo Ferrare. In the flesh. And suddenly, this giant room seemed barely large enough to contain the man to whom it belonged. The sheer presence of the guy was incredible. Joe's eyes narrowed. God, what he wouldn't give to have a pistol in his hand right now.

While the urge to blow her father away roared through him, Joe tightened his arm around Cari's shoulders protectively. She glanced up at him sideways, a quick look that was equal parts grim, grateful and scared silly.

Joe braced himself for Eduardo to bellow like a bull. But instead, the guy leaned back in his desk chair, waiting and watching as they approached. And with each step closer they took, Cari was getting stiffer and stiffer underneath Joe's arm. Man, she really was terrified of the bastard.

The two of them came to a stop in front of Eduardo's desk. Up close, the guy's eyes were blazing mad. He looked like some sort of lunatic.

But all he said was, "Explain yourself."

The silky, soft slide of the guy's voice made Joe's skin crawl. A shudder passed through Cari, too. But she said lightly, even casually, "You'll never believe what we did this evening, Daddy. Oh, and this is Joe, by the way. Joe, my father, Eduardo Ferrare."

Joe nodded politely, but daddy dearest ignored the introduction, his gaze fixed on his daughter with unblinking, reptilian intensity. Joe half expected the guy's tongue to flick out at any second, tasting the air.

A shaky breath jerked into Cari's lungs, but she continued gaily, "We got married! Isn't that the coolest? We decided to just do it, so we jumped in a car, drove over to Judge Cabot's and had him marry us."

Score one for Carina. Eduardo's jaw sagged and his stunned gaze passed back and forth between Joe and Cari several times. Joe did his absolute damndest to keep his expression happy. Stupid. Patently besotted with his new bride. Helpfully, he pulled out the rumpled copy of their marriage license and handed it across the desk to Ferrare.

Eduardo studied it intently for several seconds.

And then he found his voice. All of it. And expressed his opinion of Joe eloping with his daughter at the top of his lungs. "Do you have any idea who she is—who I am?" he bellowed, exactly as Joe had expected him to.

Time for him to go into his surfer dude act. The idea was for Joe to throw Eduardo off balance by acting too dumb to possibly be a threat to the man. "I sure do," Joe drawled. "This here's the prettiest little lady this side of the Panama Canal, and you're her daddy."

Eduardo stared at him, momentarily silenced and apparently a bit flummoxed by someone who didn't seem to know him by reputation. Joe met Eduardo's scowl head-on and nodded knowingly. "Yo, dude, I told Cari you'd be mad if we up and got married without asking your permission. I mean, there's a right way to do these things. The guy—that's me—asks the old man—"

Eduardo's brows slammed together and Joe corrected hastily "—I mean, the father, for the girl's hand. And then you get married. But, hey, at least I didn't sleep with her first—"

That brought Eduardo up out of his chair. "Whaat?" he bellowed.

Hmm. If he kept up this line of conversation, maybe he could give Eduardo a stroke and kill him that way. The guy looked positively apoplectic. Joe shrugged. "What can I say?

I'm an old-fashioned kind of guy. You marry the girl first and then you boink her."

Eduardo choked. And then spluttered. And then choked some more. Meanwhile, Cari's shoulders shook beneath Joe's arm. He looked down in alarm but was relieved to see her stifling laughter. Even Gunter was coughing conspicuously behind them.

Eduardo came out from behind his desk and stormed over to the two of them. Cari's shoulders stilled abruptly.

Eduardo leaned forward, his face no more than a foot from Joe's. "I should kill you where you stand. Give me one good reason not to, you little prick."

Joe looked Eduardo straight in the eye and answered matter-of-factly, "I love your daughter."

Eduardo studied him with the intensity of a laser. The man's ability to sniff out a lie was legendary. It was part of why he was such a successful criminal boss. Nobody pulled any stunts on him and got away with it.

"Does she love you?" Eduardo snapped back.

Joe shrugged. "Well, yeah. Why else would she have married me?"

Eduardo's gaze narrowed. He could probably think of a bunch of reasons why this arrangement benefited Joe. Like getting ahold of some of the Ferrare millions. Or riding a fast train to the heart of the Ferrare crime empire. Or simply the thrill of sleeping with the daughter of one of the most powerful men in this part of the world. But clearly, Eduardo was perplexed as to what Carina had to gain from marrying Joe. Ferrare spun away and paced a lap of the huge office before coming to stop once more in front of them.

"Let us be clear, young man. The only reason you are alive right now is because of the respect you have shown my daughter over the last several weeks. If, for any reason, I find out you are playing with her affections, I'll feed you to the sharks. In little pieces. Do you understand me?"

A speech worthy of the most devoted father. Too bad the *precious child* the bastard was protecting was his *business* and not the flesh-and-blood woman plastered against Joe's side. "I get ya," Joe mumbled. "Nothin' to worry about on that score, though. I'm not ever going to get tired of her. I mean, what a babe. Your daughter's hot—" He broke off as if realizing he was rushing headlong yet again into dangerous waters. And Cari's shoulders were shaking under his arm again.

Eduardo snapped, "Gunter, escort these two upstairs and see to it they don't wander around and get into trouble."

The German nodded impassively.

Cari turned, dragging Joe with her. Lord knew Joe was more than ready to escape. He let Cari pull him out of Eduardo's office and, as they stepped out into the dim hallway, he let out a relieved breath. They'd done it. They'd gotten past the first interview with Eduardo and were both still alive. Charlie Squad's psychiatrist had made it clear that the greatest danger lay in that first confrontation, when Ferrare was most likely to erupt into sudden violence. She'd been the one to recommend that Joe use Cari as a physical shield between himself and Ferrare. Of course, he'd have put his arm around Cari anyway to support her and protect her.

The two of them followed Gunter upstairs and down the long hallway to the east wing of the house and Cari's room. Joe noticed she became more tense with every step closer the two of them got to her room.

Gunter stopped beside the last door on the left. He opened it and stood there, waiting, while they stepped inside. The room, a study in white lace, was dim, lit only by a small bedside lamp. Joe spun at the clicking sound behind him.

Not a pistol cocking but not much better. Gunter had just locked them in. Carina gave the door a defeated look and turned to step further into the room.

"The bathroom's through that door," she said, pointing.

"Oh, and I see the goon squad is done searching your suitcase. Nice of them to bring it up here since they probably figured they'd be carrying you out of my father's office in a body bag."

Joe scanned the room quickly. Damn. In a single glance, he spotted dozens of places to hide a camera or an electronic bug. He moved swiftly to Cari and put a finger on her lips. He touched her ear and then tilted his head slightly at the walls. Impatiently, she nodded her response, as if it was a given that her room would be bugged.

He moved over to the balcony door and lifted aside the curtain to look out. "Great view," he commented.

"Go on out. You'll like it," Cari replied.

"Show me."

A tiny smile flitted across her drawn features. Poor kid was a nervous wreck. In those first weeks when he'd watched her around the clock, she'd spent a lot of time out on this balcony. He'd gotten the impression she drew strength from the ocean. Maybe it would help her relax now.

He opened the French doors and held them for her. As she brushed past him, he caught a whiff of her perfume. Exotic. Mysterious. It reminded him of a night-blooming orchid in the jungle.

The ocean was restless tonight, and waves pounded the shore, flashing whitecaps catching what little moonlight filtered through a thin layer of clouds.

Cari assumed her usual position, elbows resting on the stone balustrade, gazing out over the backyard and pool to the ocean beyond. Joe leaned on the balcony beside her, their shoulders brushing lightly. "How much privacy do we have out here?"

"Plenty, especially at night. The ocean is too noisy to hear anything over it. There are cameras watching us 24-7, but during the day, there's less privacy because Gunter can read lips."

A lip-reader, huh? Good to know. It was a hell of a note to have the civilian protectee lecturing the commando about security precautions in this little shop of horrors. It said a lot about the life she'd lived. And it said a lot about her that she wasn't all bitter and shriveled up inside.

She continued, "I'd still exercise caution at all times, though. You never know who's watching."

"Or listening," he added dryly.

"Or listening," she agreed.

Silence stretched between them. He gazed out to sea. Ironic that such a wide-open expanse should be so tantalizingly close to this gilded cage.

"Well, we got through the hard part," he commented.

"I don't know about that," she replied.

He looked over at her quickly. "You think we're still in danger?"

"I think every moment we spend in this house is dangerous," she retorted.

He'd love to reassure her, to tell her to be patient and he'd have her out of here as soon as possible. But he dared not. There was no guarantee that a microphone couldn't pick up what they were saying. He settled for mumbling, "Hang in there. He'll come around."

Joe did give in to the temptation to loop his arm around her waist, though. Gently, he drew her slender frame close. She was shivering.

"Cold?" he murmured.

She made a noncommittal noise.

"Let's go inside and get some rest. It has been a big day."

Her mouth twitched. "Indeed. My wedding day."

"*Our* wedding day," he corrected.

Her gaze lifted in surprise to meet his.

"You're not alone anymore, princess. I'm in this with you now. Till the very end."

Their eyes met. And something passed between them. It was more than shared relief that they'd lived through the confrontation with Eduardo. They were in this *together.* And it drew them close in a way that reminded him of how he felt about the rest of the guys in Charlie Squad. Facing danger together bonded a bunch of guys faster and stronger than anything else in the world. *Good Lord, the same damn thing was happening between him and Cari.* Cold alarm coursed through him. This wasn't about bonding; it was about getting her out of here alive!

A momentary but genuine smile touched her lips. "You're a good man, Joe."

He was a lot of things, but good was not one of them. Dangerous, yes. Smart, calculating, good in a fight, maybe. But in his line of work, men didn't have a lot of time for emotions like empathy or compassion—the things that made them truly good or even human. He measured himself by skills mastered or missions accomplished. But good was definitely not part of that equation.

And to prove the point, he said, "C'mon. Let's go to bed. Time to put on a show for your old man. This is our wedding night, after all."

Chapter 6

Cari's head snapped up. Was he actually suggesting they go to bed and have noisy sex for the benefit of the listening devices in her room? The idea of having noisy sex with Joe had been on her mind for most of the last few weeks, but when he put it that way, he could forget it!

His mouth tilted into a crooked grin. She stopped. Frowned. That almost looked like an apology. And then it hit her. This was more of the clueless but love-struck routine he'd pulled on her father downstairs. Knowing what a bright, sophisticated guy he actually was, she'd been shocked to the point of laughter when he'd done it the first time.

Joe took her hand to lead her inside. To her bed.

Oh, God. Her bed. She balked against the tug of his hand before she even reached the French doors.

He looked over at her with concern and mumbled, "There are cameras out here. Even if it is dark, they can still see some of what we're doing. You need to look a little more willing to go to bed with me. I won't pull anything with you, I swear."

Her first impulse was to do a little swearing herself in response to that promise. But that wasn't the point. She was scared to death of her bed. Not of being in it with Joe, but of the bed itself.

And he wanted her to climb into it. To lie where Tony had lain, where his blood had soaked her clothes and skin.... Horror bubbled through her.

"Come inside, princess. Please," he coaxed her under his breath.

Taking a deep breath, she bolstered her courage and stepped through the door. She could do this. Her freedom— heck, maybe her life—depended on it. It was just a stupid phobia. She could overcome it. She was stronger than her fear.

Joe closed the French doors behind her, bathing the room in darkness. And the memory of that devastating spill of blood flooded Cari's mind's eye, creeping across the floor to reach out and grab her. She barely suppressed an urge to jump up on the couch like a woman on a chair, hiding from a mouse.

She made out Joe's frown. Questions raged in his eyes, but he dared not voice them aloud for fear of the bugs that he rightly guessed peppered this room.

"Come to the bathroom with me," she announced. He stared at her in surprise. "I need help with my zipper. It's stuck and we'll be able to see it better in there."

"Uh, okay," he mumbled.

She turned the water on full blast in both of the sinks as soon as he closed the door behind them. She swallowed her pride and stepped close to him. She leaned forward reluctantly and confessed in a whisper, "I'm afraid of my bed. I haven't slept in it since..." Her voice cracked.

"Ahh." Enlightenment dawned in his eyes. And that looked like relief, too. "So it's not me you're afraid of?"

She blinked, startled. "Of course not!"

He exhaled hard. "Thank God. I was trying to figure out what I'd done to freak you out so bad."

Her cheeks heated up. "You're fine. It's just the idea of lying where all that blood was..."

He drew her into a hug. "Aww, baby, I understand. You don't have to explain. You're authorized to freak out over that."

She collapsed in relief against his shoulder. "I feel like such a wimp."

"That kind of a shock has broken strong men. You're no wimp, Cari."

She smiled against the warmth of his silk shirt. "You don't hate me?" she asked in a small voice.

His chest rumbled with a chuckle. "Of course not."

"So maybe you'd kiss me again?"

He went rigid beneath her. Cleared his throat. "You think that's a good idea?" he asked dubiously.

She buried her face in his neck rather than look up at him as she muttered, "I happen to think it's a great idea. But if you don't want to, I get the picture. I won't bug you again..."

A finger hooked under her chin, nudging her face up. "I happen to think it's an outstanding idea, too."

His smile positively incinerated her. And then his mouth swooped down, capturing hers with just enough aggression to make it crystal clear exactly how good an idea he thought it was. Somewhere in the background, she heard the water go off and the bathroom door open, but she didn't care.

His lips were warm and smooth, rubbing across hers with finesse. Enough of the gentleman, already! She didn't want finesse—she wanted the inferno from the nightclub.

She clenched her fists in the fine silk of his shirt and tugged him closer. "I want a real kiss, dammit!"

He laughed, deep in his throat. And complied. Oh, God, did he comply. His whole body wrapped around her, bending her backward beneath him, the heavy thickness of him pressing against her belly, his arms impossibly strong as they supported her. This was no refined gentleman, dipping his tongue in and out of her mouth in the rhythm of wet, hot sex. This was an alpha male, powerful and in control.

Oh, how she liked that. She got so sick of college boys kissing her like they were scared to death her father was going to burst in at any second and break them in half. And then there were the types that styled themselves great lovers and got so caught up in being suave they forgot to enjoy it. And, of course, she couldn't forget the selfish jerks who treated her as if she was little more than a life-size plastic doll.

Joe's hands stabbed into her hair, pulling her head back, opening her to him as he leaned down, kissing and licking and sucking his way down the column of her neck.

"You taste so good," he rasped. "I can't get enough of you."

She tugged on his hair, pulling his mouth back up to hers. "So do you," she mumbled against his mouth. "You taste like coffee with cream and a shot of whiskey."

"Baby, you taste like great sex," he growled back.

One of his hands slid up her naked thigh to her hip, pushing her flimsy skirt aside and tracing the route of her thong downward toward her throbbing center. Her thighs went soft and she moaned as she took a step, spreading her feet shoulder width apart to allow him better access.

His hand closed over her wet heat and she all but flung herself at him as lust roared through her. This man would make love to her like an adult. No adolescent fumbling around. No self-centered performances that treated her like a blowup doll. This man would take them both to the stars and back.

He stepped backward and she followed, chasing his body heat and addictive mouth shamelessly. He laughed as his thighs bumped into something. Then he grabbed her with both arms and fell backward. She started as they bounced onto the bed.

And she froze.

"You're not lying on the bed, baby," he murmured. "You're lying on me. Focus on my mouth."

And then his hands were on either side of her face, drawing

her down, down into a sweet void where nothing existed but his body cushioning hers, his arms holding her close, his mouth sliding across hers, sipping at her like a fine brandy.

She moaned her pleasure shamelessly.

And he laughed in return, a sound of exultation. Of possession. Of soul-deep pleasure. "Come here, princess. I want more of you."

"I don't think there's another inch of me that can get into more contact with you than it already is," she protested.

His hips rolled ever so slightly against hers. *Oh.*

"Well, there is that," she laughed.

He rolled over, pinning her for a moment against the mattress. And before she could finish the tensing that rippled across her shoulders, he bounded to his feet, pulling her with him.

"More," she demanded, stalking him like a tigress.

"Patience, love," he murmured. "We've got all night."

Oh, my. She liked the sound of that.

"Stay right here. I have to get something."

She looked around. "Here" was right in front of the French doors, all the way across the room from her bed. How had they gotten over here? Damn, that man did crazy things to her head. She shouldn't be having these feelings for him. But for crying out loud, the man kissed like a god.

And then there was a giant heave on the other side of the room. Her entire bed moved, the covers went flying and the top mattress slid sideways. What in the world?

She watched, bemused, as Joe grabbed an armload of blankets and pillows and carried them over to where she stood. He dumped them on the floor at her feet.

He murmured in a low voice that barely carried to where she stood only a foot away, "For what it's worth, that's a new mattress. It's not the same one as—well, the same one. There's no way to remove a bloodstain like that from a mattress, and yours is pristine."

She all but sobbed in relief at that revelation.

Joe went back to the bed and dragged the heavy queen-size mattress across to her. He dropped it with a heavy whump to the floor.

A voice called through the hallway door, "Everything all right in there?"

Joe glared over his shoulder and called out loudly, "It's our wedding night, for God's sake. We're not exactly sleeping in here, you moron!"

Cari slapped a hand over her mouth and burst into giggles.

Grinning and rolling his eyes, Joe positioned the mattress in front of the French doors and efficiently remade the bed. Then, with a flourish, he presented her with the make-shift bed.

That was possibly the sweetest thing anyone had ever done for her. She smiled up shyly at his image swimming in her tears, then whirled and headed for the dresser in the corner. She dug around, found what she was looking for and headed for the bathroom.

"I'll be right out," she called over her shoulder.

She changed quickly into a filmy, white negligee she'd ordered from Paris a few months back. It was made of silk so fine it was nearly transparent, and it weighed hardly more than a magician's handkerchief. She'd never worn it before. She hadn't been consciously saving it for a special occasion, especially since lately her love life was more monkish than not. But as she slipped it over her head and let it float down around her naked body, she had to wonder if maybe she'd known subconsciously that this night and this man were about to come into her life.

The silk fabric flowed like a warm breeze over her skin. She adjusted the tiny little rosettes of pastel ribbons that held it up at her shoulder and brushed her hair quickly. When she stepped back into the bedroom, the French doors stood wide open, letting in a cool breeze and the rhythmic pounding of the surf.

Joe was already in their bed, the covers pulled up to his waist. His chest was bare. Oh, Lord. Was he naked under there?

Her heart beat wildly at the idea. As she walked toward him, she pictured what he must look like under the sheet, and the image stole her breath away. And then she noticed the way his gaze was roaming up and down her body, absolutely inhaling the sight of her, and what little breath she had left escaped in a whoosh.

He held up the covers for her in silent invitation. And the world disappeared once more, narrowing down to this man and this moment, this dark cavern of linen and flesh, safety and—

She sank down to her knees and eased into the bed beside him. It was warm from his body heat. She was disappointed to discover he was wearing a pair of shorts, but in the next instant, he drew her against that lovely chest and everything else melted from her mind.

It all crowded in on her again, everything she'd ever wanted and more. A flesh-and-blood man holding her, protecting her, *loving* her. *Hello, reality check. Total stranger only here to rescue her. Not happily-ever-after guy.* But darned if he didn't feel like that guy as he held her close. Gradually, the dream retreated—not a lot, but enough to breathe.

He propped himself up on an elbow and gazed down at her, his body perfectly still but his eyes ablaze. "You are, without a doubt, the most stunning woman I've ever laid eyes on," he murmured.

She reached up to smooth her fingers along his jaw. "You're not so hard on the eyes yourself, Mr. Smith."

"Ah, Cari, Cari. What am I going to do with you?" he murmured.

Her lips curved into a sultry smile. "Do you want me to suggest a few answers to that question?" she replied.

"No. Definitely not," he answered almost sharply. He rolled onto his back beside her, an arm flung over his face. "Don't tempt me," he mumbled from under his elbow.

She grinned up at the ceiling. Tempting, was she? She could live with that. A cool breeze whispered across her skin and she drew the covers up. Joe's hand was there immediately, tucking the blankets in around her shoulders.

He murmured, "If you get cold, let me know and I'll close the doors. I thought you might like to hear the ocean, though. It always helps me sleep."

She replied, "If I get cold, I'll snuggle with you. I can feel your body heat all the way over here."

A pause. A clearing of the throat. "That works, too."

She smiled into the darkness. And fell asleep with a smile still on her lips.

But the next morning, along with the sun came the reality check she'd been incapable of last night. She looked over at Joe and saw a mature man lying beside her. He was *so* out of her league. Who was she trying to kid?

Besides, she hardly knew him. She had no idea what his agenda was. Bitter experience had taught her that he'd get over his infatuation with her soon enough and emotionally abandon her. She'd read books about men who stayed loyal to the women they loved, but she'd bloody well never seen any of them.

Her father's men who actually bothered to engage in relationships went through women like shoes. They put them on, wore them out, and then discarded them. According to Julia, by the time her father had gotten around to killing her mother, all Inez had felt for her husband was terror, and all he'd felt for her was contempt. As a kid herself, her father's attention had come and gone as his career and time allowed.

Love wasn't a rock; it was water. It ebbed and flowed, flooded and dried up, depending on the landscape and the capricious weather of life. It certainly wasn't something to count on.

Joe would get her out of here, and then he'd get on with his regularly scheduled life. If she let him, he'd love her and leave her like everyone else did.

She sighed. Sure he kissed amazingly well, but was it

worth getting her heart broken over? Probably not. As hot to trot as he made her feel, lust was a purely transient thing. It would pass. It always did.

"Hey, princess," Joe murmured beside her.

She rolled onto her side. His hair was tousled and a hint of whiskers shadowed his jaw. In the daylight, his bare chest was a sight to behold, wrapped in hard muscles, bronze flesh, and a sprinkling of dark hair. Okay, so in the meantime, he was a gorgeous hunk to wake up to.

"Hey," she managed to mumble back past an inexplicable constriction in her throat. If only he were real. She could fall for him like a ton of bricks.

"Sleep well?"

The question startled her. Or, rather, the answer did. For once, her dreams hadn't been inhabited by images of dead bodies and blood. Instead, they'd been filled with this man. It was perhaps the best night's sleep she'd had in her bedroom since Tony's murder.

"I actually slept great," she replied. "You?"

He smiled and shrugged, a breathtaking display of bunching muscle. "I don't need to sleep much. I spent most of the night watching over you."

Watching over her? The thought sent her stomach spinning and a warm feeling fluttering through her. Safety. That was the feeling of being *safe* racing through her. Certainly a novel sensation in her father's home.

"Ready to go face the lion?" she asked.

Joe rolled onto his back and stared up at the deep-blue sky overhead. "I dunno. I see him as more of a shark than a lion. Maybe it's the gray color of his hair."

She added dryly, "Or maybe it's the way he always seems to be testing the waters for the smell of blood."

Joe nodded. "Good point."

He got up and she was surprised when he dragged a sheet with him, holding it around his lower body like he was naked.

But then he stepped outside onto the balcony and called "Good morning" down to someone out by the pool.

Gunter's curt voice floated back up. He didn't sound too happy. But then, he was grumpy most of the time, anyway.

Joe stepped inside, grinning, and closed the door behind him.

"What was that all about?" she asked.

"Gunter was hiding in the bushes down there and was annoyed that I spotted him."

"He was actually hiding in the bushes?"

"Yup. Right in among those oleanders that head over toward your father's office."

Cari grinned. "He's actually a really nice guy if you give him half a chance."

"Gunter?" Joe retorted. "The *Terminator?* Nice?"

Her grin widened. "Relative to the other guards around here, he's a veritable saint."

Joe shook his head and suggested, "Why don't you go take a nice, hot shower. You'll feel better."

She felt just fine, thank you very much. Except he was giving her a significant look and even jerked his head ever so slightly in the direction of the bathroom.

"Come with me?" she purred.

His eyebrows shot up. "I beg your pardon?"

She laughed. "We *are* married. It is allowed, you know."

"Uh, right," he mumbled. "Are you sure?"

"Positive," she said firmly.

Joe frowned. Clearly, Cari had something in mind other than a shower. But what it was, he had no idea. She was in a strange mood this morning. Last night, she'd been all over him. And in all fairness, he'd been all over her. It had taken all of his willpower not to pick up where they'd left off once she climbed into bed.

Two things he was sure of, though. One was that her room was under surveillance, and the other was that they'd had an avid audience of guards at the other end of those bugs and cameras. At least, his and Cari's romp on the bed had probably satisfied the bastards that the two of them were really married.

And then a disturbing thought occurred to him. Maybe last night had been just another piece of Academy Award-caliber acting for her. He wouldn't put it past her to be capable of it or to have done it. So where did that leave him?

Fine. He'd go into the damned bathroom with her and see what she wanted. But disquiet filled him at the idea of once again closing himself in that little room with her. And taking a shower with Carina Ferrare *certainly* wasn't part of the game plan. It had been hard enough to look at her in that transparent wisp of cloth she called a nightgown without leaping all over her, not to mention lying beside her in it all night long. Sleep had been entirely out of the question. His nerves were stretched plenty thin right now. The thought of warm water running all over that luscious, naked body was almost more than his formidable self-control could contemplate. He wasn't about to make a fool of himself again.

"C'mon," she beckoned with a smile that was both ladylike and a siren song—a combination he'd never been able to resist. And then it hit him. The minx was playing him! As smoothly as she'd played Freddie and Neddie yesterday, and as smoothly as she'd played her father. Damn, the woman was a barracuda when it came to manipulating men. She already had his number and they barely knew each other!

In minor shock, he followed her to the bathroom. Twice more, she looked over her shoulder, smiling encouragingly at him. He stepped into the bathroom cautiously, not sure where to point his gaze. When did the walls close in and turn this place into a shoe box, anyway? Heaven help him if she stripped and climbed into the shower in front of him. But thankfully, she only turned on the jets and stood back to wait. Perplexed, he leaned against the counter, his arms crossed in self-defense against what she was planning to do to him.

Clouds of white mist rolled out of the shower enclosure—

it must be a steam shower—and in a few moments, the mirrors fogged up. And then Cari did something strange. She relaxed. Truly, completely relaxed for the first time since she'd set foot in this house last night.

She leaned close and murmured, "This room is free of bugs and cameras. I meant to mention it last night, but we got…distracted."

"How can you be sure?" he asked skeptically.

"Because I've wired a jamming system into the electrical outlets, and I've done a thorough check for cameras. Plus, the steam will fog up any camera lens in here."

"You've wired a jamming system?" he repeated in disbelief. "How in the hell did you learn how to do that?"

"I have a degree in electrical engineering from the University of Miami."

He stared at her, openmouthed. How in the bloody hell had their research on the Ferrare clan missed that one? "You're kidding," he finally managed to blurt out.

She grinned sheepishly. "While everyone thought I was sleeping off the wild nights in South Beach, I went to college during the days. I specialized in microelectronics. It wasn't hard to build a transmitter to interfere with the equipment my father uses in the house."

"When's the last time you checked to make sure there hasn't been a frequency or baud-rate change in the transmissions?"

"Two days ago," she replied easily. "And most of the stuff around here isn't digital. Straight EM transmissions work better with all the steel in the walls."

Okay, then. Maybe she really was an engineer. Holy cow.

She continued. "I check my father's equipment about twice a week in this room. I don't mess with the stuff in my bedroom because that would draw too much suspicion. Although, I have been gradually changing where the cameras are pointed. I've got them mostly pointed away from my bed—and the French doors to the balcony—now."

There were cameras pointed at her bed? Talk about an invasion of privacy! There was such a thing as being security-conscious, and then there was plain being a sick bastard. Joe's jaw tightened into a knot of tension. But Cari continued, apparently not noticing the sudden fury rolling off him.

"In here, it's plausible that the steam, and my blow-dryer and my other electric appliances could mess up the signals. So I went ahead and jammed them. I needed someplace for a little privacy."

So that explained the wide array of hot rollers, hair-straightening irons, hair-curling irons, electric toothbrushes and the like cluttering her counter. He nodded, impressed as hell.

She went on, "Anytime we need to talk, we can come in here and turn on the shower. And in case you want to check out the system…" She moved over to one of the electrical outlets by the sink and popped out the whole plug face.

Except it was damned hard to concentrate with her leaning over the counter like that, her perfect tush jutting out and the fine silk of her gown clinging to the curve of her hips.

Over her shoulder, she explained, "I installed fake screws with springs behind them so it's easy and fast to get in behind these and adjust my gear. I did this on my summer break a few years ago—once I knew how—so the equipment might not be totally modern. But it gets the job done."

She turned around, showing him a full-blown circuit board wired behind the plug, a red light blinking on its surface. But his eyes strayed to the delicious curve of her breast, the faint, rosy shadow of a nipple beneath the silk.

She pointed down at the little red light with the tip of her French-manicured fingernail. "That means the jamming system is active. You deactivate it by flipping this toggle here." She pointed to a tiny black switch. "Sometimes when I come in just to put on makeup, I turn off the system. I figure if no signal ever gets out of here, someone will get suspicious. But I've got Gunter convinced this is just a bad reception area."

"Sweet setup," he commented warmly, adding, "Well, aren't you just a bundle of surprises?"

The grin she threw him was positively impish. "I like to keep my men off balance."

No kidding. She turned to replace the plug in the wall and the side of her breast was outlined clearly by a patch of damp silk. The way her negligee kept going completely see-through as it clung to various parts of her anatomy had Joe way beyond off balance. He was positively reeling. He had to get out of there before he embarrassed them both.

He mumbled, "Uh, why don't you take a shower for real? I've got a couple of things I need to do in the bedroom and there's no reason to risk you getting caught, too."

She frowned and opened her mouth, but he cut her off gently. "Don't ask. Just trust me, okay?"

She nodded doubtfully. "Okay. But be careful. The guards are going to be watching your every move."

"Thanks for the advice," he muttered.

He spun and bolted from the bathroom, closing the door between them fast. He leaned, literally panting, against the wall to catch his breath and his equilibrium. Damn, that woman was lethal! Sexy as hell and not afraid to use it.

He shook his head to clear it. *Get your act together.* He looked around the bedroom. She said the cameras had been pointed at the bed and now weren't. That narrowed down where the suckers could be hidden. Under the guise of putting the bed back together, he scoped out possible hiding places. He identified three possible spots to conceal a camera.

He wandered around her room, examining little trinkets and doodads, and approached the likeliest spot. Bingo. A small black lens aperture poked out of a vase sitting on a bookshelf in the corner. The bastards. The amount of ire that little round eye provoked in him border-lined on shocking. But then, he was starting to get used to these bursts of violently protective feelings toward Carina.

Time to make a statement to his new father-in-law. He picked up the marble horse statuette at the other end of the bookshelf and smashed the vase. Pieces of porcelain flew in every direction.

He grabbed the camera lying in the wreckage and yanked its wires free from where they disappeared into the shelf where the vase had sat. He jammed the black box into his pocket.

A sudden motion behind him made him whirl around defensively. Cari. Rushing out of the bathroom, a towel clutched in front of her naked body. *God Almighty, look at all those miles of legs.*

"Are you all right?" she gasped. And then she took in the smashed vase behind him and her eyes widened in shock. She opened her mouth, but he waved her to silence.

"Go back and finish your shower, princess. Everything's fine out here," he said clearly.

Looking stunned, she turned, absently clutching the towel ends behind her and gifting him with a view of the slender length of her back and more of those sleek thoroughbred legs of hers. Only one coherent thought formed in his head and he voiced it aloud. "Nice tan."

Cari jerked, looking over her shoulder in surprise. She stared at him for a moment and then burst out laughing. She disappeared into the bathroom.

Cari stepped back into her shower. Nice tan, indeed. The man was incorrigible. His glib tongue was going to get him in trouble as surely as she was standing here. She tipped her head back and hot water sluiced over her face in a cleansing rush. Her hair pulled, heavy and wet at her neck, like the steady tug of Joe at her emotions. His intelligence and compassion filled her mind, and the way his dark eyes lit when they looked at her filled her heart.

Back off, girlfriend. He was a strict look-but-don't-touch proposition. Damn! Okay, maybe a look-but-don't-fall-head-over-heels proposition!

It was almost difficult to remember what a force to be reckoned with Eduardo was because Joe so commanded all of her attention. But she had to be careful. Eduardo was a cobra. You never turned your back on him or he'd strike to kill in a heartbeat.

And then a new thought sent an icy chill rippling through her. If she developed real feelings for Joe, she'd be handing a lethal weapon to her father. Eduardo would jump all over that weakness the second he saw it. Not only would he use it to manipulate her, but caring about Joe would put him at just that much more risk of being killed. The lesson of Tony's death was not lost on her. Oh, no. Not by a long shot. She could let herself be in *lust* with Joe, but never in *love* with him.

Joe. Abrupt awareness of time passing made her lurch. Knowing him, he was already downstairs at breakfast with her father, saying something outrageous and all but daring Eduardo to kill him. She hustled out of the shower and dried off hastily. Eduardo was as grumpy as a bear in the morning and wouldn't take kindly to Joe's antics.

She rushed out into the bedroom, wrapped in a towel, and stopped cold as Joe turned around. He was standing in the corner, his back plastered against the juncture of the walls, apparently studying her room for more cameras. She'd only found two cameras in all her searches. She watched as he sidled along the sidewall toward the pale-pink Renoir sketch of a little girl hanging in its gilded frame.

"There's a motion alarm on that," she warned, nodding significantly in the direction of the painting.

Joe nodded his understanding. "I'm not planning on stealing it," he remarked aloud. He reached up and took the painting down and, sure enough, an ear-splitting alarm made her slap her hands over her ears. But it didn't prevent her from seeing Joe reach up and tear the camera off the back of the painting and its wires out of the wall. The device was wired right into the spotlight that shone down on the painting.

"Get dressed," Joe ordered her shortly over the din of the alarm. "It's time to go downstairs and have a little talk with your father."

But she continued to stand there and watch in dismay as he snatched a towel out of the bathroom and wrapped it around the jumble of wires and cameras. A pounding noise added to the chaos and it took her a second to realize it was a fist slamming against her door. Joe rehung the Renoir and headed for the door, jerking his head sharply in the direction of her closet. Right. Clothes. She hustled off toward her dressing area.

As she crossed the open space, she felt Joe's gaze on her as surely as if he'd reached out and touched the warmth between her shoulder blades with his fingertips. A purely sexual thrill whispered across her skin.

Ducking into her closet, she stopped just inside the door to catch her breath and heard Joe talking to someone outside.

"What the hell's that noise?" he complained to Gunter. "Man. I just kissed Cari and that thing went nuts. You got some sort of sex alarm installed in here, or what?"

Cari giggled and pushed away from the wall. Clothes. She needed to get some clothes on. She hustled into a tennis skirt and matching top while Gunter explained curtly that there was a motion sensor on the priceless painting.

Joe harrumphed. "You got any more of those damned things in here? I mean, we're likely to make a whole lot of stuff shake, rattle and roll, if you get my meaning…."

She grinned as she tied her shoes. She'd better go rescue the poor German from her irrepressible spouse.

"Thanks for turning that thing off, Gunter," she said as she stepped into the room.

Both men turned to look at her, one in exasperation and the other in frank male appreciation.

Joe commented to the older man, "Is she a knockout, or what?"

Gunter blinked in surprise, and his features softened. "Miss Ferrare is quite beautiful, yes."

"Why Gunter! Thank you!" she exclaimed.

Joe held out his arm to her and she grasped his forearm, looping her fingers around rock-solid muscles that were surprisingly tense. She noticed the rolled towel tucked under his other arm. Damn. What outrageous stunt did he have up his sleeve now? He escorted her to the doorway and paused beside Gunter.

All kidding erased from his voice, Joe spoke to Gunter in deadly earnest. "The name's Mrs. Smith now. Don't forget it."

On that note, he moved gracefully past the stunned German and hauled her down the hall while she stumbled in shock.

"Are you nuts?" she murmured under her breath. "You practically threatened Gunter!"

Joe murmured back, "There's no 'practically' about it, princess. That was flat-out meant as a threat."

"I'll say it again. Are you nuts?"

He smiled down at her gently. "Trust me, baby. I know what I'm doing. I know guys like him and I know what it takes to establish respect with them."

She frowned up at him. She knew so very little about him. If, indeed, he was a member of Charlie Squad, he certainly did know about men like Gunter. He *was* a man like Gunter.

But then Joe derailed her train of thought completely by announcing, "C'mon. I need to teach your old man a little respect, next."

Oh, God. What was he going to do now?

Chapter 7

Carina eyed Joe apprehensively. "What are you planning to do?" she asked cautiously. "Do I need to talk you out of it?"

Although Joe smiled casually, there was a distinctly icy glint in his eyes. Loudly and, no doubt, for Gunter's benefit behind them, he announced, "C'mon, babe. I'm hungry."

Rico, the thug from Colonel Folly's car window last night, was lounging against the wall at the end of the hallway leading to her suite, chewing a toothpick. When they approached him, he pushed vertical without comment and led the way downstairs to a large dining room.

A wooden table stretched the length of the room, a dozen tall, ornate chairs in the shape of narrow thrones arranged around it. A wrought-iron chandelier and hand-painted tiles around the walls lent the room a powerfully Spanish feel. Her mother had decorated this space, and Cari had always loved its calm, elegant feel. She liked to imagine that her mother had been as calm and elegant.

Her father already sat at the head of the table, reading a newspaper and sipping a cup of coffee. He didn't look up as Joe held her chair at Eduardo's left and then took a seat beside her. She winced as Joe unobtrusively slid the rolled towel underneath his chair.

She ate in silence and was abjectly grateful when Joe followed suit and didn't pop out with any outrageous comments directed at her father.

Throughout the meal, Eduardo, his lawyer, Sevi Gallegos, and Gunter talked about the business climate in South America, which was a relief to Cari. She doubted Joe would, in dumb gigolo mode, dive into that particular conversation. All in all, it wasn't a bad first meal with her father and the unpredictable American at the same table.

But she'd let down her guard too soon. As a maid cleared away their dishes, Joe leaned down under his chair and grabbed the towel. *Oh, God.* She caught herself looking around surreptitiously for someplace to take cover if this thing exploded into a firefight.

Joe stepped toward Eduardo and Rico tensed, leaping to Eduardo's side. But Joe glided forward so fast that he brushed right past Rico before the guy could actually block him. Joe moved so fluidly and so quickly that he didn't look like he'd done anything extraordinary. Rico stared, apparently confounded as to how Joe had just gotten past him to Eduardo's side.

She watched in sick apprehension as Joe raised the towel high in the air and let go of all but the end of it. It unrolled rapidly and the jumble of wires and cameras fell into his free hand.

He laid the handful of electronics beside her father's plate and said casually, "Obviously, there wasn't time last night to remove these before we took occupancy of our room. I took the liberty of doing it for your people."

Eduardo looked at Joe sharply. Reassessing. Joe had just shown himself to be a much brighter cookie than Eduardo had initially given him credit for.

But then Joe shrugged and grinned. "I mean, if you're planning to put us on the Internet doing the horizontal mamba—you know, to make a little extra cash on the side—you should've asked. I mean, you gotta have the right moves, play to the cameras, stuff like that."

Eduardo choked on his coffee and only narrowly avoided spewing it all over his shirt. Cari gaped. If she didn't know better, she'd say Joe had timed that remark to coincide exactly with the moment when her father had taken that big mouthful of coffee. Her mouth snapped shut. She didn't dare smile.

"C'mon, baby. Let's go practice some moves in case your old man—uhh, daddy—decides to cash in on us."

Now it was her turn to choke. She sputtered, and he pounded her good-naturedly on the back.

Rico leered at Joe. "Give it your best shot, buddy. You still never know when you'll be on camera."

Joe turned slowly. Real slowly. Took a leisurely step forward until he stood right in front of the bodyguard. And then something funny happened. Joe didn't move a muscle, but it was almost as if he grew by a couple of inches. The room went dead silent. This bunch knew a challenge when they saw one.

Joe practically whispered, "You put one second of Cari and me, or Cari, or even her bedroom on film, and I'll break you in half. Carina's my *wife*. And you will treat her with utmost respect at all times."

He didn't have to utter the "or else" hanging in the air. It was almost louder for his not having said it. Rico obviously couldn't decide whether to puff up in threat response or yield the field for now and just walk away.

In consequence, he ended up just staring openmouthed at Joe's back as he turned casually toward her, returned to his normal size and said, "On second thought, let's go for a swim, princess. I feel a sudden need to clean up."

Amazed that he'd walked away from that confrontation

alive, Cari followed Joe outside to the crystalline pool gleaming under the late-morning sun. The ocean was vivid turquoise today, the beach a strip of pale gold. The lawn was emerald, the pool deck stark white and the pool itself nearly as blue as the sea. The quality of the light was extraordinary, glowing with an almost surreal intensity. Or maybe it was the exhilaration of having witnessed someone, anyone, stand up to one of her father's meanest thugs. Ah, Joe was good for her soul.

She left him in a chaise lounge by the pool and excused herself to head upstairs and change into a bikini. Joe, with outstanding foresight, had worn a pair of baggy swim shorts down to breakfast.

She dug out the skimpiest Rio thong bikini she owned, looked at it for a second, and shocked herself by putting it back in the drawer. Instead, she pulled out a white one-piece suit that was a hundred times more conservative and, truth be told, a great deal more complimentary to her figure and her golden tan. Sometimes a girl just wanted to look her best. Today was one of those days. Besides, her father would croak if she wore something classy for once. Maybe he'd rightly credit Joe for the change.

She took a critical look at herself in the full-length mirror in her closet. Generally in the past, she'd thought of her extraordinary looks as merely one more weapon to wield in her private war against her father. But today...today they meant more. They were a gift. Something she could bestow on Joe to thank him for risking his life for her. She reached for the bottle of sunblock on the shelf beside her floppy sun hats and array of sunglasses. And smiled. She tossed the bottle into a canvas bag, along with a book and a beach towel.

When she stepped outside through the doors in the dining room, Joe lifted his head lazily to glance at her. And he froze, his head several inches off the lounge chair. "Kowabunga," he exclaimed.

Warmed all over by that ridiculous little greeting, she put on her best high-fashion catwalk and sashayed over to him, gifting him with a full display of her long legs and curving body.

"Could you put some lotion on me, darling?" she purred, holding out the bottle of sunblock and sinking down into his chaise.

That wiped the smirk off his face fast. "Uh, sure," he mumbled, glancing over at Gunter, who made no secret of watching them from a chair in the shade of the covered porch in front of the TV room.

And then Joe's hands touched her and all else fled before the onslaught of images and sensations that rolled over her. The smooth glide of his warm palms down the curve of her spine provoked blatantly sexual thoughts. And despite the heat of the sun baking her, a chill shivered across her skin, nearly orgasmic in the shuddering shower of tingles shooting through her. How was it that lust and worship could be one and the same? Sin and absolution as one?

No matter how chaste the hand gliding up the back of her thigh, she wished for it to slide off the slope of her thigh and between her legs, to plunge into her darkest, most secret places and stroke them to a screaming release. She ached to let her legs fall open, to invite him to do it. It was unnatural, nearly criminal, to keep her knees pressed tightly together against her rampant lust, her lips pressed shut against a moan of welcome, an invitation of longing.

His fingertips trailed down her arms toward her hands and she marveled at the impromptu anatomy lesson of the nervous system. Who would have guessed that every single inch of the underside of her arm was peppered with sensitive nerve endings that shimmered and sparkled under the gentlest of caresses?

And then the lesson changed. His hands grasped her shoulders, rolling the muscles of her neck and upper back under the heels of his hands, and her moans of need became groans of pleasure escaping against her will to mingle with the pounding rhythm of the ocean nearby.

His hands lifted away from her and she nearly cried aloud at the sudden void left behind. His weight shifted on the chaise beside her and she nearly jumped out of her skin as his hands settled on her right calf. He massaged his way down the limb, circling her ankle and digging his thumbs into exactly the right spot in the arch of her foot to send melting pleasure rushing through her.

Her other foot got the same treatment, and not a solid bone remained anywhere in her body. She was a formless mass of heat and desire, molded helplessly like melting cookie dough to the lounge supporting her. The sun radiated its own brand of heat, twining in and around the moment like a molten ribbon of gold, binding it irrevocably into her memory. She whimpered faintly. Joe's hands stilled on her skin.

Cari turned her head to look at him and caught a flash of movement over his shoulder. And fear speared through everything else she was feeling to pierce her heart like an arrow of ice. "Don't stop," she mumbled. "My father's watching."

Without moving his lips, Joe murmured, "Where is he?"

"In his office."

Joe reached for the bottle of sunblock and tipped more of the lotion into his palm. His hands began their smooth slide across her skin once more. "Let him watch."

Her eyelids drifted closed in spite of themselves. On a long exhalation, she placed her trust in Joe and let him worry about her father for the moment. She simply enjoyed, savoring the warmth of the sun and Joe's magic hands on her body.

A blissful eternity later, his hands lifted off her flesh and she cracked open one eyelid enough to see him stretch out on the chaise beside her, his face turned up to the sun and his eyes closed.

"Are the office windows bulletproof?" Joe mumbled, so low that Cari could barely hear him.

"Yeah," she replied. "Worried about him shooting you?"

"Nah. Was thinking about shooting him. It would make our exit from here a whole lot easier."

She jolted. Her eyes flew open and she stared at Joe in shock. "You're serious?"

Joe's eyes opened lazily and a single eyebrow arched at her. He didn't bother to answer her question. He didn't need to. She saw the answer in his eyes. It wasn't a *threat* of death; it was a solemn *promise* of it. Hatred so thick she could barely breathe past it rolled off of Joe.

And then it was gone. As quickly as it had flashed out of him, the emotion was erased. But it left her shaken. Even more frightened because of the tremendous control he had over it.

"What?" Joe murmured. "What's that look on your face?"

She answered, stiff-lipped, aware that Gunter was still watching and could read her words if she wasn't careful. "Who are you?"

Joe's mouth turned up in a smile, but his words, uttered past clenched teeth, were all but snarled. "I'm the guy who's going to set you free."

With her body still singing its need for him, it was hard to ignore the siren call of her desire, hard to reconcile the cold knot in her stomach with the heat zinging across her skin. What was wrong with her? She desperately wanted to get away from her father. She wanted to live her own life, to be free of the web of crime and violence all around her. Joe had promised to take her away from all of this. But at what cost?

Was she willing to pay his price?

She'd certainly known in her head that Joe would do whatever it took to get her out, but she'd been naive to ignore what that *really* meant. If even a fraction of the stories her father told about Charlie Squad were true, every member of Joe's team was only one step shy of insane when it came to accomplishing the mission.

And she'd just brought one of the chief nutcases into her father's home.

She started when Joe announced abruptly, "I'm no good at just sitting around. I'm going for a swim. Wanna come?"

The mere thought of cool water and Joe flowing over her heated skin evoked almost unbearable sexual pleasure. "Uh, I think I'll pass," she mumbled.

Joe shrugged and stood up. He took two quick, powerful steps and made a running dive into the swimming pool, knifing cleanly into the water in a shallow dive. He emerged nearly at the other end of the pool, executed a neat flip turn, and took off stroking toward her. Fifty easy laps later of her father's twenty-five-meter-long pool, and showing no sign of tiring, she quit counting. Well, that explained where the gorgeous physique came from.

Even Gunter was openly watching Joe's smooth, powerful strokes. He glided through the water like a porpoise, with water streaming off his sleek body in a V-shaped wake as every pull of his arm rocketed him forward. A constant forward momentum not attributable to his upper body and turbulence just under the surface of the water behind him gave testament to the strength of his legs as he kicked pistonlike from the hips. His was the beauty of a true athlete.

She was almost sad when, well over a hundred laps later, he popped out of the pool. Mesmerized, she drank in the sight of him strolling toward her, his body flushed from exertion, his hair standing up every which way like he'd just gotten out of bed and his eyes so alive she could hardly stand to look at them without exploding.

She handed him a towel as she asked, "How far did you go?"

"'Bout two miles," he answered casually from underneath the snowy terry cloth as he dried his hair.

"Where did you learn to swim?" she asked.

"Duh. In a swimming pool," he answered drolly in his best beach bum voice.

Suddenly suspicious, she glanced over her shoulder and, sure enough, Gunter was standing there. The German threw an assessing look at Joe and said shortly, "Mr. Ferrare wants to see you. Now."

Chapter 8

Joe padded into Eduardo's office behind Gunter. The air-conditioning was cold against his bare skin, especially after the tropical sun outside. Although he'd have preferred not to show Eduardo any reaction to it, there was no help for the goose bumps on his chest and arms, nor the occasional shiver that rattled through him. A transparent tactic by Eduardo to drag him in here like this, wearing nothing but a pair of swim trunks and a towel around his neck. It was, no doubt, meant to make him feel naked and vulnerable before the grandeur of the great man. *Whatever.*

He dug his toes into the thick carpet and did his damndest to strike a casual pose. "Yo, Mr. F," he drawled at Eduardo, "you really gotta get outta this mausoleum and hit the waves. It's gorgeous out there."

Ferrare scowled. "Your arrival has caused me substantial unexpected work that keeps me at my desk."

He'd bet. He could just imagine the mad scramble by Ferrare's people to figure out who in the heck had just blown into their midst like a minor hurricane. He just prayed they ran into the fake life history Charlie Squad had hastily planted for Ferrare's people to find.

"Hey, man. I'm not a high-maintenance guy, I swear. I'm totally willing to pull my weight around here if I'm gonna be a burden to you. I used to clean pools, and I'm pretty good with plumbing. You got any johns backed up? Flushing sluggish, maybe?"

Eduardo looked taken aback at the turn this conversation had taken. "My plumbing is fine."

Joe grinned and opened his mouth to speak, but Eduardo cut him off, correcting hastily, "Rather, my house's plumbing is fine."

That was more like it. The guy was off balance now. Joe pressed his advantage and perched a hip on the edge of Ferrare's desk. Gunter gaped, appalled at the nerve of such a thing. Good. Wouldn't hurt to have *him* off-kilter, either. Joe drawled, "This is a pretty nice spread you got here, Dad. Mind if I call you Dad?"

"Yes, I mind!" Eduardo bellowed.

Joe shrugged. "Yeah, you're right. That does feel kinda weird. How 'bout Ed?"

"How about Mr. Ferrare?" Eduardo ground out between his teeth.

"It's your name. Your call. So what's up? Big G said you wanted to see me."

It took Eduardo a second to figure out that Big G was Gunter. And it didn't take the German too long after that to level a dire scowl in Joe's direction. Finally, Eduardo seemed to recall that there was actually a purpose behind this farce. He cleared his throat. Placed his palms flat on his desk. Seemed to be having trouble regaining his mental focus, let alone control of the conversation. Yup, upgrade his dimwitted son-in-law act from category 1 to category 2 hurricane.

Joe held back a grin. Hell, torturing Eduardo was turning out to be a whole lot more entertaining than he'd ever imagined it could be.

"I have your dossier here," Eduardo announced. "My people assembled it last night."

That snapped his mind back to business fast. "I have a dossier?" he echoed. "Cool! What does it say?"

"It says you've had a little trouble with the law."

"Shucks, don't believe everything you read, Mr. F. The cops said some ugly things about me, but they never proved anything."

Eduardo leaned back in his chair, his gaze keen. Assessing.

Assess away, buddy. I've been trained by the top shrinks in the business to lie like an angel. Heck, he could even fool a lie detector if he worked hard at it. And standing in front of Eduardo Ferrare, who could order him killed in an instant, he was working damned hard.

"It says here you are a firefighter."

"Well, I've been through fire school and I passed the advanced course for chemical fires and hazardous-material burns last year. And, yeah, I've worked my share of fires. But mostly, I'm an EMT. I'm the guy who peels folks out of car wrecks and wraps blankets around people when they stumble out of burning buildings."

"It also says here that you've been implicated in causing several suspicious fires."

Joe shrugged. "Like I said. Nobody ever proved a thing. It's all smoke and mirrors. Good one, huh? Smoke and mirrors?" He guffawed at his own joke.

Eduardo lashed out, "What does my daughter see in you?"

Good try. Abrupt and shocking shift of topic to startle a straight answer out of a suspect. Too bad Joe had been trained by the top police and FBI interrogators in the United States. He looked Eduardo dead in the eye. "That's easy. I love her." And damned if that didn't almost feel like the truth rolling off his tongue. Hell, he hardly knew Cari. And the more he did get to know her, the more he realized how little he really knew her.

Eduardo leaned forward, glaring. "I think you're a small-time punk. A cheap wanna-be. And I think you seduced my daughter in a feeble attempt to get inside my organization."

"Hey!" Joe protested. "I told you. There was no seducing going on until after the wedding!"

"Nonetheless," Eduardo forged on, "if you thought you just caught the fast train to the top of the wise-guy pyramid, you thought wrong. Nobody gets a job—or respect—from me unless they earn it. You got that?"

Yeah, he got it. Like Charlie Squad. They'd kicked Eduardo's butt enough times for him not only to respect them, but to fear them. And the biggest dropkick of all was standing right under his nose. Asshole. Joe answered casually, "Sure thing. And that's the way it ought to be, too, if you ask me."

Gunter cleared his throat loudly as Joe caught a flurry of movement out of the corner of his eye, a flash of long, tanned legs and white bathing suit at the patio door. Then the diamond ring on Eduardo's finger caught the sunlight streaming in the windows. The ring was a gaudy piece, sporting a large kite-shaped diamond set in a massive gold band. It threw sparkling prisms all over the white room as its owner hastily stuffed the papers strewn across his desk into a file folder.

Carina strolled over to Joe and looped her arm through his. "You boys having a nice talk?" she asked lightly.

Eduardo opened his desk drawer to put the papers away.

"You don't have to bother hiding that, Daddy. I know you checked out Joe. Oh, and I hope you thanked Judge Cabot and his wife for their hospitality to us."

Eduardo's eyes narrowed. *Easy, Cari,* Joe thought loudly, in hopes that she'd catch his brain waves.

She continued. "I mean, I up and drag some stranger home with me. Of course, you'll check him out. I hope you didn't get too upset over that whole business about starting those fires. Joe would never do anything like that. And even if he had, nobody was hurt. All the buildings they accused him of torching were abandoned. A bunch of bored kids probably did it."

Eduardo snapped, "What else did he tell you about his past?"

Joe whispered loudly, "I didn't tell her the part about fixing toilets. I mean, how unsexy is poo?"

Cari went rigid beside him, as though she was waging a mighty battle not to burst out laughing.

Eduardo growled, "Get out of here. Go surf or whatever it is you young people do."

Joe wiggled his eyebrows suggestively at Cari. "Let's go do a little whatever, eh?"

She slapped him lightly on the arm. "Behave yourself!"

He wrapped an arm around her waist and dropped a kiss on the tip of her nose. "Never," he said, laughing back.

In one smooth move, he turned her around and started for the door. Trading smooches with her, Joe wandered out of Eduardo's office, for all appearances having completely forgotten about his father-in-law's existence in the midst of the various love nibbles he was busy trading with Cari.

Gunter closed the door more firmly than necessary behind them, staying inside with his boss. *Still sore over the Big G remark, apparently.*

Joe dropped his head onto Cari's shoulder in a moment's relief. "Thanks for charging in to the rescue like that. I owe you one."

Her arms tightened around his waist briefly and she murmured, "You're welcome. I'll be sure to collect later."

Hmm. *That* sounded interesting. *Time-out. The op, Romeo. Focus on the op.* Yeah, except this gorgeous, smart—and brave—woman *was* the op. How cool was that?

Cari rubbed her arms against the chilly night air as she stepped out onto the balcony. Joe's silhouette was a darker shade of black against the inky night. Thick, angry-looking clouds scudded across the sky, threatening to burst into a major squall at any moment.

Finally, after a long evening of supper with her father and then movies in the media room, they were alone. Truly alone, without microphones picking up their every whisper.

Joe sat on the wide stone balustrade, staring pensively out to sea. His stillness drew her to him, pulling at her heartstrings as surely as she knew she shouldn't let it. All that silence he'd wrapped himself in made her want to charge out and rescue him from it.

"What are you thinking about?" she murmured as she perched on the balcony beside him.

"I'm watching the cameras out here. There's a weakness in the system."

"Do tell."

"They sweep back and forth to achieve full coverage of the grounds. Wherever there are moving cameras, there are blind spots. It would be possible to slip in behind the arc of movement of any one of them and make our way anywhere we needed to go on the grounds."

She loved hearing his voice. Listening to him talk soothed her. Made her feel safe. More to keep him talking than because she really cared about the answer, she asked, "And where do we need to go?"

"I'm thinking the ocean is our best bet to get out of here. I can arrange to have a fast boat sit offshore and we could swim out to it."

She frowned. "Gunter has radar watching the water. No vessels are allowed within a mile of this place."

"What happens if some tourist strays into this mile-wide zone?"

"A couple of my father's men go out in a boat and tell them this is a private beach. They're invited to leave in however strong terms it takes to get rid of them."

"So how do you feel about swimming a mile in the ocean?"

She grimaced, remembering that terrible night she'd swum out into the ocean and run into Joe. "It would be awfully cold."

"Yeah, it would," he agreed, obviously thinking hard. "I wonder if we could get ahold of a couple of wet suits."

"Gunter keeps all the diving gear locked up."

Joe frowned. "Maybe I could get a couple of wet suits dumped on the beach and hidden where we could get at them."

"Motion detectors all the way to the water," Cari replied.

Joe nodded. "Yeah, I saw those when I was watching the place."

"You watched this place?" she asked, surprised. "For how long?"

"A couple weeks. Technically, I was watching you. But I also scoped out possible ways to pull you out of here."

"And found none," she added bitterly.

He smiled gently. "Don't knock it. How else would I have managed to convince you to marry me?"

Startled by the sincerity in his voice, she replied, "Don't sell yourself short. If I'd have met you under perfectly normal circumstances, I'd have been interested in you."

He shrugged. "Under normal circumstances, our paths would never have crossed."

Her gaze narrowed. "You see me as some spoiled little rich girl, don't you? You think I run around with the jet set, partying the nights away and being generally useless."

"I didn't say that," he replied evenly.

No, but he thought it. They all did. Everyone who lived outside her world and looked at it from afar thought she had some great life. But outsiders didn't live with bodyguards dictating their every movement, with the constant threat of kidnapping or murder hanging over their heads. Outsiders didn't flinch at every loud noise or get awakened in the middle of the night and hustled down to a panic room in the basement to hide, locked in with a terrified maid for hours on end while God knows what transpired upstairs.

She said defensively, "You think it's been a bed of roses growing up in this house because my father has so much money, don't you? You think wealth makes it all better?"

His back went stiff. "It sure as hell beats growing up without any money at all."

She paused, arrested. He'd just given her a rare glimpse at the real man behind the facade he kept so carefully in place. Grew up poor, did he? "Did you have two parents when you were a kid?" she asked.

"Yeah. Why?"

"Did they love you?"

"Of course they did."

She reached out and trailed her fingers across his cheek gently. "Ah, Joe. I'd have traded all this luxury in a heartbeat to remember what my mother looked like. To know what a hug from her felt like. To know that something other than my father's jealousy and rage cost me my mother."

He muttered dangerously, "What do you mean? What exactly happened to your mother?"

"Eduardo killed her when I was a toddler. He decided she was having an affair and broke her neck with his bare hands. Julia overheard him bragging about it once."

Joe stared. Then his brow grew thunderous. Then, finally, the tension left his shoulders and he moved, shifting to sit behind her, wrapping his arms around her and pulling her back against his solid warmth. "I'm sorry, princess. I keep forgetting to look past the surface with you."

"Past the surface?" she repeated.

"There's so much more to you than meets the eye. You're so dazzlingly beautiful it's easy to get caught up in just looking at you. I keep having to remind myself not to underestimate the woman behind the looks."

Warmth that went beyond shared body heat flowed through her. "That's possibly the nicest thing anyone has ever said to me," she murmured.

"Then you're going to be one easy lady to romance," he laughed. "I haven't even begun to ply you with real flattery yet."

She snuggled deeper into his arms. "Sounds yummy."

He chuckled and, if she wasn't mistaken, buried his nose in her hair for an instant. But then the light touch of his breath on her ear withdrew and he said quietly, "Tell me about your childhood. What was it like growing up here?"

"We didn't really grow up here. We spent most of the time at the main compound. It's on the other side of St. George at the edge of the jungle—"

"I know the place."

He did? How was that? Her mind spun with possible answers to that one. Belatedly, she continued. "I was two when my mother died. Julia—she's five years older than me— mostly raised me. The servants were too afraid of my father to do much more than feed and clothe us."

"What about Eduardo? Was he around a lot?"

"No. He traveled all the time. The thing was, nobody ever knew when he might come or go. By the time I was ten or so, though, he had his organization pretty well established and started to spend more time at home."

"What kind of father was he?" Joe prompted.

"He never failed to provide for us. We always had new clothes and went to good schools. I wouldn't go so far as to say he openly loved us. But in his own way, he showed us he cared. I think he always regretted that we weren't boys."

Joe's arms tightened briefly and he mumbled, "I, for one, am thrilled that you're a girl."

She laughed.

"Tell me more."

She couldn't tell if this was some sort of subtle interrogation for the purposes of doing his job or whether Joe was simply interested in her life. Either way, she continued speaking. "He always brought us gifts when he'd been out of the country. Sometimes a stuffed toy or a box of expensive chocolates. Once, he brought us both silk dresses from Paris. He had us wear them to a big party he threw for the leaders of the drug cartel he was trying to hook up with."

"And did he?"

She frowned. "Did he what?"

"Did he hook up with the drug cartel?"

"Oh. Sort of. A couple of the members didn't want to do business with him. They said he was too violent. So he killed them and then asked to join the cartel again. The survivors let him in."

"Did he talk about business around you and your sister?"

"Actually, he was pretty careful about not talking around us. I think he liked pretending we didn't know what he did. He always told us he owned a bunch of coffee plantations. When we were young, most of what Julia and I knew we learned from eavesdropping on the servants."

Joe snorted. "How old were you girls when you figured out what he really did?"

She had to think about that one. She searched her memory for a time when she didn't know what and who her father was. "I can't remember ever not knowing that Daddy killed people and sold drugs that make people sick."

"What did you think about that?"

"I used to lie in bed at night and pray that no one would come to our house and kill us to get even with Daddy for killing someone they loved. Which is to say, I had a lot of nightmares and insomnia, even as a little kid."

"Wow. That's some burden to carry around," he commented.

"You know, the worst of it wasn't the fear. It was the guilt." She hadn't thought about this stuff in a long time. The old pain seared across her stomach like an ulcer.

"Guilt? Why?" Joe asked when she didn't continue.

She considered her words before answering slowly, "I used to think that if Julia and I hadn't been born, Daddy wouldn't have needed to turn to crime to support us. I figured it was all our fault. To get the money to take care of us, he had to do the things he did."

"And how old were you when you grew out of that illusion?"

She gazed out at the ocean, a vague, growling mass out there in the dark. "My head grew out of the notion before I hit my teens. But I don't know if the heart ever grows out of something like that."

Joe lurched behind her. "You don't honestly think your father's life of crime is your fault, do you?"

She shrugged. "I know it sounds stupid. Like I said, the head gets over it. But you have to admit, there is a certain element of truth to our part in all of this. If Julia and I had ever gone to the authorities, maybe he could've been stopped. Maybe a lot of lives could've been saved. Maybe she and I are as guilty, in our own way, as he is."

"Julia's disappearance has caused a major blow to your father's activities. She very much wants to do whatever she can to stop him further."

She couldn't keep the bitterness out of her voice. "Right. While I partied the night away and let her take all the heat. And the guilt train just keeps on rolling."

"Your sister was in a unique position by being your father's banker. You didn't have the luxury of having her insider knowledge."

She snapped, "I may not be his banker, but that doesn't mean I don't know any inside stuff."

"Like what?" he challenged. "What do you know that could be of use to the authorities?"

"Well, I know when he's going to have important meetings. He always wants me to put in an appearance at them. To serve drinks to his guests and let them grab a quick feel or two."

Joe's arms tightened at that.

She shrugged. "At least he never made me sleep with any of them. I hear that some of the men in the cartel make their wives and daughters service important clients."

"Sick bastards," Joe said.

"Lucky for you, Eduardo told me I didn't have to show up for tonight's meeting. I guess he figured you might go nuts if someone touched me, and he doesn't want a scene with this bunch."

"There's a meeting? Tonight?"

"Yeah. An important one. He's had it planned for weeks. He's been really antsy to meet whoever's coming."

"When's the meeting?"

"Two in the morning or so. They're having late drinks at a nightclub and then coming back here to discuss business."

"Who's he meeting with?"

"I have no idea. Someone new with whom he's never done business. I got the impression these guys deal in something he's never dabbled in before."

"So Eduardo's diversifying?"

She shrugged. "I couldn't tell you for sure. But that's my impression."

"I'm inclined to trust your impressions. And my own impression is that I need to find out who's at this meeting. I'm going to need your help. Are you game?"

"To do what? Spy on my own father?"

"Exactly. Will you help me?"

Cari gulped. "I'm not so sure that's a good idea. We could get in a lot of trouble if we got caught."

Joe shrugged. "So we don't get caught."

Right. Like that was an easy thing. But then, if Joe was as good as the rest of Charlie Squad, he probably could spy on the meeting without getting caught. He'd already figured out how to get around the security cameras watching the grounds below. She'd lived here on and off for most of her life and had never figured that one out.

Except something was still making her terribly uncomfortable about the whole idea of spying on tonight's meeting. Something besides the risk. Something having to do with…

Oh, my God. Something having to do with not wanting to spy on her father *because it would be disloyal to him.* Disloyal? Why in the world was she worried about being disloyal? It wasn't like Eduardo had ever done anything to earn her loyalty. Except be her father. Except let her live. Except provide for her in his own way.

And then the terrible, awful, horrible truth dawned on her. The same truth that had been staring her right in the face ever since Tony's death. The truth that had made Tony's murder hurt so bad. How could she not have seen it before now?

She'd never truly intended to run away from her father at all. She'd been running away from something else all that time. She'd been running away as fast as she could from the fact that *she still loved her father.*

And here she was, bound to a man who'd sworn to take her away from Eduardo at all costs. What in the hell was she supposed to do now?

Chapter 9

A sick feeling settled in the pit of Joe's stomach at the look on Cari's face. Buyer's remorse. Damn! He was as much a prisoner in this house as she was. She couldn't back out now or he could kiss his butt goodbye.

He'd known it was one of the risks going in. Her sister had pulled a stunt like this nearly a decade ago. Julia had agreed to help Charlie Squad arrest her father, only to back out of the deal at the last minute. While she was at it, she'd gone on to set up the team for an ambush by Eduardo's men.

Thankfully, when Julia contacted them a few months ago, she *had* followed through on her promise to help Charlie Squad. But even then, Dutch, the team member who'd been her primary contact on the op, said she'd had periods of doubt about going through with handing over incriminating information about her father.

What was it about Eduardo Ferrare that commanded such loyalty from his daughters? Neither Julia nor Carina had any illusions about what a monster he could be, nor of the crimes he was capable of. Both of them had feared for their own lives at his hands. How could they still love him? Surely, that was the only reason either woman would remain loyal to the guy.

Was it really as simple as them both living lives so deprived of love that the occasional scraps of attention Eduardo threw at them were all they knew? Is that why they clung to him like they did? Talk about tragic.

Now the question was, could Carina be lured away from her father? Dutch and Julia had been in love once before and fell in love again when they reunited. Unfortunately, Joe didn't have that past history with Cari to call upon. All he had was the here and now. And he had precious little leverage to use to pry Cari from Eduardo's clutches.

The only real bond they had at this point was the attraction leaping and twisting between them, and that was a fragile thing, at best. Damn. He'd just have to make what use of it he could.

Over Cari's head, he glanced at his watch. A little before midnight. He had about an hour to distract her, to get her back on board with the idea of helping him spy on her old man. He hated having to play her like this, but she gave him no choice.

He leaned down slightly, inhaling the clean, sweet citrus scent of her hair. "How long has it been since I told you how beautiful you are?" he murmured.

She replied, "I think it's been at least an hour."

"You know, the thing about beauty," he reflected, "is that when you actually get to know a physically attractive person, they either get a lot more or a lot less beautiful in your eyes."

She snuggled a little closer to him but said nothing.

He continued, "Before I met you, I thought you were stunning to look at. But now that I'm starting to know you, you absolutely take my breath away."

Her breath hitched on a little gasp and he dropped a kiss, little more than a light touch of the lips, just below her ear.

"You're a miracle," he whispered.

And that did it. She turned in his arms to face him, flowing into him like silk, all but offering herself up for the taking. God, he was a bastard. Here he was romancing an innocent young woman to get her to work for him. How despicable was that?

He started as her mouth captured his in a hungry kiss. She still tasted faintly of the orange she'd peeled and eaten earlier in a sticky, drippy orgy of pleasure that had left him hard as a rock. Just thinking about how she'd sucked on the juicy sections made him hard again.

He tilted his head to better fit their mouths together. He slid one hand behind her neck under her hair, savoring the warmth beneath his fingertips. She tasted like an orange Creamsicle bar, all sweet and smooth. He could eat her up until he was drunk on her.

Her hands roamed his chest and she moaned in the back of her throat. He swept his tongue into her mouth, searching for the source of that delicious sound, breathing it into his chest like pure oxygen.

She came to him with her whole body, flinging herself against him in abandon, breasts smashed against his chest, her thigh wedged between his and rubbing parts of him that didn't need any encouragement at the moment. He tried to resist her. Tried to hold himself separate. But, dammit, she was all tropical heat and steamy nights, the roar of the ocean and pounding of the surf. Hell, sex on a beach.

And he was the biggest jerk in the world. Here he was, letting her drape herself all over him, *enjoying* her draping herself all over him. He didn't want to hurt her, to damage her self-esteem, to turn her off sex or men. He shouldn't be doing this. He…should…not…be doing this.

Aw, hell. He wrapped his arms around her, gathering her into him, kissing her like there was no tomorrow. He kissed her eyes, her cheeks, her ears, her neck. He sucked her lips, laved her tongue with his, hauled her up against him more tightly, her breasts pressing against him, her thighs giving against the hardness of his. Oh, yeah. He could do this nonstop for a couple of lifetimes.

Her fingertips crept underneath his waistband, hot against his skin. *Hello.* Parts of him that were already alert zeroed in on those questing fingers. He ripped his mouth free, groaning, and grasped her wrists.

"Slow down, baby. You're killing me here."

She laughed against his mouth. "I know the feeling. Kiss me."

He tried to take it easy, tried to be delicate and tender with her, but then she bit his lip.

He growled deep in his throat and she matched him with, swear to God, a purr. She sounded like a damned tigress as she licked the spot she'd nipped. An extremely self-satisfied tigress.

So she wanted to play rough, did she? He could definitely give as good as he got in that department. He stood up, dragging her with him, shoving his hands under her shirt and reaching between her shoulder blades for her bra hooks. And then a movement high on the wall of the house caught his eye. He swore viciously.

Cari reached up to pull his head back down to her, but he resisted. Reluctantly.

"Sorry, princess. We're on *Candid Camera*."

"I don't care," she mumbled against his mouth, arching into him.

He closed his eyes. Lord, he could smell the lust on her skin. And he could bloody well feel the lust raging across his. If that camera were a few feet closer, he'd rip it off the freaking wall.

As it was, the interruption was probably just as well. He needed to get his mind on business, and he certainly didn't need to go making this a real marriage. A real—

Well, hell. And wasn't *that* thought a big bucket of cold water on a guy's libido?

"It's cold out here, honey. Let's go inside."

Still draped around him much more than he could safely ignore, Cari dropped her head against his shoulder and mumbled, "While I appreciate your gentlemanly urges, next time could you not find them for a little while longer?"

He laughed ruefully. "I'm no gentleman, darlin'. I just don't like the idea of giving Gunter and Rico a free peep show."

"Screw Gunter and Rico," she grumbled.

He grinned but wiped the expression off his face fast as she glanced up at him.

"And I'm *not* cold," she stated forcefully.

"Neither am I," he replied regretfully. "But we've got places to go and things to do."

And that broke the mood, dammit. He had to be some sort of Class A idiot to walk away from Cari's obvious willingness—hell, eagerness—to engage in some seriously gnarly sex with him.

He shook his head and reached for the French doors, holding them open for her. And as he followed her inside, he turned quickly, grinned and flipped his middle finger at the camera, which was still pointed right at him.

Cari sagged on the foot of her bed, tingling from head to toe. Damn him for stopping! How long had it been since any man had treated her with enough respect to stop of his own volition? a tiny voice in her brain argued back. Hmm. That would be...never. God, how pitiful was that? What did it say about her self-esteem? Some shrink would have a field day with a revelation like that.

"Are you okay?" The deep murmur made her look up at him in the faint moonlight filtering into the room.

She sighed on a half laugh. "I'll live. But it's not nice to let a girl get all dressed up with nowhere to go, if you catch my meaning."

He smiled wryly. "Yeah, I get your drift."

Without warning, he leaned down and kissed her swiftly, his mouth pressing hard against hers. "Soon, princess, soon. When there are no cameras."

And then he was gone, moving across the room, stripping off his shirt as he went. Faint moonlight played across his back, highlighting the bulges and dips of a glorious set of deltoids and lats. He stopped in front of the chest of drawers that held most of his clothes. She started as he dropped his shorts, revealing a pair of black Lycra shorts cupping arguably the best butt she'd ogled in as long as she could remember. He turned slightly and the moonlight caught him just right. *Thank you, God.* The fabric clung to him in all the right places, outlining long, powerful thigh muscles, the deep cut up the side of his leg to his narrow hips and another bulge....

She tore her gaze away.

Well, okay, so she cheated and peeked a little. What girl wouldn't with a hunk like that changing in her bedroom? He pulled on black trousers cut like fatigue pants and a black long-sleeved turtleneck. In the dark clothing, he suddenly became difficult to see in the shadows playing across that corner of the room.

He glanced over his shoulder at her and paused, apparently arrested by the realization that she'd sat there the whole time, watching him change. Far from reacting with embarrassment, his eyes blazed so hot she could see the fire in them from here.

"Go change out of your clothes," he said roughly. "Put on something black for me."

Right. Clothes. She stumbled to her feet and across the room to her closet. She stepped into the dressing area, although she was half tempted to change out in the main room in front of Joe. The silk turtleneck she pulled on irritated her sensitized skin. She wanted hands on her body, not this damned shirt! The black cotton jeans weren't much better against her legs.

She tore her mind away from the things she couldn't have right now. Ah, but later...

Right now, she had to concentrate on helping Joe spy on her father's meeting. And the very thought sent cold shivers through her. This was not a good idea. Even if Joe could get past all the cameras and guards and other security measures, it was still a dicey stunt to pull off. And why was Joe so interested in who came to Eduardo's meeting, anyway? Was he thinking about contacting one of tonight's guests and asking for help? Surely, he knew better than that. Possibly the only more vicious, more violent criminals in this part of the world than her father were the men he did business with.

She stepped out into the bedroom. Joe was untangling a jumble of rope and thick wooden dowels. Her fire escape ladder. The same one she'd used to flee her room the night Tony was murdered. She'd been surprised Eduardo hadn't taken it away from her after she'd gone over the balcony and headed for the ocean. Maybe Gunter had convinced her father that it was better to just give her the ladder because she was wild enough to jump from the balcony without one.

She followed Joe outside to the balcony, where the noise of the ocean would mask their voices.

He moved over next to her and muttered in her ear, his mind apparently firmly on business. "We'll wait here until the meeting's started, then climb down and work our way over to the windows. You can point out to me anyone you recognize and I'll take pictures of the rest."

She nodded, the misgivings piling up in her gut. It was one thing to try to leave her father. It was another thing altogether to actively help Joe do something awful to him on the way out the door.

By bringing her to this beach house, his private killing ground, Eduardo had already hinted at doing her harm if she didn't cooperate with him. Rumor among the servants was that her father had ordered Julia killed a number of weeks back. A couple of the whispers had him pulling a gun on Julia himself in some big confrontation between the two of them. And, Lord knew, Julia was a lot more important to her father than she'd ever been. If he'd kill Julia for disobeying him, he'd certainly kill her, too. And she was going to help Joe and expose herself to this additional risk? *Why?*

Memories of Joe's hands on her skin, his mouth on hers, his body against hers, of what else she wanted from him skated through her head. It was a lousy reason to spy on her father. But it was a reason, at least. The faster they got done checking out this stupid meeting, the faster they could get back to what they'd been doing before.

She shook her head in disgust. She was smarter than to do something dumb or dangerous in the name of impressing a guy. But here she was, blithely agreeing to this insanity. Apparently, she'd decided sometime during the last twenty-four hours that she was going to ignore the inevitable pain of losing Joe in favor of wallowing in their current mutual infatuation.

At least, she hoped he shared her infatuation. He could just be putting on a big act for the cameras and bugs. Now that she thought about it, the surveillance devices always seemed to be around whenever he laid a hot kiss on her. She frowned. And still she wanted him. How lame was that?

As Joe hooked the ladder onto the side railing, tucked close to the wall of the house in a deep shadow, he said conversationally, "I'm surprised you and your sister didn't figure out how to sneak out at night when you were kids."

"We didn't spend much time here, especially after our mother—"

Joe blinked. "She died here?" he asked quietly.

She nodded. "He does most of his killing here. He likes to toss the bodies to the sharks. No messy evidence, you know." She thought of Tony and her voice broke on the last sentence.

"You really cared for Tony, didn't you?" Joe asked quietly. "What a jerk I've been. It's too soon for you to have another relationship and here I've been coming on to you." He ran a hand through his hair. "Christ, I'm sorry."

She stepped near him, capturing his restless hand in hers.

"It wasn't like that. Tony didn't have those kinds of feelings for me nor I for him."

"He had enough feelings to risk his life for you!" Joe retorted.

"Tony was gay," she explained gently. "Not-the-slightest-bit-interested-in-girls-except-to-borrow-their-clothes gay."

"Oh." Joe's jealous anger deflated in an instant. "I'm sorry."

"For what? For being jealous, or for being sensitive to the fact that I might not want a new relationship so soon after losing someone I cared about?"

He frowned. "I'm not jeal... What the hell. I'm just sorry, okay?"

"Okay," she smiled. "Look. A light just went on in my father's office."

Joe glanced at his watch and frowned. "It's not time for the meeting yet."

"Gunter will go in first and sweep the place for bugs. Then he'll lock the door and only open it again when it's time for the servants to take in the refreshments. He'll stay in the room with them until the meeting begins."

"Thorough."

She was silent as Joe reached into one of his pockets and pulled out an average-looking digital camera.

"Planning a sightseeing trip on the side, are you?" she quipped.

He grinned. "You didn't think I'd come in here to rescue you without a few cool toys, did you?"

"How'd you get them in the door?"

"By giving the thugs who searched my suitcase exactly what they were looking for. Average, everyday items. Like this camera. Looks like a middle-of-the-road model, but it can store up to a hundred high-resolution pictures taken under extremely low-light conditions. The pictures can be blown up to ten times their regular size with no appreciable loss of detail."

Wow. That was a whole lot of pixels crammed into a single image.

"What else did you sneak in here in your little bag of tricks?" she asked.

Darned if he didn't choose that very moment to wax evasive on her. "A little of this and a little of that. Of course, I wasn't able to bring in a weapon or any obvious surveillance gear. But I've got enough doodads to jerry-rig almost anything we might need to get out of here."

"You hope," she retorted.

"I hope," he amended with a boyish smile that just about knocked her knees out from under her. She gulped and tried to catch her breath as he moved with the grace of a tango dancer to one side of the porch and peered below.

She moved up behind him and stood on tiptoe to murmur in his ear, "You're almost too pretty to be a mortal man."

He mumbled indignantly, "I'm not *pretty*."

Chuckling, she slipped her hands around his waist beneath his turtleneck. Ah, yes. Rippling muscles flexed beneath her palms, his skin sliding against hers like rough satin. He felt so delicious she could practically taste him. His flavor would be a combination of woodsy and pungent. She swallowed as her mouth puddled with anticipation.

"I'm working," he muttered.

"So am I," she murmured back.

"How's that work?" he grumbled. "It feels like—"

Hmm. It felt like what? She filled in for him in a whisper, "It feels like heaven? Like you want more? Like sweaty sex on satin sheets?"

He jerked beneath her hands. Tension thrummed through him. "Jeez, woman. Do you take pleasure in torturing me?"

"I might," she murmured, her lips pressed against the back of his neck. Oh, yes. He did, indeed, taste like bergamot and fine wine. "I'm game to find out."

He jerked completely away from her this time, turning sharply to stare down at her.

She stared right back. "You keep treating me like some

naive little girl. I'm not, Joe. I'm a grown woman and I know what I want. And I'm not afraid to go after it."

The next words hung unspoken between them. And what she wanted was *him*. All of him. For some of that sweaty sex on satin sheets.

He cursed under his breath and spun back toward her father's windows. If she wasn't mistaken, he was breathing hard. She satisfied herself with standing right behind him, not touching him, looking out over his shoulder on tiptoe at her father's office. It was almost sexier standing here not touching him than it had been to put her hands on him. This way, she could imagine putting her mouth on all the places where her hands had been and more. And darned if her breathing didn't take on a heavy quality, too.

Joe had waited out some tense vigils in his day, but this one topped them all. By a lot. The sound of Cari all but panting over his shoulder was going to kill him soon. Assuming his imagination didn't get the job done first. The memory of her soft, warm hands roaming over his flesh refused to go away. It was all he could do not to turn around, rip off her clothes and bury himself in all that sexual energy all but exploding from her.

The mission, dammit, the mission!

And how many times had he watched the other guys on his team struggle with that one? As many times as he'd seen them weaken and give in to the women who'd stolen their hearts. He unleashed a long string of profanities inside his head. He wasn't losing his heart to Carina Ferrare. He wasn't!

Methinks the boy doth protest too much.

Crap.

A movement from inside Eduardo's office caught his attention. A bartender setting up shop behind the stainless-steel-and-glass bar in the corner. Almost showtime. Praise the Lord. He couldn't take much more of Cari's fast breaths tickling the back of his neck like this.

Yup, there he was. Ferrare had just walked into the room. Bingo. He paced around the room a couple of times. Damned if the bastard didn't look nervous. Oh yeah. Joe definitely had to find out who Eduardo was meeting with tonight.

"When your father's guests arrive, we'll go," Joe muttered. He felt Cari nod behind him.

There they were. Four men had just walked into Eduardo's office, accompanied by a phalanx of security types. The thugs looked around and then backed out of the room.

"Ready?" he murmured.

Another silent nod at his back.

"On the next sweep of the nearest camera, all the cameras will be looking away from the balcony. We'll have about fifteen seconds."

She tensed against his back.

He did his best to ignore the hands that settled nervously on his waist. "Three…two…one…"

He moved fast, flipping the end of the ladder over the balcony. It snaked down into the darkness below. Cari crouched beside him, her eyes huge with fear.

"I'll go first," he breathed.

Lying on the balustrade on his belly, he slipped over the edge fast and down the rope ladder. He paused about six rungs down to help Cari climb over the edge. She mimicked him, keeping a low profile as she went over the railing. She'd taken about four steps down and her head was level with the floor of the balcony when she lurched violently above him. What had happened? She started back up the ladder.

"What are you doing?" he bit out.

"Someone just knocked on my door," she hissed.

Dammit!

She raced up and over the rail, tumbling to the floor of the balcony in her haste. "Just a minute," she called out. She sounded flustered and out of breath. But then, that might not be a bad thing. Whoever was knocking would think the two of them were fooling around. It would explain the long delay in answering the damn door.

As Cari jumped up and ran inside, Joe raced up the ladder, rolling over the balustrade, falling onto the balcony floor and popping to his feet in one frantic movement. He took off, running across the bedroom, as Cari reached for the door.

"Cari! Get some clothes on!" he called out urgently. No time to get close enough to whisper so the bugs wouldn't hear.

Cari jerked to a halt, frowning. He ripped off his turtleneck and gestured for her to do the same. He jumped for the bed and ripped the covers back, tearing a sheet off.

As she disappeared inside her black shirt, he did his damndest *not* to notice the black lace bra she wore with its little bow nestled in her cleavage, or the way her golden flesh showed in far too much detail under the flimsy lace, or the generous display of curving breasts above the lingerie—he *so* failed not to notice.

He flung the sheet at her and then jumped under the covers himself, stripping off his pants and jungle boots under the tangle of blankets as Cari wrapped the sheet around toga-style and cracked open the door an inch or so.

"What do you want, Gunter? Why aren't you downstairs with my father?"

"He changed his mind. He wants you at the meeting."

Joe froze in the act of yanking off a sock. He poked his head out of the covers. Cari voiced his exact thought aloud.

"You've got to be kidding!" she exclaimed.

"I'm to wait while you put on a dress and escort you down myself."

"I'm married now. I don't want to schmooze his clients anymore. It's not…seemly."

Gunter's reply was impassive. "I don't think he's particularly concerned about propriety. He ordered you down there and he expects you to go. Now."

Chapter 10

While Cari stared at the German in dismay and shock, Joe's brain kicked into overdrive. He didn't want to subject Cari to any unpleasantness in the form of stares or gropes. But on the other hand, he knew from the tone of Gunter's voice that this was nonnegotiable. And he wasn't ready to start an all-out war with Eduardo. Not just yet. The soldier in him gave a silent "oh yeah" at the realization that she'd be able to hear exactly what Eduardo was up to with these important strangers. It was almost too perfect an opportunity to believe. She could get names, dates, exact details of whatever they were up to—it was a stroke of extraordinary luck. He was surprised when an even fiercer voice inside of him said *Cari's safety is more important than the information.*

"Just a minute, Gunter," Cari said heavily.

She closed the door and hurried over to the bed. "Oh, God, Joe. I don't want to do this. I thought I was done with all that."

He sighed heavily as well. "I know. But your father is

testing us, testing *me,* to see how much of a threat I am to his relationship with you. He needs to know if I'll yield to his wishes. He needs to know that I won't take you away completely before he agrees to give you to me."

Cari closed her eyes for a moment in anguish. "One more time. I'll do my father's bidding one more time."

She turned toward her closet. Joe lay back on the pillows, his gut churning. He didn't like letting her go to the meeting. But Colonel Folly would put his butt in a sling if he messed up this mission because he suddenly went über-protective on this girl. He called out, "Don't wear anything too sexy. You're my wife now, not somebody else's plaything."

One thing he could do was make sure she wasn't down there all alone. He might not be able to get into the room, but he could damn well be right outside to keep an eye on her.

It appeared that Gunter was willing to wait patiently outside until Cari emerged. So Joe reversed himself and started putting his clothes back on. About the time he zipped up his second boot, Cari emerged from her dressing area. She wore a short tropical-print dress with a halter top and a floaty skirt. It was less revealing than some of the things he'd seen her wear, but there was no disguising her sex appeal.

He swore at himself. The green-eyed monster was alive and kicking, all right.

Jaw clenched, he got out of bed. She paused in front of the door and Joe moved over to her side. He put his arms around her waist and mumbled, "You'll be okay. I'll be watching."

She turned around, burrowing into him, and nodded against his chest. His arms tightened around her possessively, willing her to feel him, to think of him when she went into that meeting and flirted with those other men. Her father had no right to ask this of her. Joe swore some more under his breath.

Cari slipped through the door and out into the hall. And then she was gone. Joe charged across the room, heading for the balcony, but drew up short in front of the French doors. Patience, man. Don't be stupid.

He waited until the cameras all lined up, pointing away from him, and slipped outside. Although it took good timing and speed to slip past the security measures and shimmy down the ladder, it wasn't particularly difficult to pull off. He landed on silent feet in the lush oleander bushes, with their long, narrow leaves. Interesting choice for Eduardo's garden. Oleanders were beautiful but very poisonous.

It was kid stuff to make his way through this dense cover over to Eduardo's office. The last oleander bush came right up to the end window in the wall of floor-to-ceiling windows that faced the ocean. Even better, a lower panel of the window was tilted outward from the bottom, granting him the ability to hear what was going on inside.

The bar was no more than ten feet from his position, and Eduardo and his four guests bellied up to it, grazing on the hors d'oeuvres and sipping glasses full of ice and amber liquid. None of the men were drinking much—experienced businessmen, then. They knew better than to let Eduardo get them hammered before they worked out the details of whatever deal they had cooking.

All the men's heads turned abruptly. A door opened across the room and Cari breezed in, as shiny and beautiful as a polished diamond. Joe's gut clenched at the impact of her beauty. Even though he'd been staring at her nonstop for the last two days, he couldn't get enough of her.

Eduardo's guests responded pretty much the same way. They swelled up en masse as Cari turned her dazzling smile on them. Joe restrained a serious temptation to reach through the window and roll up the jerks' tongues and stuff them back in their mouths. They could quit drooling at his wife, dammit.

She...was...not...his...wife!

Yeah, whatever. He still wanted to clobber them for ogling Cari.

Eduardo seemed a bit taken aback by Cari's dress but quickly recovered and made the introductions. "Gentlemen, this is my daughter, Carina. She's here to serve you tonight and see to your pleasure and comfort."

Joe's black gaze snapped to Ferrare. The bastard had put just enough emphasis on the words *pleasure* and *comfort* to make that sound like a sleazy offer. Cari's smile abruptly developed a fixed quality to it.

One of the men spoke. Sounded Slavic. "And do you have any sons who participate in the family business, Mr. Ferrare?"

Eduardo answered with sincere regret. "Alas, I do not. I was cursed with only daughters. And what good are they to a man in my position? Women are good for one thing only. And it isn't running a multinational business conglomerate."

Joe's gaze narrowed. *Pain.* He was going to cause Eduardo a lot of pain someday.

"Take Cari, for instance," Eduardo continued. "Why would God see fit to deny me a son and instead give me a girl who is a first-class beauty to look at but good for nothing else?"

The Slavic man gave a sage nod, then sidled up to Cari and ran his fingertips along her neckline, delving under the fabric before following the curve of her neck up to her lips. "The fates were unkind to you, Eduardo. But maybe it is possible to find a use for this beautiful mouth?" he suggested, shoving the tip of his thumb into Cari's mouth, then slowly pulling it out.

The guy's implication was clear. He was asking if Eduardo would mind if he availed himself of Cari's...attractions. Joe just about rammed his fist through the window. And then he caught sight of Cari's face and his heart wrenched. She was smiling more brilliantly than ever and looked about ready to shatter into a million pieces.

Eduardo gave a casual shrug. "She might as well make herself useful. But first, perhaps, we should begin our discussions."

God Almighty, how was Cari managing not to pick up a bottle of whiskey and break it over that bastard's head? Her own father was talking about her like she was little more than an expensive whore.

Eduardo turned away from the Slav and was now engaging a silver-haired ex-commando-looking type in quiet conversation as they all moved to the other end of the room, near Eduardo's desk. Joe couldn't hear much of what they said over the blood roaring in his ears, but from the snippets he caught, he'd guess the guy was South African. Cape Town native, maybe.

He watched in helpless rage as Cari gripped the edge of the bar until her knuckles turned white. She looked more inclined to throw up than to fight back. But maybe Cari didn't know to fight back. Maybe she thought all parents allowed their children to be treated like that. Is *this* what she thought love was? If possible, Joe's rage swelled to epic proportions. Cobralike, the focus of his fury swung away from the Slav and on to the rightful target—Eduardo. The bastard had given his guest permission to do this to his own daughter. *He* was the one at fault!

Joe's glare skewered the object of his wrath. The pompous, arrogant, sociopathic—

Something moved behind him. *Someone.* He froze, his years of training taking over by reflex. No matter how riled up he was, survival took precedence. Stay invisible. Stay still. Avoid discovery at all costs.

A flashlight swept back and forth on the other side of the bushes. Its beam pierced the foliage of the oleander like a sword, then swept away, then back. Crap! It flashed across his feet. At least his jungle boots were olive nylon and black leather.

Whoever was wielding the flashlight didn't notice his feet because the shadowy figure moved on. The guard turned his head and Joe caught the silhouette: Rico. Joe stayed frozen in place until Rico had circled the pool and gone back into the house via the dining room doors.

He turned his attention back to the meeting. Eduardo was talking and all the guests were listening intently. He couldn't hear a blessed word of it. They were too far away from the open window, and Eduardo was speaking too quietly. Joe willed Cari to use the others' distraction to leave. *Get out, baby! Ease over to that door and slip out while no one's watching.* But she didn't move. Desperately, abjectly, he begged her to go.

Instead, she glided away from the bar under the guise of collecting a couple of abandoned drinks. She picked them up and drifted back to the bar to set them down. She lifted one of the plates of hors d'oeuvres and moved forward with it in hand. She set it beside one of the heretofore silent guests who hadn't manhandled her.

She had to be hearing every detail of what her father said. Joe jolted. Here he was, flipping out in the bushes, while she was in there keeping her wits about her and collecting information. Nerves of steel, she had. He owed her no less. He reached for his camera. And heard another sound behind him.

He froze.

Not Rico again. Irritated beyond belief, he shifted into full-stealth mode—where he should have been all along, dammit!—and eased his head to the side far enough to have a look around the backyard. Freddie and Neddie were walking a slow circuit around the pool this time.

Damn. They might actually be alert enough to spot him. Worse, in a dozen more steps, they'd be in position to glance over and see the ladder hanging in the shadows of Cari's balcony. Frantically, he cast his gaze around at his feet. There. He picked up a golf-ball-size stone and, extending his arm above the top of the oleander fronds, pitched the stone across the yard.

The rock swished through some bushes and hit the ground with a muffled clatter. The cacophony of cicadas, crickets and frogs went silent. And that was almost more noticeable than the rock itself. The two guards jerked, reacting in unison to the intrusion of silence on the tropical night. They hustled off toward the other side of the pool.

Working fast, Joe stood up just far enough to peer between the leaves of his hiding spot. He pulled the digital low-light camera out of his pocket and aimed it at Eduardo's office, quickly capturing the faces of the four men with Ferrare from several different angles.

Cari picked up an armful of empty plates and glided toward the back of the room as unobtrusively as the finest of waiters. Joe kept one eye on her and the other on Freddie and Neddie as they poked around in the bushes on the other side of the pool like a couple of hogs rooting around in the mud for a truffle.

Okay. Cari was clear of the room. She'd just slipped out so subtly he'd nearly missed it. A move worthy of Charlie Squad. But then, she'd grown up having to make herself invisible if she didn't want her life to become very unpleasant. Why was it that he suddenly felt a burning compulsion to make that up to her?

Joe slithered on his belly under the oleander, inching along the long stucco wall toward the balcony. Past the dining room. Alongside the TV room and its French doors leading out to the pool.

And then he stopped. Right at ground level, a long, flat metal grate interrupted the line of the house's concrete foundation. It looked like a vent of some kind. The faintest light shone from between its narrow slats. Was there a *basement* in this house of horrors? It certainly wasn't indicated on any blueprints he'd ever seen of the place.

He had no more time to think about it. He had to get back upstairs before his absence was discovered. He crawled a few feet past the mysterious vent. He'd have to leave the cover of the bushes to cross an open stretch of lawn now, but the shadows were good. He hugged the ground, following the curves of the shadows, his entire body plastered against the cool grass. In another couple of hours, this area would be covered with dew and his passage would leave a telltale track as visible as snail slime across a sidewalk. But for now, he was okay.

He made it across the grass without incident. Grateful for the renewed cover, he eased under the next stand of oleander. Another fifteen feet and he'd be at the ladder. A short pause for the cameras to line back up and he'd be safely back where he belonged. Good Lord willing and the creek don't rise, Cari would already be waiting for him in the room.

He reached for the bottom rung of the ladder. One more sweep of the camera directly over his head and all the lenses would be aligned away from the balcony. Five…four…three…

He dived flat as lights abruptly illuminated overhead and shouts erupted from inside Cari's room.

He translated the Spanish in his head. Rico had somehow figured out that Cari and Joe were not in the room. Her absence from the meeting must have been noted and someone had gone looking for her. Obviously, she hadn't made it back to her room. She hadn't been found where she was hiding, either, or there wouldn't be all the commotion above.

He gave the ladder a yank. Hooked solid. It wasn't coming down off that balustrade anytime soon. The evidence of their little outing would be discovered in a few seconds.

He was so dead. Maybe he could draw them off. Make them think Cari had nothing to do with all this. He'd take the fall, but maybe she'd live. And just maybe Charlie Squad could find another way to get her to safety. His demise was so going to suck. He had confidence that Eduardo's thugs would torture him within an inch of his life before they finally killed him.

Crap. He had to ditch the camera, too. Maybe Cari would find it later and get the pictures out to Colonel Folly somehow. He scrabbled with his fingernails in the mulch and soft earth around the base of the landscaping, burying the camera beneath a shallow layer of dirt and pine chips. The moisture and dirt were probably going to ruin the expensive piece of equipment, but there wasn't anything he could do about it.

Time to face the music. He pulled his knees under him and

braced his hands in preparation for standing up and surrendering to whomever stuck a gun against the back of his head first. Any second now, someone would come tearing outside to see where the trail led away from the telltale ladder.

He shoved to a half crouch and prepared to stand up and show himself. Men were slamming around the room above now, calling loudly to each other as they searched the space. It wasn't like there were a whole lot of possible hiding spots. The search would take them a matter of seconds and then they'd burst out onto the porch, find the ladder and point their AK-47s down it, directly at him.

The French doors beside him burst open and he whirled reflexively, his hands reaching for the stars.

"Hurry!" Cari whispered frantically. "To the pool!"

The swimming pool? What in the world did she have in mind? He stared at her stupidly, stunned that she wasn't Gunter or one of the others come to kill him.

"Come *on*. And strip while you're at it!"

That jolted him into motion. "Say again?" he managed to say as he sprinted beside her in a crouch toward the open space of the swimming pool.

Ahead of him, she fumbled with the knot at the back of her neck as she ran. The halter top of her dress sagged and she paused by the pool just long enough to let the fine silk drop to the ground. All she had beneath it was a black thong. A flipping unbelievably skimpy thong.

He gaped in open disbelief.

She reached for his pants and tore down the zipper fly. "We used the fire rescue ladder to sneak down here for a skinny dip. But you'll have to be naked for them to believe it."

And then it dawned on him what she was up to. She'd realized they had to have a cover story for the ladder and had come up with a *brilliant* one. He tore off his shirt and flung it down. He unzipped his boots, kicking awkwardly out of them while Cari fumbled with his belt. She pulled it free as he stepped on the toes of one sock, yanking his foot free of it. She shoved the pants down around his knees while he staggered and managed to yank his foot clear of the other sock. The French doors on her balcony burst open.

The men up there wouldn't have full night vision, having just come out of a brightly lit room. But their eyes would adapt in a few seconds.

Joe sat down on the edge of the pool, pulling Cari down beside him. He slipped carefully into the water, doing his damndest to make as little noise as possible. Cari slipped in beside him.

"Can you get your shorts off?" she muttered.

"I dunno," he mumbled back. "Spandex gets real clingy when it's wet." He forced the fabric off his skin, treading water while he kicked the shorts free. He set them on the edge of the pool and gulped as Cari put a tiny scrap of black fabric beside them.

She grinned beside him. "Having fun yet?"

How in the bloody hell could she be so relaxed at a time like this? His nerves were balanced on a razor's edge.

"That's not the word I'd choose, no. But for the record, this was pure genius."

She smiled briefly, acknowledging the compliment. "C'mon," she said. "We may as well get out in the middle of the pool so there'll be no doubt as to what we're up to when they turn on the underwater lights."

He shoved off from the side. "Do me a favor. When the lights go on, move your arms around a lot and make a lot of waves."

"Why?" she murmured as she commenced treading water with a slow, rhythmic motion of her limbs. Good idea. They'd be able to keep that up for a while. Although he doubted they'd be out here more than a few more seconds by themselves.

He answered wryly, "That way, the surface of the water will be good and disturbed and nobody will be able to make out any details below the waterline."

Cari grinned at him, a flash of white in her shadowed face. "You're worried about your modesty at a time like this?"

"Hell, no. I'm worried about yours!"

She was saved from having to reply by a phalanx of armed men bursting into the backyard, followed by a blinding flash of light as the house's exterior floodlights were thrown on. The entire yard was lit up nearly as bright as day.

"Hell's bells," he complained loudly into the blackness beyond the spotlights. "Can't a guy and his girl have a little privacy around here?"

Cari paddled over to where he treaded water and draped herself around his neck, giggling. "Poor baby. You've been trying all day to have your way with me and nothing's working out!"

Gunter glared. Freddie and Neddie gaped. And Rico looked so mad, his head could explode. Must have a crush on Cari or something.

"Uh-oh," Cari mumbled against his neck. "Here comes trouble."

Joe glanced up. And looked squarely at the tailored knees of Eduardo Ferrare's suit. *Trouble, indeed.*

Chapter 11

Cari flinched as Eduardo bellowed, "What's the meaning of this?"

"What's the meaning of what?" she asked innocently. "You were busy with your meeting so we decided to take a swim."

Rico growled, "With no clothes on."

Jerk. She took Joe's advice and moved her arms vigorously, stirring up the surface of the water as much as possible. And, sure enough, the underwater spotlights popped on just then and the pool lit up like a brilliant blue topaz. It was acutely uncomfortable having a half dozen of her father's armed guards standing around, staring down at the two of them like goldfish in a bowl.

Joe groused, "What do we have to do to keep the whole student body from crashing the party?"

"Stay in your room," Eduardo snapped.

"Yeah, well that's hard to do when my wife's father is ordering her to go to his business meetings to serve drinks," Joe snapped back.

Cari froze. Nobody talked to her father like that.

"Jeez, dude," Joe continued. "If you needed me to spot you a little cash to hire a waiter, all you had to do was ask. I mean, we're family now. I'd have helped you out."

Cari inhaled and got a mouthful of water instead. She coughed and sputtered and Joe was there instantly, his strong arms around her and his incredibly powerful kicks supporting the two of them easily.

And then the rest of it registered. Joe's body—all of it— was plastered against hers. He was warm and hard in the cool water, as lithe and muscular as a dolphin. What little breath she had was stolen from her by the feel of him. She'd love nothing more than to lose herself in the sensations bombarding her from head to toe.

She glanced up at him and their gazes locked in mutual shock. He was as aware of her as she was of him! For an instant, the rest of the world disappeared and it was just the two of them, floating weightless as one. This was exactly how it would be when they made love. They would create a world all their own where nothing and no one could come between them. She'd be safe and loved and would joyfully give every bit of herself, body and soul, to him.

Then Eduardo snapped, "Enough shilly-shallying around. Out of the water, you two."

The spell was broken. She closed her eyes briefly as the pain of what could have been speared through her.

And then something equally delightful—*not*—occurred to her. She was going to have to climb out of the swimming pool, naked, in front of a crowd that had now swelled to over a dozen. It would put the cherry on top of a totally humiliating evening. First, that pervert sticking his fingers where he had no right to put them, and now this. She had no doubt Eduardo knew exactly how embarrassing this would be for her. And he didn't care one bit. It was all about power. Control. Having the ability to order people to do things that were odious to them.

With a sigh, she gathered herself to head for the side of the pool. It was no use fighting her father. But Joe's arms, which were loosely circling her, tightened, stopping her.

"Hey, Mr. Ferrare. Tell me something," Joe asked casually. "Did you ever change Cari's diapers when she was a baby?"

What was he up to *now?*

Eduardo's gaze snapped to Joe. "I beg your pardon?"

"You know, diapers. Nappies. Those cloth things you wrap around babies' butts to catch the mess."

"I know what diapers are," Eduardo snapped. "What does that have to do with anything?"

"Well, the way I see it, if you changed Cari's diapers on a regular basis when she was a baby, you can probably make a decent argument for having a right to look at her rear end now. But if you weren't a diaper kind of guy—and I have to say, Ed, you don't strike me as the butt-wiping type—then I don't think you have any business telling your daughter to get out of the pool and parade around in her birthday suit in front of you and your men."

"I have every right!" Eduardo bellowed.

"No kidding?" Joe exclaimed. "I figured you wrong, man. You came across to me as big-time diaper-challenged. How old was Cari when she finally got potty-trained, anyway?"

"I wouldn't have the slightest idea," Eduardo half shouted. "And I didn't change diapers!" he added forcefully. This last statement was blasted in the general direction of his men.

Joe tsk-tsked. "Big mistake, man. I've heard experts say it's really important for fathers to do some of that day-to-day, care-for-their-kids stuff. Helps them, like, bond, you know? I figure it helps keep the mommies from going homicidal on the daddies, too."

Eduardo stared down at them, as flummoxed as usual by Joe's rambling conversational style, which always seemed to end up someplace outrageous.

Joe prattled on. "I thought maybe since her mother died

when she was little, you might've pitched in with the whole diaper bit. How did your mother die, anyway, Cari?"

She blinked, startled at the abrupt change of topic and even more startled to be brought into this strange discussion. "Uh, she died of a broken neck," she answered cautiously. This was traditionally a taboo subject in Eduardo's household. Her mother's name was never mentioned, let alone the manner of her death.

"A broken neck? Wow. That sucks. How'd that happen?" Joe looked around expectantly, first at her and then up at Eduardo. Yikes. No way would her father care to have that particular bit of dirty laundry aired for this madman in their midst.

On cue, her father blustered, "Somebody, go get a couple of towels, for God's sake."

As one of the thugs trotted off to play fetch, Joe called after him loudly, "And bring us some bathing suits, too!" Joe continued slightly more quietly to her father, "I'm going to assume Cari is finished with your meeting for the evening, and I'm not letting my wife flash anything at your men when she climbs out of the pool. Then we are retiring to our room, and I trust we won't be disturbed again. I'm sure Cari represented you well this evening as your daughter. But tonight, she is my wife."

Eduardo scowled, unsure of how this situation had spun so completely out of his control. He pivoted on his expensively clad heel and stomped inside, leaving her and Joe to the tender mercies of Gunter and crew.

While they all waited for towels and swimsuits to arrive, an awkward silence fell. Joe's hand on the small of her back strayed lower, his fingers grazing the crevice defining the terminus of her spine. She gasped, startled. Whoa. Heretofore undiscovered erogenous-zone alert! And then his hand cupped her derriere gently, possessively, almost as if he were marking the spot as his and his alone. She exhaled softly, melting closer against him.

It was all a matter of intent. How Joe managed to convey such respect while cupping her behind, she had no idea, but there wasn't the slightest doubt in her mind that he would never take advantage of her. In a strange way, his gentle caress wiped away the Slav's minor invasion, sanctifying her, making everything okay again. She looked through her lashes at Joe, grateful yet again for his unfailing consideration of her,

He smiled down at her apologetically.

He had nothing to apologize for. He was a gentleman—with a capital *G*. It was an honor to be the object of his respect and caring. She didn't deserve him. Once this whole mess was over, she'd give anything to be able to stay with him, to be his wife or, at least, his girlfriend in reality. But he'd never look twice at her.

Every now and then, she caught a glimpse of just how much Joe despised Eduardo and what he stood for. He couldn't help but see her as an extension of her father. Why did she have to be Eduardo Ferrare's daughter?

She reached up with one hand and laid her palm on his cheek. "You're such a good man," she murmured.

He snorted. "You said that before, and you've got to know that I'm a lot of things, but *good* surely isn't one of them."

"Then you're not looking at yourself through my eyes," she replied with conviction. "From where I stand, you're practically sainthood material."

He blinked at her, looking nearly as flummoxed as her father had just been. "You're looking through rose-colored glasses, princess. Seeing what you want to see."

"Then here's to wearing those suckers forever," she said.

"I'm the one who doesn't deserve *you*," he muttered back.

She'd just opened her mouth to deny the truth of his statement when Gunter spoke from beside the pool. "In answer to your earlier question, Mr. Smith, Cari was potty-trained for daytime when she was two-and-a-half years old and fully trained by her third birthday."

Cari looked up at him, surprised. "How in the world do you know that?" she asked.

He gazed down at her, the expression in his eyes as close to human as any she'd ever seen. An infinitesimal smile cracked his lips. And then he shrugged, turning away.

"Son of a gun," Joe breathed in her ear. "Who'd have guessed. Big G has a heart."

Shock rendered her unable to reply. Gunter? He cared enough for her to remember details like that? But as she thought back, he did, indeed, treat her like his own daughter much of the time. Who'd have guessed, indeed?

Joe interrupted her stunned train of thought, murmuring in her ear, "You are one truly incredible lady. Spine of steel."

"Who, me?" she blinked.

"Yeah, you. You blow me away. I've never seen anyone who can take a punch like you can. You roll with it and just get back on your feet and press on. You're amazing."

Her cheeks felt hot. Nobody had ever said anything remotely like that to her before. Ever. When he put it like that, she suddenly did feel strong and in charge of herself and her life. And wasn't *that* a change from the status quo?

She glanced up at him. There it was again. That sense of shared, intimate understanding of one another. It was like having their own secret garden to retreat to in the midst of everyone else around them.

Finally, the towels and bathing suits arrived. She snagged the white one-piece suit that got tossed out to her and shimmied into it while she treaded water. It was a trick to do without drowning herself. Joe pulled on a pair of baggy surfing shorts beside her and then helped her untwist the straps across her back.

Although their entire swim probably took less than ten minutes, it felt like she'd been in this water for an eternity. It was so nice to finally climb out of the pool—clothed. Gunter held a big beach towel out to her and she smiled shyly at him. He ducked his head, embarrassed, and looked away as she took the big cloth and wrapped it around herself.

Tucking in the free end over her bosom, she murmured, "Thanks, Gunter. You're the best."

He nodded and turned away without making eye contact with her. Well, weren't the macho images just toppling left and right tonight?

"Let's go, princess. I swear, when we get to our room, I'm locking the door and not letting anyone in for a week!"

"Sounds like a great plan to me," she agreed as Joe looped his arm around her shoulders.

They didn't see her father on the way upstairs. No doubt, he was busy pondering his lack of bonding with his daughters because of his failure to wipe their bottoms as babies. She bit back a grin. Where did Joe come up with that stuff?

Never in her entire life had she seen anyone manage to turn Eduardo inside out and tie him in knots like Joe did. It was a gift.

Gunter escorted them upstairs and let them inside with a quiet admonition. "Stay inside at night from now on."

Joe grinned at the security man. "Can I quote you on that?"

Gunter's gaze flickered over to her. "Keep her safe, eh?"

Joe's voice shifted, taking on a tone she didn't hear often outside of this room. One of deadly seriousness. "With my life."

Gunter nodded as if the two of them had just come to some huge understanding. Must be some sort of guy thing. Passing the torch for the care and feeding of the weak, needy female. She rolled her eyes and stepped into the room.

While Joe did, in fact, lock the door securely, she turned off the lights. All of them. It had suddenly hit her that Joe had seen what had happened in her father's office. He'd witnessed the Slav's disgusting suggestions as well as her father's response. It had been so personal. So…degrading. And she didn't want to talk about it, thank you very much!

In an effort to distract him, she said, "I need a shower. To get the chlorine from our swim out of my hair. Join me?"

Joe glanced at the bathroom and then back at her. The understanding that she wanted to talk and didn't want to be overheard dawned on his face.

He nodded crisply but drawled easily, "You got it, baby. I'll scrub your back if you'll scrub mine."

"Deal."

When the bathroom door was securely closed and the water running full steam, Joe turned to her. "What's up?"

"I thought you might be interested in exactly what it was my father was buying tonight."

"He's buying something?"

She leaned her hip against the blue granite counter and crossed her arms. "Yup. Information."

Joe cocked a questioning eyebrow.

"Turns out the Slavic jerk has access to his country's intelligence documents. And the South African guy buys information from a spy satellite the South African government still has in orbit. I don't know where the other two get their stuff from, but they're information brokers, too."

"Okay, I'll bite. What's your old man trying so hard to get his mitts on?"

She paused for a moment to let the dramatic tension build.

"Well?" Joe prompted.

"He's buying the names and home addresses of everyone on Charlie Squad."

Joe lurched up off the toilet, where he was seated. "What?"

"I said—"

"I heard you the first time. Tell me everything he said."

She shrugged. "There wasn't much to hear. My father offered a million dollars to the first man to bring him the complete roster of Charlie Squad operators and where they live."

"And what's he planning to do with that information?" Joe snapped.

"I have no idea. The South African asked the same thing in a roundabout way, and in just as roundabout a way, my father told him to mind his own business."

Joe unleashed a long string of profanities. "I've got to get that camera back."

"What camera?" she asked, confused.

"The one I used to take pictures of all your father's guests. I hid it under the bushes below your balcony when I thought your father's men were going to shoot me."

The thought of him taking a bullet made her shudder.

Joe was speaking again. "Did you catch their names?"

She nodded.

"The first order of business is to relay this information to some friends of mine who'll know what to do with it."

That was interesting. He didn't come right out and name himself a member of Charlie Squad, nor did he acknowledge the existence of the squad by so much as a flicker of an eyelash.

"Have you got any ideas on how I could send out a message without it being intercepted?" he asked.

"I can modify your cell phone. Tighten up the transmission frequency and change it so the regular scans Gunter uses won't pick it up. Would that work?" she asked.

He nodded. "Especially after I get the camera back. I'll send the pictures digitally over my phone."

"Let's go get the camera now," she said eagerly, already thinking about how to change up his phone.

He laughed. "Slow down, honey. We won't get an inch outside this room for the rest of the night without a horde of your father's men landing on us. Maybe tomorrow."

She deflated rapidly. He was right. Apparently, the adrenaline still surging through her after their close encounter in the pool had left some sort of residue in its wake. An afterglow of wildness that was tearing at her for release.

"Besides," Joe continued, "I'm exhausted. Go ahead and grab a shower. I'll wait for you in the bedroom."

As Cari took a quick shower and dried her hair, she doubted Joe's supposed fatigue. He just didn't want her coming on to him. She *knew* he was attracted to her, but why wouldn't he do anything about it? Obvious answer: work. He felt a need to be on guard all the time. All she had to do was get him to relax. Let down his hair for a little while and then his real feelings would come through and he would finally get around to making love to her! It was worth a try, at any rate. She couldn't take too much more of this frustration.

When she left the bathroom, Joe was surfing TV channels. He stopped on a music video station and turned it up loud. And then he reached for the bed covers, which had been remade from where he'd ripped them up earlier. Cari bet a maid had been sent in to repair the damage while she and Joe were trapped in the pool.

She never could get used to the total lack of privacy in her father's home—the way others came in and out of her room, manhandling her possessions as if they were public property. Yet another reason to get out of here as soon as possible.

Joe invited her with a sweep of the hand to climb in. And, shockingly, she was okay with doing just that. Maybe it was the knowledge that this was a new mattress. Or maybe it was Joe's comforting presence. But whatever it was, she was actually going to sleep in her bed again! Exultation at the victory filled her. It was a small thing—stupid, really—but she'd overcome her fears. And *that* was huge.

She crawled between the smooth, cool sheets, more grateful to have dodged disaster in the pool than alarmed at the prospect of sleeping in her own bed again.

"Way to go, tiger," Joe murmured. "I told you. Spine of steel. You're a brave woman."

She smiled up at him. "Don't be too impressed. I only borrowed some courage from you."

"Consider it a gift," he replied. Joe pulled the covers up around her chin and leaned over to turn off the little lamp on her bedside table. The room went dark.

Beneath the blaring music, she murmured, "Hold me?"

"Are you sure?" he replied cautiously.

"Please."

Thankfully, he didn't require any more invitation than that. His warmth encircled her even before his arms did. Oh, my, he felt nice.

His hand cupped the back of her head as her cheek found the perfect spot to nestle at the base of his neck. He'd pulled on a T-shirt and a pair of dry shorts and the soft cotton rubbed lightly against her skin. Her palms itched to get under it to the warm man beneath.

Why not? They were technically married, after all. All the cameras were gone and nobody was going to hear anything over that music channel. Besides, tonight she'd earned a little of what *she* wanted for a change.

She reached down and ran her hand up inside the front of his shirt. Joe tensed.

"I don't bite," she commented.

"Damn," he mumbled. "I was hoping you did."

"Don't tempt me," she laughed. "You look pretty tasty."

"Be my guest," he replied. "I'm all yours. Anything you want."

That comment shot her pulse up. A lot. Going to sit back and let her call the shots tonight, was he? Whoa. Well, that was just fine. She knew *exactly* what she wanted from him.

Chapter 12

"Anything I want?" Cari echoed. She wanted to make sure she'd heard him correctly before she made her request.

"Well, within reason," he amended. "It's not like we can walk out of here tonight, for example. The hornet's nest is too stirred up for that."

"That's not what I want anyway."

"What do you want, princess?" He sounded extremely wary as he asked that.

"Tell me your real name," she said.

"It's Joe."

"Seriously."

"Seriously," he repeated. "My real name is Joe."

"Joe what?"

"Ah, Cari. Let's not go there."

"Why not?"

"Some things are best left alone. If you knew my last name,

you could research all kinds of unpleasant things about me and my past. And trust me, you don't want to know the details."

"Are you a criminal?" she asked.

He answered reluctantly. "I suppose in some people's minds I am. I'd like to think there's always a good reason for anything I do. I certainly don't think of myself as a criminal."

That was an interesting answer. Open to several possible interpretations. She cut to the chase. "Are you a member of Charlie Squad?"

He leaned back far enough to look down at her.

Stalling, was he?

"If I were a member of that group, I'd have to say no, and if I weren't a member, I'd say no, too. So my answer to that one is…no."

That had to be the most unconvincing no she'd ever heard. And maybe that was as close to an honest answer as he was allowed to give her.

"Where did you learn how to do spooky stuff?"

"Spooky stuff?"

Stalling again. She clarified. "Finding weaknesses in security systems, climbing off balconies and lurking in the bushes with high-tech cameras."

He chuckled. "You make me sound like the perfect paparazzo."

She smiled against his neck. "Believe me, I've been the target of paparazzi before and you're not nearly aggressive enough to be one of them."

"Wow," he responded. "That bad?"

"If you want to see firsthand, go out in public with me. By now, the rumors of our secret wedding have to be flying like crazy."

"You know, that's not a bad idea. I wonder if daddy dearest would go for it."

"After tonight's little expedition, probably not. He'll want to yank the leash hard for a couple of days. Make us remember who's in charge."

Joe shrugged beneath her ear. "If you pull the leash too short, the dog can bite you."

She raised herself up on one elbow in alarm. "Don't do anything stupid, Joe. You've gotten away with the surfer bum act so far, but he's got plenty of bite of his own."

Joe reached up and urged her head back down onto his shoulder. She subsided, but reluctantly. She *had* to convince him not to push her father too far. And then it hit her. He'd done it again! He'd adroitly turned the conversation away from whether or not he was involved with Charlie Squad. Dang, he was good. She could reopen the subject and push the matter, but he'd just distract her again. He'd probably given her all the answers he was going to. And maybe, ultimately, that was more revealing than hearing him actually admit to being in Charlie Squad.

She lay there thoughtfully and started when Joe's hand closed over hers. She hadn't been paying attention, but she'd been stroking his chest beneath his T-shirt and twining her fingers in the sprinkling of chest hairs there.

Sudden vibrating tension raced up her arm and down to her core. Without a word and hardly a movement, he'd totally changed the tenor of the moment. It was as if he had flipped on a sex-appeal switch and, all of a sudden, steaming sensuality was rolling off him. Not that she was *complaining* about it, of course. But as distractions went, it was pretty bloody effective.

An answering surge welled up inside her, rising to meet him halfway.

"God Almighty, woman," he muttered as he half rolled to face her. "What am I going to do with you?"

He felt it, too, huh? "Do you want me to actually answer that question?" she replied laughingly.

He laughed ruefully. "No, I don't. I've got too many ideas of my own already."

A chink in the gentleman's armor, eh? "Really? Like what?"

His free arm went around her and he gathered her close. "Nothing I'm going to act on right now. You've had a rough night and I'm not going to pile more emotional baggage on top of everything else."

Her right hand crept around his waist. This guy didn't carry an ounce of fat on him. He was solid muscle. "Look. That Slav was a bigger asshole than most of them, but it's not like stuff like that hasn't happened to me before. And I'm still okay."

"Are you?" he whispered. "Are you really?"

The pain in his voice arrested her. He was really upset by the incident.

"Yes, Joe, I really am." She leaned back and wormed her arms free so she could reach up and put her hands on either side of his face. "I've survived worse."

"Oh, Lord. Don't tell me that. I'm going to have to go out and kill every bastard who's ever laid a hand on you."

"My own knight in shining armor," she murmured. "You can't slay all the dragons by yourself, you know."

"No, but I *can* kill the biggest, baddest one of the bunch," he growled. "You just say the word."

She froze. If she wasn't mistaken, he'd just offered to kill her father for her. The thought sent a cold chill down her spine. Her father was just doing business, using all available tools at hand to get the job done. It was nothing personal.

"Joe, my father has always used my looks to distract men in meetings. It's no big deal."

"Honey, I'm sorry, but I have to disagree. It *is* a big deal. That guy was all over you. And your father *let* it happen, even implied it could go further. No parent who loves his child would use her in that way."

Joe broke off sharply as if his anger was about to get the best of him. He took a couple of long, deep breaths, exhaling hard.

"It's okay, Joe. Really."

"No, it's not okay!" He exploded, sitting up abruptly and yanking his arm out from beneath her.

"Shh," she cautioned him in alarm, sitting up as well.

"I'm serious," he continued in a lower voice. "At a minimum, it should infuriate you."

Should it? She looked inside herself. Was there a kernel of anger inside her somewhere that she'd missed or ignored? *Anger* wasn't the word for it. *Hurt* was a better description. She wanted to please her father, to do what made him happy. She wanted his approval. If letting his business associates paw her a little made her father proud, then she would put up with it. Except, tonight her father had gone further than before. But she was sure he didn't mean it. And he would have made sure the Slav kept away from her once the meeting was over. Of course, he would have. She frowned. Viewed through Joe's eyes, it seemed like she was letting her father prostitute her body in a calculated and debasing way. Maybe she *should* be angry.

"Maybe I'm not strong enough to get mad over it," she said carefully.

"Bull," he snorted. "I wasn't kidding when I said you're the strongest woman I've ever met." He shoved a hand through his dark hair. "You just don't know to get mad about it. That bastard has you believing he loves you because you do crap like that for him. And it's a lie. He's using you. He's treating you with no more respect than a cheap hooker. Jeez—" Joe broke off and took a deep breath "—Cari, that's not love. It's—"

Anger flared in her. "It's what, Joe? Go ahead and say it. What does that make me?"

It was his turn to look at the walls in alarm and shush her.

"Don't go telling me to be quiet. You're the one who brought this up. You can damn well finish this conversation."

His eyes closed in acute pain. When he finally opened them, sorrow shone in their dark depths. He spoke gently. "I'm sorry, Cari. I was wrong to open this can of worms. It's your life and I have no right to intrude. I just hate to see you get hurt."

And that did it. The dam broke and the tears came. Thank God the room was dark because she had never learned how to cry prettily. Her eyes turned red and swelled and her nose ran, and she snorted ungracefully while ugly sobs racked her. She didn't even make decent crying noises. She sounded like a bull moose with a cold.

She *wanted* him to claim the right to intrude! Why did he refuse to see that? Why did he make her face this pain? What purpose did it serve? It all closed in on her—the hurt, the fear and the shame—and she sobbed all the more.

But through it all, Joe held her, offering her tissues and pushing her hair off her face to wipe away the tears.

"Better?" he finally murmured.

"God, I don't know," she mumbled. "I'm not even sure what I was crying about."

"Why don't you just chalk it up to stress relief," he suggested.

A comforting thought, but there was more to it than that. Much more. Tonight, Joe had torn away part of the blinders she wore to get through her life with a measure of sanity. She didn't want to see her world as it really was, dammit! Didn't Joe understand that? She had to let a layer of fog obscure the sharp corners and harsh realities of it all. Her illusions were all she had.

"Come here, baby," Joe murmured.

She rolled into his arms and clung to him tightly. She ought to be embarrassed by her complete breakdown, but Joe seemed to have taken it in stride.

"I'll make it better, I swear," he muttered into her hair.

Was he saying that to her or to himself? She couldn't exactly tell.

"You already have," she mumbled against his chest.

"How's that?"

"Just by being here. By caring enough to make me face something ugly about myself."

"There's nothing ugly about you, Cari," he said slowly. "Your father has brainwashed you into believing his bull. But now you're growing up. You can look at what he says and does and see it more clearly."

"You make me sound like some kid."

"You *are* a kid," he replied.

"I'm twenty-four. That's not so young. And you have to admit that growing up in this house has exposed me to stuff most twenty-four-year-olds never have to deal with."

He drew her even closer in a protective gesture. "In some ways, you're more worldly than most fifty-year-olds. But your life has isolated you from certain lessons, as well. I don't mean to insult you. You're incredibly bright and wise for your age. But there's no way around the fact that twenty-four is damned young."

Too young for him? Was that what he was saying with such regret in his voice?

"How old are you?" she asked.

"Thirty-seven."

"Wow. You're just about ready for the old-folks' home. Do you need help taking your teeth out and brushing them or can you still manage that by yourself?"

"Hey!" he laughed. "I still get around. It's just that—"

"I'm too young for you?" she suggested with a certain edge in her voice.

"Well, thirteen years *is* a big age difference."

"Thirty years is a big age difference," she retorted. "Thirteen isn't that huge a chasm. Besides, when has love ever stopped to look at birth certificates? It happens where it wills. If two people are meant to be together, age is mean-ingless."

"Aha, the truth comes out. She's a closet romantic!" Silence fell between them.

"Joe?"

"Hmm?"

"There's something else I want tonight."

Instant caution zinged through his voice. "What's that?"

"Make love to me."

He jolted beneath her.

She raised herself up on one elbow and stared down at him in the dark. "You know, by refusing to make love to me, you might just give me more of that emotional baggage you mentioned earlier. It would probably be best just to give in to what's between us."

He frowned at her. "There's something between us?"

She raised her eyebrows. "Not much experience with women, Joseph?"

He scowled and she laughed at him. And then she leaned down and kissed him. That was more like it. The wildness she'd been feeling ever since she first met this man surged to the fore once more. Her hands skimmed across Joe's shoulders, his neck and his face as her tongue swept into his mouth, inviting him in no uncertain terms to come play with her.

His arms came up around her as if to stop her from rubbing herself against him, but she groaned deep in her throat and Joe froze. The nature of the embrace changed. Answering hunger rattled in the back of his throat.

"We shouldn't do this," he gasped, tearing his mouth away from hers.

Gee, wasn't that supposed to be the girl's line? She tried to remember what the guys said to get past that particular protest but drew a blank. So she kissed him some more. And it was hot. No way would she ever get enough of this man. If she could figure out a way to inhale him, she would.

She crawled on top of him, reveling in his powerful body, rejoicing in the feeling of her breasts smashed against his hard chest. His hands roamed all over her back, up her ribs and brushed the sides of her breasts. Liquid heat sprang between her legs and she buried her face against the corded column of his neck.

"I can't believe what you do to me," she laughed. "You're killing me."

He reared up at that one, rolling her off him abruptly. But blessedly, he followed after her body with his, never breaking contact between them. His weight pressed her down into the mattress.

Desperate to have him fill her, one of her legs crept up, wrapping around his thighs in naked invitation.

"You're the one who's killing me, here," he muttered.

"Then make love to me and we'll die together," she breathed up at him, her throat too tight to make any more noise than that.

He grinned. "Hey, that's my line."

"Well, you seemed to need a little help remembering what comes next."

His eyebrows shot straight up.

She continued blithely, "I mean, seeing as you've had so little experience with women and all, I thought maybe I'd better help you along."

"I don't need any help, thank you," he growled.

She studied him in mock seriousness. "I don't know," she said doubtfully. "Do you need me to tell you where everything goes?"

He laughed aloud at that. "Let's see if I can figure it out for myself, shall we?"

She speared her hands deep into his hair and tugged his head down close to hers. "I'm all yours," she whispered.

He sank into her by slow degrees, his mouth soft against hers, kissing her sweetly at first. His hands traced lightly over her skin, awakening her body, nerve by nerve. He kissed her deeply, but he was still holding back. A lot.

He was going to drive her crazy to get even with her for starting this thing. But what a way to go. She closed her eyes and savored the tingling progress of his fingertips. And when he'd finished with his hands, he began with his mouth. She had to give him credit for being thorough—he didn't miss one inch of her body. He licked and nipped and sucked his way from paradise to hell and back, driving her steadily out of her mind with need.

And when he pushed her knees apart and sampled the sweetest fruits of her desire, she was sure she'd died. She trembled around the electrical currents building higher and higher within her, robbing her of breath. She raised her head off the pillows, her entire body taut as his tongue circled and teased her to the very edge of release.

And then he rose up over her, as dark and mysterious as the night around her, and plunged into the molten depths of her until she couldn't tell where he ended and she began. She let out a cry as she exploded, and a great black void of nothing but incredible sensation burst over her, showering her in tingling pulsations that nearly tore her apart.

She opened her eyes, staring up in disbelief. Oh, she'd enjoyed sex before, but nothing like *that* had ever happened to her!

A slow smile broke across his face. "Do I have everything in the right place?"

She nodded, too out of breath to speak.

"Let's see what happens when I do this." And then he began to move again, a slow, gentle rocking that built and built until it became a hot, hard, driving thrust of flesh on slick flesh.

And the tension began to build again, stretching her out tighter and tighter until she thought she couldn't stand it anymore. She surged up beneath him, straining toward release. She heard her own voice, husky with need, begging him for more.

And then a glittering explosion of pleasure filled the black void once more, rushing out to the very ends of her fingertips. In that endless moment, Joe buried his face against her neck and cried out against her skin, shuddering powerfully against her body. It was perfect.

She fell back against the mattress, panting. *Oh. My. God.*

How long they lay there, their limbs twisted together and their hearts pounding as one, she had no idea. But, eventually, she managed to mumble, "You've ruined me."

Joe's head jerked up off the pillow above her shoulder and he stared down at her. "I didn't hurt you, did I?"

"No! But after that, I won't be able to make love to anyone else for as long as I live."

He frowned, looking alarmed.

She clarified. "Nobody else could ever top that. If you ever leave me, I'll just have to swear off sex altogether. Because nothing less than that would ever do again."

He rolled over, finally disengaging their bodies from one another. She missed the feeling of him deep inside her already.

"You may have spoiled me for any other woman, too," he muttered, so quietly she wasn't sure she was supposed to have heard it.

"Good thing we're already married," she said lightly.

Joe tensed beside her. Cursed.

She propped herself up in alarm. "What's wrong?"

"I just may have negated our ability to get an annulment. I'm sorry, Cari. This means we might have to get a divorce when you finally get sick of me."

She blinked a couple of times. Did he know what he'd just said? He'd just acknowledged that this was a real marriage. Furthermore, he'd said, "when you get sick of me." Not the other way around. Was he starting to harbor thoughts of a long-term relationship with her? Could it be?

Aloud, she said fervently, "Remind me to thank Julia the next time I see her for sending you to me."

Joe grinned. "I will. And remind *me* to thank her for sending me, too."

A moment of silence fell. It lay there comfortably between them. A good thing, given what they'd just shared together. She figured it would either draw them closer together or send him running for the hills.

"Get some sleep," he murmured. "You've had a big day."

"What's on the agenda for tomorrow?" she mumbled. "Can we do more of this, please?"

Joe's finger traced her lips lazily. "That sounds like a plan." But then he sighed. "I'd love to stick around here and find out what Eduardo plans to do with the information he's buying, but after what we just—" he broke off. "Let's just say, it's more important than ever to get you out of here."

"How are you going to do that?" she asked.

"Good question. I still have to figure out some of the features of the house's security system."

In other words, *butt out*. It was too late to press the issue, but tomorrow she'd demand to know the details. And, speaking of late, she was getting sleepy.

She sighed, "The only person in the house who knows more about the security system than I do is Gunter. He used to show me all the controls and how they worked. Tomorrow, you can ask me anything you want to know."

"Answer me one thing and then I really am going to let you go to sleep. Is there a basement in this place?"

"Mmm-hmm," she replied, already half-unconscious.

Joe went stiff beneath her. His mind raced, *finally* emerging from the spell of their lovemaking, as Cari drifted off to sleep on his shoulder. God, she felt good, curled up against him like that.

She continued to amaze him with her resilience. She'd made good progress tonight toward breaking off her dependence on her old man. It had to be hard to let go of the only parent she'd ever had.

And he was a schmuck. It was cruel to make love to her— hell, to manipulate her emotions this way. She was a living, breathing woman with real feelings and real pain, and he was playing it all like a violin to his own advantage. He was worse than a schmuck.

The hell of it was, he really did care for Cari. Even if they hadn't just shared the most mind-blowing sex of his adult life, he'd still be concerned about the way her father was using her. He'd still worry that she had no idea what love was or how it appropriately ought to be expressed.

He was falling for this woman—hard—despite his best

efforts not to. Every time he turned around, she showed him some new facet to her personality. Yeah, sure, she had some problems. She was clueless about how to stand up for herself and, although she knew sisterly love, she clearly didn't understand parental love. Plus, the whole idea of mutual respect between a man and a woman seemed to have escaped her experience. He didn't even want to *think* about the men she'd dated before.

It didn't matter what wrong lessons in love they'd taught her, dammit. It wasn't his job to fix her misconceptions.

Yeah, but if she offered him the assignment, he'd be hard-pressed to turn it down. He had it bad for her, all right. And the list of reasons not to let there be a repeat of tonight went on for miles. Topping the list was the fact that it went against all standards of proper military behavior. Right behind that was that the last thing he wanted to do was hurt Cari. And, surely he would if he let her fall in love with him.

One day soon, this mission would end and he'd walk away from her. The next op would beckon and he'd be out the door to God knows where for God knows how long with no guarantee of returning alive. He couldn't ask her to wait for him. Her life was already too unstable. She needed someone she could depend on. Someone who'd be there for her every day and every night.

Hell, he'd drive himself crazy with jealousy if he left a girl as beautiful as Cari behind every time he went on the road. He'd seen so many long-distance relationships crumble between soldiers and the girls back home that he couldn't count them all. It took a special woman to wait alone on the home front and remain loyal through all the long absences his line of work dished out.

A little voice at the back of his brain nagged at him. How could he be so sure Cari wasn't that special a woman? She'd shown him a hell of a lot of character so far. The kind of fortitude a guy could come to believe in and trust for the times apart.

Maybe making their marriage the real deal wasn't so far-fetched an idea, after all....

Cari shifted against him, mumbling in her sleep and draping her leg across his thighs. Her arm settled across his chest. Inexplicable panic speared through him.

Trapped. He was trapped.

He had to get out of here. And where was "here," exactly? Was he freaking out about getting away from the irresistible lure of Cari, or was his sudden and overwhelming claustrophobia a result of being trapped in his enemy's home? It didn't matter. Either way, he couldn't lie here one more second.

He eased out from under Cari and breathed a sigh of relief as she slept on. Silently, he changed into the black pants and turtleneck he'd worn earlier. Time to go have a look at the basement.

He cracked open the hallway door. Thank God. No guard standing outside it tonight. Everyone must have figured that he and Cari would have the good sense to stay in for the rest of the night after their disastrous excursion earlier.

He moved quickly down the hallway. In his exploration of the house so far, he'd determined that there weren't many security cameras in the public areas of the interior. He had found them only around doorways leading in and out of the house. He guessed that the majority of the cameras were reserved for the guest bedrooms and Cari's room, of course. It was the great weakness of the home. The place was wired to keep intruders out but not to keep intruders *in*.

He paused, crouching, at the end of the hall. He watched the foyer for a couple of minutes. He knew that guards roamed the house and grounds all night long, but he had no idea what their routine was. He was working blind here. And that meant he had to go slow and be extra careful.

He waited until a guard passed through the entry hall downstairs. The guy was walking slowly, looking around, bored.

Definitely the patrolling duty guard. Joe gave the guy a couple minutes to move on and then raced on ballet-dancer-light feet down the sweeping staircase.

His best guess was that the basement entry would be near the kitchen. From the blueprints that they had gotten from a classified source he recalled a couple of pantries and a small office were off the kitchen. Charlie Squad had always assumed that office was where Eduardo's security men were based. But now that he was inside the mansion and saw the true extent of the operation here, that office wasn't nearly big enough to house all the electronics, let alone the other monitors and gadgets that had to go with this fortress's security system.

Besides, if he got caught by the kitchen, he could always claim to be on a refrigerator raid. In fact, he probably ought to grab a snack to act as his cover. He glided across the expanse of the commercial kitchen and opened the big stainless-steel refrigerator. He spied a plate of individually wrapped subs. Perfect. He grabbed one.

Now, to find that basement. He headed for the office next to the kitchen and stopped in front of the closed door. A faint light seeped underneath it. No noise. Impossible to tell if there was someone on the other side of that door or not. His best bet was probably just to open it right up and act like he was snooping if there was someone there.

He unwrapped one end of his sandwich and, armed only with the hoagie, threw open the door.

Nada.

There was a small desk with a newspaper spread out across it. A monitor was perched on one side of the desk. Right now, it showed a view of the dark swimming pool. This must be where the roving guard parked between circuits of the estate. And beyond the desk, bingo.

An open door with a downward staircase. Footsteps slapped on the kitchen floor behind him. The guard returning to his post! Joe bolted for the stairwell and ran most of the way down before he stopped and lay down on the steps to reduce his profile.

Whoever had just entered the little office didn't poke his head down the stairs. Damn, that had been a close one!

He turned his attention to the other end of the stairwell and eased the rest of the way down the flight of steps. He plastered himself against the wall and stuck one eye out just far enough to peer at what lay beyond.

A long hallway. With doors opening off each side. The floor and walls were unfinished concrete, and row after row of heavy, black cable ran overhead between the wooden beams of the ceiling supports. Those electrical wires were good candidates for cutting if he ever needed to throw the house into chaos. He'd bet a good chunk of the house's power—and probably the security system's power—was routed through those lines. A few narrow, brightly colored lines were strung up there, as well—probably phones.

The far end of the hall ended in what looked like a commercial freezer. The big, horizontal stainless-steel bar handle and insulated metal door screamed meat locker. The estate was well outside of town, a long way from the nearest market. They must keep a pretty hefty supply of food, given the number of mouths that had to be fed each day.

Joe eased out into the hall. The first door on his right was cracked open just enough for him to glimpse a wall of television monitors and the back of a man's head seated before them. The main nerve center of the security operation. *Roger, ops, we have primary target acquisition.*

This was just the Achilles' heel he'd been looking for. Knock out that room full of toys and he and Cari could stroll right out of there while everyone ran around like chickens with their heads cut off.

The guy at the video console started to turn and Joe ducked past the doorway quickly. He stopped at the next door, which was closed. He tested the knob. Locked. No time to pick it just now.

A third door revealed a storage room lined with shelves and crammed with the usual junk that houses accumulate in their basements—Christmas decorations, garden tools, assorted camping gear and sports equipment, old lamps and lots of dust. In the back, he found a large heating-and-cooling unit and a half-dozen water heaters. No surprise, a large electrical generator sat there, too. It was silent now, though. Must be the backup system for power outages.

He checked the hallway before heading out again. The coast was clear. He opened the fourth door and stepped into—

Holy crap! A torture chamber. It couldn't be anything else. The walls and ceiling of the room were completely upholstered in thick, padded blankets, the same kind used in food-processing plants to wrap around frozen food while it was shipped. A plain wooden table and a couple of wooden chairs were the only furniture. The lights were naked bulbs behind wire-mesh cages. There was a small drain grate set into the floor in one corner of the room. Probably served as both prisoner toilet and drain when it was time to hose away the blood. As his eyes adjusted to the dark, he noticed big, dark blotches on the walls. He'd bet his next paycheck those were bloodstains.

God, what a gruesome place. He'd sure as hell hate to end up in here as a client on the receiving end of the twisted services offered within these walls.

The only door left down here was to the freezer. What the hell. He might as well have a look in it, too. He peeked out into the hallway in time to see a figure disappearing into the security office. He waited a few minutes and, when no one emerged again, sprinted down the hall to the freezer. He eased open the latch and pulled the heavy door open far enough to slip inside. A blast of Arctic air slammed into him.

Before he pulled the door shut behind himself, he checked

to make sure there was a latch on the inside, too. Yup. He closed himself in, pulled out his pocket flashlight and shined it around the space, which was huge and cavernous.

He spied a light switch beside the door and flipped it on. The room was maybe twenty feet across and at least that deep. Damn. Eduardo could feed a small army out of this place. Maybe the guy was afraid of a siege or something.

Joe moved between the rows of tall shelves, stacked high with all kinds of food. In the back of the freezer, there was a large open area, maybe eight feet deep and running the width of the freezer. A long, coffin-shaped box sat on the floor in one corner. Surely, Eduardo didn't store dead bodies down here. Not when he could dispose of them so easily by tossing them out into the ocean for the plentiful sharks to consume. Joe tried the lid on the box, but it was padlocked shut at both ends. Weird. Maybe it was just a side of beef or something. But in that case, the locks made no sense. He shrugged and moved on.

Most of the rest of the space was lined with boxes that, as soon as he got close to them, were self-explanatory. They were explosives and ammunition. Crate after crate of the stuff.

It wasn't necessary to store explosives in a cold environment in this day and age. Not since nitroglycerin was bouncing around in stagecoaches had explosives been that unstable. Perhaps the thick cement walls and steel-reinforced ceiling of the freezer were the real reason this stuff was stacked in here. The meat locker did make an excellent ammo dump, now that he thought about it.

He took a last look at the coffin-shaped box. He grabbed a corner of it and tried to lift it. Very heavy. Maybe there were weapons in there.

The seeds of an escape plan were beginning to take shape in his mind. He'd pry open the box, grab a weapon if there were any inside, maybe snag a little C-4. He'd set up a timed charge to blow a couple bundles of those wires in the ceiling…. It could definitely work….

He headed back to the big storage room. He raided the toolbox he found, pulling out pliers, wire and wire cutters. He snagged an old windup alarm clock off one of the shelves, too, and went to work. He wired the clock to the ignition controls of the backup generator. It took several minutes, and he was careful to get it right. His life and Cari's might depend on this rig working.

Then he added a crowbar to his cache of tools and headed back down to the meat locker. Quickly, he stashed the tools behind the crates of ammunition. When it was time to escape, he wouldn't have to root around in the storage room, looking for what he needed. It would be right here. Now, all he had to do was pray he and Cari got a chance to use this stuff sometime soon.

In the meantime, he'd better head back to bed. It would start getting light before long and, with sunrise, the guards would perk up and be more alert.

Quickly and carefully, he retraced his steps down the hall and to the stairs. He made his way up them on his belly and stopped just shy of the little office at the top. Damn. The guard was sitting there, eating. His position on the stairs was completely exposed and he had nowhere else to go.

He lay there for ten interminable minutes. He was starting to contemplate jumping the guard from behind and knocking him out in order to get past him when finally, thankfully, the guy stood up. Joe's heart about stopped as the guy turned toward the stairs. But all he did was pitch a balled-up sandwich wrapper in the trash can. He turned away, gave his rear end a scratch and left.

Thank God.

All Joe had to do was make it to the kitchen. From there, he could stroll upstairs with his trusty hoagie in hand, without the slightest need for secrecy. He darted into the kitchen. Safe.

He unwrapped the sandwich, took a big bite and headed for bed. Tomorrow night, he and Cari would blow this Popsicle stand once and for all and get on with their lives. A little voice whispered in the back of his head, *our lives together.*

He narrowly avoided bolting for the front door in panic.

Chapter 13

Joe must have fallen asleep after he slipped back in beside Cari because he experienced a definite moment of waking up later that morning. A moment of registering a soft, warm body plastered against him from shoulder to knee. A moment of roaring response by his own body, and an infinitely worse moment of chagrined realization that there was no way in hell he got to roll over and relieve his rock-hard need on the sumptuous female form beside him. Yeah, he could wake up to her every morning for the rest of his life and not complain about it a bit.

He lay there for a few minutes, soaking in the intensely feminine vibe of white lace all around him. A month ago, he'd have said a room like this would drive him crazy. But, now he had to admit, the fringe benefits weren't bad at all.

Asleep, Cari looked even younger than he knew her to be, and even more innocent. Hell, downright angelic. He tried to slip out from underneath her without waking her up, but she opened her eyes and smiled up at him sleepily as soon as he moved his arm.

"I'm sorry," he murmured. "Go back to sleep."

Her mouth curved up into a smile. "Mmm, I'm not tired."

She made no move to let him up, no move to roll away from him and relieve his suffering. If anything, she was snuggling even more tightly against him. He closed his eyes. *Strength, man. Fortitude.*

Her hand crept up to his neck. Slid into his hair. And brought her naked breast into unabashed contact with his bare chest.

Fortitude, be damned. He angled his head down and captured her mouth in a full-contact, wet-tongued, tonsil-probing good-morning-to-you kiss. And, Sweet Lord, if she didn't taste good. Like peaches. How did she do that? He probably tasted like mouth surgery gone putrid. And that was the only thing that caused him to drag his mouth away from hers and come up gasping for air.

"More," she panted.

He squeezed his eyes shut. He shouldn't do this. It was *such* a bad idea. He'd seen more than one of his own teammates dragged to hell and back by a woman during a mission. He'd regret it for the rest of his life....

And he'd regret it more if he didn't kiss her this very second. He surged up over her, kissing her like there was no tomorrow. He all but inhaled her, sucking at her mouth, groaning as their tongues scraped together. He couldn't get enough of her.

"More, Joe. Oh, please. More...."

Her hands were straying again, skimming downward toward places that didn't need any attention right now.

"Easy does it, princess," he gasped. "We can't—"

"Says who?" she grumbled, kissing her way down his neck.

Oh, God. Oh, God, oh, God. Her mouth was following the path of her hands—down, down toward parts of him that ached to have her taste him. And he wasn't stopping her.

He. Had. To. Stop. Her.

It was worse than running in thigh-deep water with an

eighty-pound pack on his back, but he managed to drag his hands downward, forced his fingers to wrap around her wrists. He reached deep for the last dregs of his willpower and pulled her hands gently away from him. So *that* would be what shooting yourself in some vital organ felt like. It sucked, plain and simple.

She moaned in frustration.

"Honey, I know your pain," he half laughed, half groaned.

"Then why do we have to stop?" she demanded.

"Because I've got work to do and—" another gut check and deep reach for discipline "—and it's not right."

Her hands came to rest on his chest once more. "What's so wrong about this?" she murmured. "It feels pretty darn right to me."

His gut was ablaze with need. He really shouldn't. Except he didn't want to further scar her when it came to men and rejection. Yeah, that was it. That was his story and he was sticking to it, dammit. That was why he leaned forward and planted another searing kiss on her mouth, lest he let those luscious lips wander where they willed, surrounding him and sucking at him, licking and teasing…

"What work do you have to do?" Cari asked.

"I beg your pardon?" He could barely remember his name past the pounding pulse in his crotch.

"Work. You said you had work to do," she said breathlessly. At least she had the good grace to sound hot and bothered, too. "Uh, right. Gotta ask your father about an outing for you and me. Gotta have a look at the perimeter security along the fences," he whispered in her ear.

"Outing?" she repeated, sounding nearly as distracted as he was.

He sat up. Swung his feet over the side of the bed. Stared at the white carpet between his feet and did his damndest to form complete sentences. "Right. Outing. Like shopping. Or dancing."

"Sounds good."

"Which?" he mumbled.

"Either," she mumbled back, sitting up as well.

"I'll get on it, then."

Except when he finally managed to get dressed and stumble downstairs, he was informed that Eduardo was absent today. Out of the house this morning on a business errand. That news cleared his head fast. Was Ferrare out collecting the names and addresses of him and his colleagues in Charlie Squad already, perhaps? *He had to get the word out to Folly about this latest development.*

After breakfast, Joe headed back to Cari's bedroom or, more accurately, her bathroom to see how she was making out with reconfiguring his cell-phone signal. She'd skipped the meal to get to work on it for him.

Carrying a muffin and a glass of orange juice, he shouldered open her bathroom door after calling through the panel to announce himself.

"I brought you breakfast," he murmured. "How's it coming?"

"Close the door," she muttered absently.

He complied and she commented, "Almost done. I'll need you to attempt a phone call in a minute."

It was actually less than a minute before she passed him his cell phone, minus its impact-resistant case. "If it rings," Cari said, "then it's working. You'll be transmitting outside the range of my father's surveillance-system frequencies and the jamming setup in here."

He used his fingernail to carefully press the buttons and dial Folly's cell-phone number. There was a clicking in his ear and he asked quickly, "The frequency definitely won't be monitored? I can talk freely?"

"Definitely."

"It's ringing," he announced. She was good.

It picked up on the third ring. "Go ahead," a male voice snapped.

Thank God. Folly. "Hey, it's me," Joe said. "I'm in the clear on my end. Can you talk?"

"Yeah, I'm in the clear here. What's up?" his boss replied.

"Cari rigged my phone so it won't be monitored by her father's men. We've got news."

"News? About what?" The surprise in Folly's voice ratcheted up a notch.

"Eduardo had guests last night. Turns out they're information brokers and he's trying to buy the complete roster and home addresses of a certain group of people we both know and love."

A long pause greeted that announcement. Thunderous silence out of Tom Folly was never a good thing. It either meant he was cooking up some diabolical scheme or tightly reining in his temper.

"And he's planning to do what with this information?" Folly finally bit out.

"No idea. But it doesn't take a rocket scientist to guess, now, does it?"

"No, it doesn't." A good case of galloping mad was growing in his boss's gut. Joe could hear it in the clipped way he was pronouncing words.

Joe continued. "I got pictures of the players last night, but I had to hide the camera. When I retrieve it, I'll send you the—"

Joe broke off. Cari was holding out his camera, which still had bits of damp mud clinging to it.

"You didn't climb down and get that while I was downstairs, did you?" he asked in dawning horror.

In his right ear, Folly said, "Come again?"

And in his left ear, Cari replied gaily, "Nope. I just paid one of the maids a hundred dollars to fetch it for me."

"Jeez, Cari," Joe complained. "She could go straight to your father and tell him about it. Or she might've been seen, or told Gunter about the camera and let *him* find it. We can't afford to take crazy chances like that!"

In his right ear, Folly asked, "Who's Gunter?"

In his left, Cari retorted, "I've known Grace forever. She's always done favors for me, and she never tells. The extra money helps keep her family fed."

Joe scowled at her, his heart pounding in delayed reaction.

"Doc?" Folly said in his ear again. "What's going on?"

Joe sighed. "Cari took a risk but seems to have gotten away with it. She had a maid retrieve the camera. When we're done talking, I'll call again and send you digital files of the photos from last night's meeting. An ID on the visitors would be useful."

"I can't wait," Folly replied dryly. "When are you two out of there?"

"Working on it. Possibly as early as tonight. I'm scoping out the perimeter systems today to make sure there are no additional security measures on this side of the fence that I didn't spot in my previous surveillance outside. We'll need a pickup, either by car on the coast road or by fast boat. And it'll *have* to be fast. Guards patrol the water with radar and respond in armed speedboats."

"Got it," Folly answered. "We'll cover both egress routes and be standing by on this end for a call."

Joe continued. "Gunter—he's Eduardo's chief of security, probably ex German secret police—runs a tight ship. We're going to have to do something creative to get out from under his thumb."

"Mac and Tex are here. Howdy comes in this evening. Let us know what we can do to help."

That was good news. Knowing that most of his teammates were nearby was reassuring. And it gave him more options when it came time to break out of this glorified jail.

"Any luck tracking down the mole?" Joe asked.

"Nada. Whoever it is, they've gone to ground and have quit sending out any information for now, as far as we can tell."

Joe's jaw tightened. That mole was one of the main reasons this op was so risky. He stood in grave jeopardy of being exposed and killed if the mole figured out Charlie Squad actually had one of its operators inside Ferrare's house and then relayed that news to Eduardo.

"Now that we've got communication," Folly said, "call me if you need anything. We're here to help you two. We've got round-the-clock eyes on the compound."

"Are you operating out of the same house I did down the beach?" Joe asked.

"Yup. We've still got the Caddy, and Tex scored us a boat yesterday, so we've got a ride, either way."

"Outstanding," Joe replied, relieved. All he had to do was get outside the fence with Cari and Charlie Squad would take care of the rest.

"Just out of curiosity, did you say *Cari* reconfigured your cell phone?"

Joe laughed. "Yeah. Turns out, she has a degree in engineering. Specialized in microelectronics."

"You're kidding," Folly blurted in patent disbelief.

"As I live and breathe," Joe replied.

"I'll be damned. These Ferrare girls are just full of surprises."

"There's a lot more to them than meets the eye," Joe agreed.

Folly snorted. "I don't know. They've both got a hell of a lot to recommend them to the eye."

Joe smiled across the small space of the bathroom at Cari. "They do, indeed."

"Watch your tail, champ. And I'll be standing by to download those pictures."

"Roger. Will do."

They hung up and Joe immediately called the same number back. When the colonel picked up on the other end, Joe extracted a tiny cord from a compartment in the camera and plugged its universal cord into his cell phone. He hit the Send button.

"That could take a few minutes," Cari commented. "Photo files are big, and that phone has limited capacity. Wanna take a shower with me while we wait?"

Lord, that sounded tempting. "I need to walk the fence line while your father's out. Gunter will relax while the boss is away. He'll take care of administrative stuff he can't do when your old man's around and he's stuck on bodyguard duty."

Cari looked disappointed but said cheerfully enough, "I guess *I'll* take a shower, then. We've got to do something to cover up why one of us is staying in here for the next twenty minutes or so."

He pushed away from the counter and couldn't resist planting a quick kiss on her cheek. "You're a peach," he murmured.

She laughed aloud. "A fruit, am I? I'll have to work on my image, I see."

He stepped closer again but refrained from touching her. He said roughly, "Don't knock it. I adore peaches."

Then he spun around and left the room. He dared not stay in close proximity any longer or he'd be in grave danger of showing her just how much he loved the sweet, juicy fruit.

With Eduardo gone and Gunter occupied somewhere inside the house, checking out the fence was a piece of cake. Joe just took a walk and stumbled across a path running along the inside of the fence line—no doubt worn into the dirt by security guards walking perimeter patrols. The good news was, he didn't find any new security measures that he wasn't already aware of.

Of course, the stuff he knew about was impressive enough—heat sensors, motion detectors, cameras, and infrared beams, not to mention the fact that the fence itself was twelve feet tall, made of heavy cast iron and topped with numerous pointed spikes. And he was sure the code to the gate leading out to the beach had been changed. Hopping the fence wasn't going to be an option for him and Cari, either. Maybe a little C-4 to blow a hole through it. They weren't likely to be able to sneak all the way out of this place undiscovered, so they might as well leave in a blaze of glory.

After his little nature hike around the estate, which encompassed nearly ten acres, he headed for the swimming pool. Might as well get a little exercise while he waited for Eduardo to come home so the two of them could talk.

He swam for a solid hour, losing count of how many laps he'd done. It helped burn off a little of his immediate sexual frustration, but it didn't touch the overall tension thrumming through him at the mere thought of Cari in his arms again.

When he finally climbed out, he was pleased to see that Cari had come out to the pool, wearing a fire-engine red bikini that was an absolute knockout. He flopped down on a chaise lounge next to her and let the sun warm his skin.

He felt a presence approaching and lifted his head lazily. Rico. The thug who'd gotten so mad at finding him and Cari skinny-dipping in the pool last night. He didn't look much happier today. The set of his meaty shoulders was distinctly aggressive. The guy was looking to increase his status within the organization and was jonesing to find someone weaker than himself to rough up a little. Joe sighed. Rico stopped at the foot of Joe's lounge chair and stared down at him.

Joe gazed back impassively. "Can I do something for you?" he asked evenly.

"Yeah. Quit flaunting the fact that you're sleeping with the boss's daughter," Rico growled.

Joe smiled easily. "I don't have to flaunt it. That's what married people do. I have a piece of paper that says I can sleep with her whenever I feel like it."

"Yeah, well, who the hell are you? You waltz in here and steal her right out from under her father's nose and think you can get away with it?"

Joe shrugged. "I didn't steal her. Eduardo knew we were seeing each other. And I'm sure he knew we were getting serious. Besides, he gave our marriage his blessing."

What was this guy's angle? He was acting acutely jealous. Like a big brother. Or a jilted lover? Joe eyed Rico afresh. He wasn't a bad-looking guy, in a linebacker sort of way. Was this beefcake Cari's type? She must think *he* was a scrawny little wimp, then.

He glanced over at Cari. She was frowning uncertainly at Rico, but she didn't look guilty or irritated, like she might if an old flame stirred up trouble with her new husband.

Hell, he was her husband. He had the right to ask the question. "Cari, were you and this guy ever an item?"

That was genuine surprise on her face. Hallelujah. "Good Lord, no! I was never allowed to date my father's men," she added hastily as Rico scowled darkly.

Hmm. She, too, sensed something dangerous in Rico's manner. Not good. Should he stay sprawled out on his back on the assumption that Rico wouldn't attack a man in no position to defend himself, or should he be moseying to his feet?

Getting up won out. He wanted to move far enough away from Cari so if Rico did something stupid there was no chance she'd get caught in the fray and get hurt.

Joe sat up, wiping the sweat off his face in a leisurely fashion with a towel. He eyed the bulge under the guy's left armpit beneath the light jacket he wore unzipped. A gun, no doubt. Right-handed, then. Probably wouldn't pull it, though because Gunter and the other guards would have to respond aggressively to a brandished weapon. It could get Rico in trouble or fired or, around here, worse. He might end up as shark bait.

The look in Rico's eyes said he didn't just want to bloody Joe; he wanted to kill him. The guy wouldn't come in unarmed using only his fists. A knife, then.

Rico's hands flexed into a fist. Opened. Oh, yeah. Going to reach for a weapon any second.

"Look, man," Joe said calmly. "I don't want any trouble. Why don't we go inside and get a drink. Sit down and talk about what's on your mind. I'm willing to listen to what you have to say."

Rico bared his teeth. *Definitely* not interested in talking.

Joe spoke quietly. With the calm assurance of a man speaking the truth. "I've got to warn you, Rico. I can handle myself in a fight. This isn't going to go down easy the way you think it will. You're going to come out of this with mud on your face. Cari's going to be furious that you attacked me. This is not going to win you any points with her. She's going to demand that you be fired, and Eduardo might very well kill you."

Out of the corner of his eye, he saw Cari open her mouth to speak, but he made a subtle cutting gesture with his hand, ordering her to be silent. She caught the signal and subsided, frowning. Thank God. He needed to keep all of Rico's attention on him and away from doing something stupid like grabbing Cari and putting a knife to her neck or a gun to her head.

"Think, Rico. There's nothing but downside potential to this scenario. Walk away from it now. No harm, no foul."

"I don't think so," the big man snarled. "You think you're so smart and can talk circles around me. But you're a little pissant punk in need of a lesson on the way things run around here. You can't just stroll in and take over the joint."

"I have no interest in taking over the joint," Joe replied flatly. "I'm telling you again. Turn around and walk away from this. You've got nothing to gain and everything to lose."

"That's where you're wrong, pretty boy. The boss rewards initiative. He wants to be rid of you. And the guy who steps up to the plate and takes care of the problem is going to be rewarded richly."

If that was Rico's reasoning, there was going to be no way around dropping this guy by force. Several movements behind the windows caught Joe's eye. They'd already collected an audience inside the house. Now there was no way whatsoever that Rico would back down.

Joe spoke to Cari without taking his eyes off the bigger man. "Princess, is there some sort of first aid kit around here? A crash kit, maybe?"

"What's that?" she asked, her voice vibrating with desperation. Lord, he hoped he could spare her the violence to come, but his gut said Rico wasn't going to be that considerate. He did the next best thing. He tried to get her out of there.

"A crash kit is an extensive first aid kit," he explained over his shoulder. "It usually comes in a good-size canvas bag or backpack, or maybe a box the size of a small trunk."

She replied in dawning understanding, "Yes, of course. We're a long way from the nearest hospital. We have all kinds of medical supplies."

"I need you to go inside, sweetheart. Tell the first person you see to fetch the crash kit and bring it out here. I'm going to need it to patch this numskull back together when I'm done with him." Joe's eyes narrowed. "That is, assuming he doesn't piss me off enough that I decide to just kill him and be done with it."

It was never good to go into a fight with the opponent sure that you wouldn't kill them. Fear worked on a man's mind. Ate at it. And Rico needed to taste fear today. A lot of it. Enough to scare the ever-loving crap out of him. Or else, someday soon, he'd be back for more of the same.

Cari eased up out of her chaise and sidled away from the pool. When she was several yards away, she turned and ran for the house. Thank God. She was clear of the danger zone. And if he was really lucky, she wouldn't have to witness what he was about to do.

He turned back to Rico. "Okay, Einstein. Let's get this over with. Show me what you've got."

Chapter 14

Joe eyed Rico carefully. His opponent would most certainly underestimate him, but he wasn't about to make the same mistake. Rico hesitated, seemingly unsure as to how to begin.

"C'mon, buddy," Joe said conversationally. "Let's get this show on the road. I don't want to fight in front of Cari, and she'll be back soon with the med kit. Drop your knife out of that wrist sheath and bring it already."

Rico's eyes narrowed. Without further ado, he jumped forward. A wink of metal flashed in his right palm. All right, then. The show was on. The thug held the knife reversed, the blade lying back along his forearm with the tip pointing toward his elbow. Ol' Rico had a little experience fighting with a knife, did he? Joe wrapped the towel around his left forearm, casually tucking the two ends of it in tightly. The fluffy terry cloth made a great impromptu gauntlet.

"Let's dance, shall we?" Joe invited lightly. He circled to

his right, forcing Rico to follow him in an arc to bring the knife into play.

Normally, he wouldn't talk much in a fight. The necessary breathing rhythms of speaking telegraphed too much to an experienced fighter. But today wasn't only about taking Rico down; it was also about minimizing the desire of anyone else in the Ferrare household to tangle with him. Hence, a certain amount of verbal psychological warfare was necessary.

He had no doubt that all of Eduardo's office windows were open and that the light breeze was carrying every word he said to the ears of the avid crowd that were practically pressing their noses against the giant glass wall.

Rico growled, "You think you're going talk your way out of this, pretty boy?"

Joe shrugged. "I'd rather not have to go through with this stupidity, but it was your call. And I gave you ample opportunity to reconsider. But now you've ticked me off and I *am* going to kick your ass."

"Hah."

"Already out of brilliant repartee, are you?" Joe taunted gently. "Maybe you should stick to fighting, then. Speaking of which, you can give it your best shot any day now. I'm getting bored." Joe's message was clear. He wasn't going to start this fight, but he was damn well going to finish it.

Rico finally leaped forward, swinging viciously with his right arm. Joe ducked the wild blow easily, coming up with a hard fist to the guy's solar plexus before he danced back lightly on the balls of his feet.

Rico gasped for air, eyeing Joe in surprise. No more talk. Time to get to business. Now that Rico had taken the first shot, Joe went on the offensive, pursuing Rico aggressively. The thug eyed Joe's right hand warily. Didn't like that gut shot, eh? There was more of that where the first punch came from.

Joe waited until all of Rico's weight was on his left foot and then swept his right leg forward, kicking the weight-bearing leg out from under Rico before the guy had any idea what hit him. The big man went down on the concrete with a heavy thud.

Joe took a step back and grinned down at his opponent. "Don't go taking a nap on me, dude! Get up and get busy before you embarrass yourself."

Rico climbed to his feet in a not-particularly-nimble fashion. His face was red now, his eyes slits of rage. He'd do something wild next, a big offensive move designed to overpower Joe since pure skill wasn't looking promising against the American.

Joe balanced lightly, waiting for the big move. Sure enough, Rico lowered his right shoulder and made a charge worthy of a bull in a matador's ring. Joe waited till the last moment and stepped out of the way, his movement blindingly fast and smooth as silk. As Rico barged past, Joe planted a hand in the middle of the big man's back and gave him a solid shove. Down he went again, on his face this time.

Rico rolled onto his back—a colossally stupid move in a legitimate knife fight.

Joe commented, in his best instructor's voice, "You shouldn't roll over like that when you're getting up. You're exposing your vital organs to me while you're down and defenseless. You'd be better off pushing up to your hands and knees and then jumping to your feet. That way, all you ever give me is your back. If I had a knife, I'd have a hard time killing you through all that backbone and muscle."

Rico was already halfway to his feet but actually paused as if he might roll back over and get up the right way. But then he hitched back into motion and finished standing, scowling. He charged again. And again. And each time, Joe slipped out of the way, landing a punishing blow somewhere on Rico's body as he slammed past.

By now, it had to be patently evident to even the most casual observer that Joe was toying with Rico and was a vastly more skilled fighter.

After one particularly ugly pass, Rico stood with his head hanging down, blood dripping from his split lip, panting hard.

"Give it up, Rico. Just walk away. I don't want to hurt you anymore."

"F— you," Rico snarled. He charged again and, this time, Joe didn't sidestep him. He stepped into Rico, slamming his fists into Rico's sternum in a pair of powerful blows. The thug doubled over and slammed, chin first, into Joe's fist. The guy's teeth clacked together loud enough to be heard across the yard.

Joe followed up with a vicious blow to the guy's nose and felt the bone give way with a grinding sensation beneath his knuckles.

Rico surprised him by reversing his grip on the knife and lunging at Joe, knife point first. In a reflex move honed over years of combat training, Joe crowded in fast and hard, grabbing Rico's wrist and twisting it violently. The knife dropped out of useless fingers as both wrist bones gave way with an audible crack that sounded like a rib of celery snapping in two.

Joe bent to scoop up the knife. But desperation made Rico fast and the thug's fist met his at the knife. Rico got his fingers around the handle and shoved up with all his remaining strength, which was formidable, and Joe had no choice. He had to deflect the blow into Rico's gut. The blade buried itself in Rico's abdomen with a sickening slide of slippery guts giving way before hard, cold steel.

Thankfully, the thug knew when to give up. He fell to his knees, his hands clutched around the hilt of the knife sticking out of his belly.

Joe stepped back and took a couple of deep breaths. He didn't take his eyes off Rico, though. More than one good man had had a fight won, only to take his eyes off the downed opponent and die from a sneak attack from the ground.

"You finished?" Joe demanded.

"Yeah," Rico grunted.

"You ready to let me treat that wound and keep you from dying?"

Rico glanced up in surprise. Blood was starting to seep between his fingers. A lot of it. The whole front of his shirt was turning red quickly. "For real?" he panted.

"Yes. Now lie down. The way you're bleeding, I might've nicked an artery."

"That ain't good, is it?" Rico grunted.

"No, it isn't," Joe snapped. This idiot could bleed out in a matter of minutes if that artery wasn't found and clamped off.

While Rico rolled clumsily onto his side and then his back, Joe glanced up, looking around for Cari and that med kit. There she was, standing over by the dining room door. Gunter was standing beside her and had her upper arm in a firm grip. Good man. The last thing he'd needed would have been Cari diving into the middle of the fight.

"Bring me the first aid kit," Joe called sharply. "And call an ambulance if you have them in this godforsaken country."

Gunter grabbed the heavy canvas pack from Cari and both of them hurried over to Joe. The German dropped the kit on the ground beside Joe. "What can I do?"

"Open that up and get out a scalpel and a big wad of gauze pads," Joe answered. "And surgical gloves, if you've got any. I don't trust this yahoo not to have AIDS."

He glanced up at Cari. "Put on a pair of gloves, then place your hand here and press down as hard as you can." He placed her gloved hand on the towel he'd unwrapped from his wrist and used as a makeshift pressure bandage.

She complied and he grabbed the gloves Gunter held out, snapping them over his wrists with the speed of long experience.

"Gunter, grab the knife and, when I tell you, pull it out. Lean it back against the unsharpened side. We don't need to slice him up even more on the way out."

Gunter nodded and put his hand on the protruding knife.

Joe pushed his fingers into the top of the wound on either

side of the blade, preparatory to prying the wound open to have a look for that artery. Hopefully, it wouldn't be buried deep. Rico groaned. No time to sedate the guy, assuming this kit even had the right drugs to knock him out.

"Do it," Joe ordered.

Gunter eased the knife out and a gush of blood flowed over Joe's fingers. Working by feel, he wedged his fingertips into the wound and held it open.

"Cari, use that wad of gauze to mop up the blood. I've got to see where the blood's coming from. Gunter, get me a locking clamp. It's the one that looks like a cross between scissors and pliers."

Cari leaned over his arm, sopping up the copious blood. She pulled the gauze away and, for a second, he had a clear view of the wound. Hallelujah. He'd spotted the bleeder. It wasn't cut all the way through; it was merely torn. A simple clamp should hold it for long enough to get this jerk to a hospital.

"Bring that clamp over here, Gunter, right by the wound. Okay, Cari. One more time."

She mopped up the blood again and, as she lifted the soaked mess away, he used his left hand to hold the wound open and his right hand to grab the clamp and slap it onto the arterial tear. The blood flow from the wound diminished noticeably.

He grabbed one last handful of gauze and cleaned up the wound. He packed it open for the surgeon, who would finish cleaning and repairing the stab wound, then field-dressed it quickly.

God, he couldn't count how many wounds like this he'd treated over the course of his career. The guys in Charlie Squad usually did a pretty good job of not getting themselves hurt, but civilians who bumbled into the cross fire and nimrod bad guys like Rico were a dime a dozen. No common sense at all.

He sat back on his heels and had a look at the rest of his patient. The wrist wasn't in too bad a shape, although it would need to be pinned while the surgeons had him under anesthesia. Joe slapped a quick splint on the wrist to keep Rico from doing something stupid like poking the broken wrist bones through the skin.

A couple wads of cotton stuffed up Rico's broken nose to keep it from swelling shut and that was about all he could do for his patient for now. He was actually capable of doing the required surgery to clean and repair the knife damage to Rico's intestine, but he'd rather leave it to a surgeon in a nice, sterile hospital. Meatball surgery always carried a certain amount of risk, and guts were filthy places to mess around without the proper equipment.

He looked up at Gunter. "This idiot's going to need minor surgery to repair the damage in his gut and set his wrist. He'll also need a heavy-duty antibiotic to keep him from getting peritonitis from all the gunk that's leaking out of his intestine into his abdominal cavity right now. Make sure both things happen—surgery to repair the gut and wrist, followed by antibiotics to combat the infection. He'll die if he doesn't get both treatments, got it?"

Gunter nodded briskly. "Got it." The German looked up candidly for a moment. "Thanks."

Joe retorted wryly, "For not slitting his throat or for patching him up?"

"Both."

He shrugged. "No sweat. I told him I knew how to fight. But did he believe me? Nooo."

Cari caught his gaze, some strong emotion swimming in her eyes, but damned if he could name it. Awe? Dismay? Disbelief? Hard to tell. She was good at masking her real thoughts when she wanted to. After a few minutes, she went inside, mumbling about getting dressed.

He stayed on his knees by Rico, monitoring the guy's vitals for the next half hour while an ambulance made its way from St. George to the seaside estate. Several of the guards brought out a stretcher and carried Rico through the house to the ambulance when it finally arrived. Joe picked up the sterile packaging that was strewn all over the ground by the pool and bundled up the gauze, wrapping the whole lot in the bloody towel.

A maid scuttled out to help him, looking scared. He handed it to her and said kindly, "Just throw all this stuff out, okay?"

She nodded and hurried away. He needed a shower. He was sweaty and covered in sticky blood. Heading for the house, he peeled off the rubber gloves as he went. And drew up short as Gunter stepped in front of him.

"Mr. Ferrare would like to see you."

Joe blinked. "He's home? I thought he was in town on business."

"He got back in time to witness the...excitement."

Joe slapped Gunter on the shoulder and laughed. "Excitement, huh? Where I come from, it's called an ass whupping."

Gunter grinned. "It's called that where I come from, too."

"Can the boss cool his jets long enough for me to take a shower? I'm covered in blood, and who knows if Rico practices safe sex? He's not bright enough to bother with condoms, if you ask me. Wouldn't want to expose my father-in-law to any nasty diseases or anything."

Gunter opened his mouth to answer, but Eduardo spoke from the doorway to his office. "Go take your shower. I can wait."

Joe blinked. Eduardo almost sounded friendly there, for a second. "I'll be down in a jiffy."

Eduardo nodded and turned, disappearing into his office.

Cari looked up as Joe burst into the bedroom.

"Oh, hi," he said. He sounded mildly distracted.

Apparently, it was an everyday occurrence for him to nearly knife a man to death and then patch him back together. Abruptly, just how little she really knew him hit her squarely between the eyes.

He stripped off his bloody T-shirt and carried it into the bathroom. "If you're here when the maids pick up these clothes," he called out over the sound of the shower turning on, "tell them to burn 'em. Rico's blood has to count as hazardous biomedical waste, don't you think?"

He was joking? *Joking?* He'd just about killed a man a few minutes ago. Appalled, she stood up and walked across the room. Joe had pushed the bathroom door closed but hadn't locked it. That was all the invitation she needed to barge in.

He spun around fast, his hands out in front of him like he was going to grab her. Some reflexes he had, there. The reflexes of a killer. Normally, she'd be riveted by the sight of him wearing nothing. But now, visions of him circling Rico, toying with her father's guard, delivering blow after punishing blow to the man, danced through her head. And then the final moment. She'd never forget the sight of Joe grabbing Rico's fist, twisting that knife up and back into Rico's gut. The mere thought of it now made her sick.

Joe straightened. Relaxed. "What's up?" he asked casually. As if he hadn't a care in the world.

"You almost killed Rico," she accused.

He shrugged. "What do you want me to say? I tried to talk him out of it, but he jumped me. It's no crime to defend myself."

"You didn't defend yourself. You crushed him."

Joe frowned. "If you mean that I beat him soundly, yes, I did. I've studied armed and unarmed combat practically since I was a kid. If you mean that I crushed Rico's feelings, that's too damn bad."

Her eyes narrowed. Anger stirred in her belly. "You knew you'd make mincemeat out of him, but you still got into a fight with him."

"*He* got into a fight with me. All I did was make the point to every wanna-be hero in the house not to come sneaking into your room late at night with the bright idea of taking me out."

"Nobody would sneak into my room to kill you."

"Oh, yeah? Then how in the hell did Tony die in your bed?"

The air whooshed out of her like he'd just buried a fist in

her stomach. She gasped a couple of times, but no air went into her lungs. Finally, she managed to draw a shaky breath. "That was a low blow."

"That's the truth, Cari. Wake up and look around you. This is a house full of killers working for a killer. One of them got froggy and decided to test me and I had to prove that I'm not someone who can be trampled all over. I did no more than I absolutely had to out there."

His voice was sharp as a whip, cutting into her skin and flaying her heart. She heard the truth of his words, knew in her head that he was right, but she just couldn't accept the idea that he'd turned out to be no better than her father. Both men lashed out in violence whenever their dominance was challenged.

"How can you measure violence so precisely? What differentiates I-had-to-do-it violence from It-felt-good-to-show-how-strong-I-am violence?"

Joe snorted. "You don't know the first thing about measuring violence."

"Oh, but you do, don't you?" she snapped.

He took an aggressive step forward and she backed up fast, slamming her shoulder blades against the tiled wall at her back.

"Yes, honey, I do. I've forgotten more about violence than you'll ever begin to know."

And she could see it in his eyes. The knife fights he'd been in before. The men he *hadn't* stopped fighting with to treat their wounds. The men he'd *killed*.

"How many men?" she whispered in horror.

"How many men what?" he repeated.

"How many have you killed?"

"I have no idea. I don't keep count. More than I'd like and less than you think."

"You're just like him," she accused.

"Like who?"

"My father," she spit out, turning her back on him in fury.

Joe's hand, powerful and angry, grabbed her upper arm and spun her around. His voice was cold. Flat. Furious. "I've got plenty of flaws, and I've done stuff that would curl your toes, but don't *ever* compare me to that bastard again."

She'd compare him to whomever she wanted to, dammit. And if she saw her father in him, tough. The thought arrested her. Was that why she was falling for Joe? Was he just a younger version of her father? Was she repeating the same mistake she'd made her whole life of trusting a man to whom everyone—including her—and everything was merely a tool to be used and discarded at his convenience? "What do you want, Joe? Why are you here?"

He scowled. "You know why I'm here. I'm getting you out of here. Away from your father."

"Yeah, and you've really made huge progress in that direction, haven't you?" Cari snapped. "You've learned all kinds of things about my father and his organization and haven't done a damn thing to spring us out of here."

"It's been less than forty-eight hours since I slipped that ring on your finger, Cari. But I'll be ready to leave tonight. And don't bother packing. We'll be traveling light."

"You got me away from my father's men once so we could get married. Why did we come back here? What is it you want so badly in this house?"

He stared at her, his gaze blazing hot. "I'll say it one more time," he ground out. "I'm here to get you out." And with that, he stepped into the shower.

She so wanted to scream! To rage against what he'd done. To force him to allay her doubts about him. To swear to her that he was different from her father. To convince her that his brand of violence was somehow better. Noble.

But at the end of the day, it was all the same thing. He'd harmed a weaker opponent in cold blood because it helped establish his macho reputation. If she didn't know better, she'd say he was trying to worm his way into her father's good graces and leapfrog to the top of her father's crime empire, just like Eduardo had accused him of doing yesterday.

She slid down the cool wall at her back as the room slowly filled with steam. Hugging her knees close to her chest, she finally let the tears flow. Tears of the abject terror she'd felt, standing there watching Joe fight for his life against a much larger, much stronger opponent. Tears of frustration that he wasn't being forthcoming with her and that she had no way of knowing for sure if he *was* telling the truth.

And for once, she shed tears of sorrow for herself. Just for once, she wanted to be a normal person and have normal problems and live a normal life and love a normal guy.

A normal guy—her personal misery derailed as yet another distressing thought burst into her head. Speaking of normal guys, surely it was against Charlie Squad's rules of engagement to attack and knife bystanders for the hell of it. Was Joe really a member of Charlie Squad, after all? Had he hoodwinked Julia into believing he was a good guy when he really wasn't? Had Cari seen a heroic soldier in Joe because she so desperately wanted him to be one?

He'd steadfastly denied being in Charlie Squad from the very beginning. Even last night, when she'd told him her father was out to kill every member of the team, he'd denied being one of them.

Her whole life was unraveling around her, and no matter what she did, she couldn't seem to hold it all together. The threads were slipping through her fingers faster than she could gather them back up. She just wanted Joe to be who he said he was, needed him to be a good guy, to love her back.

Was that too much to ask?

Chapter 15

Cari was gone when Joe got out of the shower. He dried off quickly, wrapped the towel around his hips and walked out into the bedroom to get some clothes. Cari wasn't in the bedroom, either. Probably just as well. She was still pretty freaked out by the knife fight.

He had a fair bit of damage control to do with her. He needed to track her down and talk with her. Calmly. When he wasn't so on edge. The shower helped release a lot of the pent-up violence still racing through his blood. He was still mad as hell at Rico for picking the damned fight in the first place, but his gut-pounding anger had receded to manageable proportions. Unfortunately, her father was waiting for him right now. First, Eduardo, then Cari.

He dressed, toweled his hair dry and combed it into place. Time to go beard the lion in his den. He walked downstairs and headed for Eduardo's office, keeping an eye out for Cari. He didn't see her out and about. He knocked on the office door and Eduardo called for him to enter. As he stepped inside, all his attention zeroed in on the man seated at the desk across the room. A person didn't deal with Eduardo Ferrare without every brain cell on high alert. Not if he wanted to live for long.

As he approached the desk, Eduardo waved at a chair and said, "Have a seat, Joe."

That was the first time Eduardo had ever used his name. And he was inviting Joe to actually sit down? Whoa. What was up with that? He took the proffered seat.

"Did you see Gunter on your way down here?" Eduardo snapped.

"No."

Eduardo stood up impatiently. "He's not answering his cell phone. I'll be back in a minute."

The second Eduardo left the room, Joe stood up and went around to the far side of Eduardo's desk. A thin stack of file folders sat on the glass desktop. They hadn't been there the last time Joe was in this office. Could these be the files that Eduardo had paid his informants so handsomely for?

He didn't have much time. Joe flipped open the first file folder. And stared in complete and utter horror…*at his own military personnel file.*

Shock exploded in his brain, nearly blinding him. He struggled to focus, to make out the words blurring together on the page. His job qualifications, physical description, home address, for God's sake! At least there wasn't a freaking picture in there, too!

Quickly, he flipped through the other folders. Mac, Tex, Howdy, Dutch and even the colonel. They were all here. All the important details of their training and personal lives were sitting on their archenemy's desk.

As he understood it, these personnel files were classified at roughly the same level as U.S. nuclear information. How had anybody sneaked this information out of Charlie Squad headquarters? To his knowledge, there were only a handful of places in the entire armed forces where any record of their existence was kept, let alone all these details.

Had Eduardo figured out who he was? Was that the purpose of this little tête-à-tête with his father-in-law?

Every nerve in his body screamed at him to run. *Now.* As far away and as fast as he could go. Except he couldn't leave Cari behind. He'd promised Julia and, more importantly, he'd promised Cari. He *wouldn't* abandon her to her father's tender mercies, under any circumstances. He'd sneak out of this office. Go upstairs and get her right now. They'd have to press ahead with the escape plan immediately. It would be a hundred times more dangerous in daylight, but what choice did they have?

Voices spoke on the other side of the office door. Joe scuttled out from behind the desk and flopped down in one of the chairs in front, just as Eduardo opened the door and walked in. He watched in silence as the older man crossed the room and sat down at his desk.

"You said you wanted to talk to me?" Joe said cautiously.

Eduardo leaned back in his chair and swiveled to face the ocean before answering. He gazed out the wall of windows for a minute before saying, "I caught the little sideshow out by the pool."

Joe sighed. "I'm sorry about that. I swear, I didn't start it. I tried to talk him out of it—"

Eduardo interrupted. "I heard you."

"Oh." Joe sat there in silence. Okay, then. Why he wasn't dead already, he hadn't the foggiest idea. Was it possible that Eduardo hadn't made the connection between him and Joe Rodriguez? Ferrare wasn't stupid.

Guilty people had a tendency to babble. He had to keep his cool. Continue to act like he had nothing to hide. As if he had not a care in the world.

He sat back, telegraphing to Eduardo that he'd have to initiate the conversation. After all, he'd called this little meeting in the first place. Joe wasn't going to carry the ball, here.

Eduardo read the signal and picked up the ball right on cue. "You handled yourself well out there today. Where'd you learn to fight like that?"

Joe shrugged. "There are places in the States where the streets are still pretty tough. I grew up in one of them."

"And the medical stuff?"

"I learned that in firefighter school. I thought I told you before that I'm an EMT. I've been scraping people off concrete for a while now."

"Is that why you were so calm under pressure?"

Joe laughed. "You didn't see the part where I went upstairs and cleaned out my shorts."

Eduardo leaned back in his chair. He steepled his fingers together under his chin and studied Joe intently. "I may have underestimated you."

Joe leaned back, as well, sprawling casually, his feet outstretched and his arms hanging loosely over the sides of the chair. But his mind was racing a mile a minute. Where was Ferrare going with this conversation?

It could not possibly be good to have drawn the man's attention in this way, particularly by displaying some of the extremely specialized skills he'd acquired as a member of Charlie Squad. He had to get out of here. The sooner the better.

"The only thing you may have underestimated was how much I truly love your daughter. And even though I'm really digging this father-son bonding bit, I gotta split, man. If you don't mind, I really need to get back to Cari and calm her down a little bit. She's still pretty freaked out."

"She'll get over it," Eduardo replied carelessly. "If you see Gunter on your way out, send him in here."

Joe did his damndest not to clench his jaw at the callous tone from Cari's own father. He stepped into the hallway and practically ran into Gunter, who looked to be heading for Ferrare's office already.

"Hey! Just the guy I was looking for," Joe said jovially. "The boss man wants to talk to you." He didn't stop to chat but rather headed straight for the stairs and his overwrought wife.

Gunter watched Joe go. *Good-looking young man. A lot smarter than he acted.* He could see why Cari was head over heels for him. The good news was, Joe seemed to feel the same way about her, too. Lord knows, she deserved a little happiness after growing up in this hellhole.

He shook himself out of his reverie and stepped into Eduardo's office. "You wanted to see me, sir?"

Eduardo gestured for him to close the door and waved him into one of the chairs in front of his desk. When he'd sat down, his boss asked, "What do you make of all the shenanigans by the pool this afternoon?"

"I think Rico's damned lucky to be alive right now."

"The American handled him pretty easily, didn't he?"

Gunter snorted. "He owned Rico. He could've disarmed Rico and slit the boy's throat anytime he wanted to."

Eduardo's eyes narrowed. If Gunter wasn't mistaken—and he usually wasn't—his boss was working his way into a cold, killing rage. Those were the worst ones of all. When Eduardo shouted and broke things, one or two people bought the farm and then he was appeased. But when Eduardo went ice-cold like this, Gunter had seen dozens of people die before Eduardo's rage was assuaged.

Had the fight between Rico and Joe set him off? Why in the world would that make him this angry? Rico would die slowly and painfully and Joe…

Hmm. That was a conundrum now, wasn't it? Did Eduardo dare kill Cari's husband? Especially because she was so obviously besotted with him. Eduardo's hold over his daughter was tenuous at best these days, and the old man knew it. If he killed Joe, Eduardo would, without question, lose Cari, too.

He'd already lost Julia and, in doing so, had nearly lost his proverbial shirt. Despite the outward appearances of normalcy around here, Eduardo's elder daughter had taken off with almost every bit of cash in the till. Ferrare was quietly selling art pieces and vacation homes fast to raise the capital to keep his empire afloat.

Desperate men did desperate things. Eduardo's next move could be absolutely anything. Literally. There was nothing Gunter wouldn't put past his boss to do.

His gut twisted with a need to protect Cari from whatever came next. If she really cared for Joe and, more importantly, if Joe really cared for her, she'd earned a shot at true love with him. Lord knows, the poor girl had had little of that in her life, so far.

"Take a look at this." Eduardo pulled a folder off the top of a small stack of files sitting in the middle of his desk and pushed it across the glass surface.

Gunter frowned and picked it up. Opened it. Scanned through its rather meager contents.

Joseph Rodriguez, nicknamed Doc. Member of Charlie Squad since…

Gunter did the math in his head. Almost ten years.

Native Spanish speaker, field medic. Height: Six feet two inches. Weight: 180 pounds. Black hair, dark-brown eyes, olive complexion. Highly intelligent, very handsome, thinks well on his feet. Current location: Unknown. Subject is working an undercover assignment at an undisclosed location. Single, never married. Home address…

Gunter frowned. He didn't like this. Didn't like this *at all*. His gut was fluttering with one of those unpleasant intuitions that never presaged anything good.

Eduardo's voice was positively silky. "Sound like anyone we know?"

Gunter closed his eyes. Opened them. And nothing but a continuous string of curses came to his mind. The bastard had *used* Cari to get to her father. *It had been an act all along.* Cold, killing rage of his own began to bubble up in his gut. Finally, he was able to collect himself enough to mutter, "Are you absolutely sure? It'll kill her, you know."

Eduardo bellowed, "It may get me killed! The viper is nestled within my very bosom!"

Poor Cari. Poor, poor Cari. She was going to die when her father killed the one man she'd thought really loved her. The one man who'd cravenly and completely betrayed her. *If* he had betrayed her.

Gunter leaned forward. "You've got to be dead sure be-fore you do anything!" he admonished desperately. "For Cari's sake."

"To hell with Cari," Eduardo snarled.

Gunter leaped to his feet. He had to get through Eduardo's rage. Make him hear reason. He couldn't go off half-cocked here and just start killing without verifying the facts. It was too important to the young woman crying her eyes out in her maid's room in the servants' quarters right now. That's where he'd been when the summons had come from Eduardo. He'd been standing around like a damn fool, being generally useless while he tried to figure out some way to comfort Cari. The maids kept murmuring about love hurting and how all men were dogs. He didn't see how *that* was going to do any good. He needed Cari to tell him exactly what Joe had done to upset her. Then he could go pound some sense into her young man and fix her pain. Action. He needed to *do* something to make it better.

Meanwhile, here was her father not giving a tinker's damn about her and talking himself into destroying what might be the one bright and shining light in her life. Gunter gritted his teeth. He mustn't let Eduardo do anything disastrous.

He took a deep, calming breath. It didn't help one blessed bit. He ground out, "Cari's all you've got left. Make the damn call. It'll take you two minutes to talk to your mole and find out where this Rodriguez guy is operating at the moment. And then we'll know for sure."

Eduardo's eyes narrowed. He glared at the interference from his number one lieutenant.

Gunter watched his employer gather himself with difficulty. He'd never taken well to anyone contradicting him, and it was a tribute to Gunter's decades of unswervingly loyal service that Eduardo didn't pull the pistol out of his drawer and shoot him on the spot. Hell, Gunter was almost more surprised that Eduardo *didn't* do it.

"Fine," Eduardo snapped. "I'll verify the damned information. Are you satisfied?"

Gunter subsided in his chair. "Yes, sir. And if it turns out he's in Charlie Squad, I'll kill him for you myself."

That garnered a brief flash of Eduardo's teeth that was more snarl than smile. "If he's Charlie Squad, I'll kill him myself. *After* I make him suffer a great deal."

Gunter watched apprehensively as Eduardo pulled out his address book and dialed a phone number with great deliberation.

"Hello, it's me. I need you to get me a piece of information right away. Yes, now. Where is Joe Rodriguez working undercover at this very moment?"

Gunter waited in suspense so thick he thought it might choke him.

"Then find out!" Eduardo shouted into the phone. "This is life or death! I'll give you ten thousand dollars extra on your next payment if you get the information within the next hour. If you don't call me with my answer by midnight tonight, I'll kill you. Understood?"

Gunter winced. He'd taught the old silver-or-lead trick to Eduardo himself. Bribe the informants handsomely, but kill them if they don't produce. The Stasi had found it to be the most effective formula by far for extracting information from coerced informants. And they'd tested every method in the book. Hell, the Stasi had *written* the book.

Eduardo slammed down the phone. "Now we wait, my old friend."

Gunter stared at his boss in dismay. Now they waited, indeed.

Chapter 16

Cari's feet dragged as she headed reluctantly for dinner. She didn't want to face either her father or Joe right now. But Gunter had been clear when he'd fetched her out of Grace's room in the servants' quarters. Tonight's meal was a command performance. Her eyes narrowed bitterly. *Performance* being the operative word. She would be expected to paint on a cheerful face, to act as if everything was okay when her mind was in turmoil, her heart in an uproar.

She needed straight talk from Joe. Honesty. *Answers*. Who was he? What was he really here to do? And, most importantly, how did he really feel about her?

While she was busy stewing over such things, she might as well stew over how *she* really felt about *him*. Her primary reaction to the knife fight had been pure, unadulterated panic that Joe would be hurt or even killed. That thought still sent her heart up into her throat and made her palms clammy with the cold sweat of terror. It had even crossed her mind to jump into the fight and throw herself on Rico's knife to save Joe. She closed her eyes on pain so sharp at the thought of losing Joe that a knife might as well have slipped between her ribs.

He kept telling her she had no idea what love was. But dammit, if being willing to sacrifice herself to keep him safe wasn't love, she gave up. Whether she liked it or not—and whether *he* liked it or not—she loved Joe whatever-his-name-was.

No matter that he was capable of explosive violence. No matter whether he did the things he did in the name of serving his country or to advance his own nefarious ambitions. The identity of his master made no difference whatsoever to her heart. And, frankly, that scared the hell out of her.

She'd loved her father through all of the atrocities he'd committed. Was she repeating the same colossal mistake? Was she simply blind when it came to the men she loved?

And maybe that was her answer. Maybe love was, indeed, blind. She'd told Joe before that the heart loves where it wills. She'd urged him to follow his heart, despite their age difference. Maybe she should just follow her heart in spite of her concerns over Joe's alignment with the law.

And maybe she was working too darned hard to justify why she ought to give herself permission to love Joe. Maybe if she'd just stop analyzing for a second, she'd look herself square in the eye and admit that all these arguments were moot. She loved him. End of discussion.

The question was, what to do about it?

Did she dare pursue a relationship with him? Was she stepping out from between Eduardo and Julia's feud only to land in the middle of a private war between Eduardo and Joe? Would she live a life of fear, waiting at home alone for an ominous knock on the door from a stranger to tell her Joe had died?

Overthinking again, darn it.

If she'd learned nothing else growing up around her volatile father and the deadly world he lived in, it was to take each day as it came. To enjoy the richness of the moment at hand and not dwell on a past that couldn't be changed or a future that might or might not ever arrive.

Sure, a future with Joe would have its uncertainties. If he *was* in Charlie Squad, she'd have to wait out the long absences that came with the job. If he was a wanna-be crime lord… Been there, done that, got the T-shirt.

But deep inside, Cari knew Joe was no crime lord. He was one of the good guys, and her father—as much as she loved him—was definitely one of the bad guys. Joe had put Rico back together; Eduardo would have fed him to the sharks.

It occurred to her that *this* was what unconditional love was all about! Loving someone no matter what he did or who he was. Like her father, like Joe. But loving them didn't mean you had to like them or respect them or be loyal to them. Those things had to be *earned*. And from everything Cari had seen, Joe had earned them, her father had not. In fact, the part of her that didn't love Eduardo loathed and hated him and was filled with a blackness so deep she didn't know if she'd ever find the bottom of it…. Until she'd met Joe.

Suddenly, Cari wasn't scared at all. She loved Joe, not knowing the identity of his master but knowing that whomever it was, it was a positive. Julia wouldn't have sent him to rescue her if it wasn't.

Never in a million years would she have guessed she'd meet a man she could love enough to accept no matter what he did or who he was. So this was what unconditional love was all about! She'd heard people talk about it, but now she finally grasped what they were talking about. Go figure.

She reached the bottom of the sweeping staircase and headed for the dining room, her heart immeasurably lighter at having made peace with her feelings for Joe and her father.

The long table was full tonight. Eduardo was already seated at the head of the table. The place on his right was empty, presumably for her. Joe sat at Eduardo's left. Gunter sat in the seat to the right of hers, and the rest of the table was lined with Eduardo's primary lieutenants.

She frowned. Was this going to be a working supper? She couldn't believe her father planned to talk business in front of Joe. Had the way Joe handled himself today made that big an impression on her father? Had Joe passed some sort of unspoken test out there by the pool?

Cautiously, Cari sat down at the table. One of the maids placed a salad in front of her and she picked up her fork.

She looked up at Joe, who was staring fixedly at her, clearly trying to figure out her mood. She smiled shyly at him, glad she didn't have to talk to him just yet. Even if they *had* been alone, without a camera or bug in sight, she wouldn't have known where to begin with him. It wasn't like she could just blurt out a proposal to him; they were already married.

Joe smiled back, more with his eyes than any change of facial expression, but it was enough. His gaze spoke volumes to her, silently communicating that they were still okay, that he cared for her in spite of her earlier outburst, that he forgave her for her doubts and hoped she forgave him for the fight and for scaring her.

Her gaze softened even more and she let her eyes fill with all the love she was feeling for him.

His eyes widened in turn, and then a full-blown smile broke across his face.

Jubilation erupted in her belly. She didn't need words to know he loved her back. No man could look at a woman like that and *not* be in love with her.

Sudden, overwhelming impatience to get out of there, to be alone with him, to tell him everything in her heart overcame her. She ate faster, speeding the moment when they could make their exit, go upstairs and fall into each other's arms.

The candles flickering down the length of the table seemed to burn brighter, and the food even tasted better. Everything was going to turn out right. They might just get a shot at happily ever after together.

Even Eduardo was in a jovial mood tonight. He talked and joked with his men freely. Over the platters of fresh fruit the maids carried out next, he even told a couple of stories about his boyhood in the streets of Gavarone. The moral of his misspent youth usually had to do with needing to be tough and smart to survive, and tonight was no different.

A plate of succulent prime rib was placed before her, and she cut into it with relish.

"Cari."

She looked up, surprised at her father.

"I got you something for your help at my meeting yesterday. You earned it. Vasily said he's looking forward to doing business with me again and is especially looking forward to working with you. I apologized for your hasty retreat last night but assured him you'd be more accommodating next time."

She froze, the smile on her face as rigid and fragile as handblown glass. Disbelief at what Eduardo was saying swept over her. He was blatantly trying to pay her off to sleep with that disgusting pervert. And he had the gall to do it in front of her husband! What a gigantic… She couldn't think of a horrible-enough word to describe Eduardo. And, oh God, Joe. What must he be thinking? She couldn't bring herself to look over at him, afraid that if he saw the panic in her eyes, he would attack Eduardo on the spot.

Eduardo reached carelessly into his sports coat and pulled out a long, flat jeweler's box. He set it on the table beside Cari's plate. "I guess you can still be of some use to me."

Her face felt hot. Surely, the mask of ice would melt off any second and she'd be able to move again. To open her mouth and scream her outrage at this humiliation. The only thing that kept her in one piece was the knowledge that soon she and Joe would be out of there, and her father would have no more control over her life!

"Open it," her father snapped. "It cost a lot. You should at least look at the damned thing."

Woodenly, she reached out and picked up the box. She lifted the lid. Inside lay a necklace made of twin slashes of gold, each nearly as long as her finger. They crossed asymmetrically in the middle. From one of them hung a row of teardrop-shaped ruby pendants that increased in size until the final thumbnail-size drop, which trembled from the very tip of the golden rod.

How very appropriate. The rubies looked just like drops of blood hanging off a big stick.

Blood money.

How many times had she accepted gifts like this from her father and thought that they were a sign of his esteem for her? How many times had she misinterpreted these *bribes* as a show of affection? Why was it that only now she finally saw them for what they really were—payoffs for silences kept or services rendered? It made her ill to even look at the row of red droplets.

"Well?" Eduardo demanded.

She closed the lid carefully. Set the box back down on the table. Pushed it away from her toward her father's plate. "I can't accept it."

"Why the hell not?" Eduardo's eyes narrowed in displeasure.

"I'm not planning to earn it."

Eduardo stopped eating. Stared. And his brows drew together like twin thunderheads. Daddy didn't like it when people didn't fall in line like they were supposed to. "Hmm, well, perhaps you will change your mind," he mumbled softly before picking up his fork again.

Cari finally gathered the courage to glance over at Joe. Undisguised pride in her shone in his dark gaze. He got it. He knew what that necklace represented, and he definitely knew what her refusal of the necklace meant.

And then a strange thing happened. Of all people, Gunter

reached beneath the table and gave her hand a quick squeeze. It happened so fast she didn't even really register the slight pressure on her fingers until it was gone.

She'd done it. She'd made the break with her father. She'd finally seen him for what he was and rejected the notion of being used by him any longer. She'd grown up.

And she owed it all to Joe. Without him, she might never have seen her father clearly, might never have known what real love acted like. She smiled brilliantly across the table at her husband, her gratitude for his lessons in love boundless. He nodded infinitesimally in return, a smile playing around the corners of his eyes.

Dessert was served: crepes stuffed with flambéed plantains and fresh pineapple. The whole thing was smothered in a sinful pecan-caramel sauce and topped with whipped cream. And tonight, she was going to eat every last bite of it!

Her spoon bit into the delicious confection, and the first sticky, tempting bite was halfway to her mouth when she heard a sudden disturbance from the direction of the front door. Someone—a man—was talking excitedly, demanding entrance and claiming to need to see Eduardo immediately.

Every head turned toward the noise. The bodyguards at the far end of the table, closest to the commotion, reached under their coats for their weapons.

Cari frowned as the South African information broker from the day before burst into the dining room, accompanied by two very agitated guards.

"Señor Ferrare, I apologize for coming to you this way, but it is a matter of greatest urgency."

Eduardo frowned. "I've already gotten the information I was looking for from another source. The money has already been collected."

The South African waved a hand impatiently. "It's not that. In attempting to acquire that information for you, I ran across something much more important."

Cari's frown deepened as Eduardo leaned forward, alert and eager. "What did you find?" her father asked aggressively.

A horrifying thought overwhelmed Cari. Had this guy figured out that Charlie Squad had a man inside Eduardo's house, eating supper at his table at this very moment?

She interjected, with desperate calm, "Daddy, why don't you and your associate adjourn this conversation to somewhere more private, like your office?" Maybe that would give Joe a few minutes to make a run for it. Give him a fighting chance to get out of here alive.

Her father slashed a decisive hand through the air. "No, I want to hear it right now."

The South African gulped. Took a big swallow. Not good. Not good at all. He was getting ready to reveal something bad. Something that would make her father angry. It had to be Joe. Frantic, she glanced over at Joe, willing him to excuse himself from the table. To pretend to go to the bathroom or something. To *get out of here!*

But Joe just sat there, a faint frown between his eyes, staring at the South African. If the table hadn't been so wide, she'd have kicked his foot under the table to get his attention. Heck, she all but threw her napkin at him to get him to look at her so she could motion him to flee.

The South African cleared his throat. "My…sources…intercepted this message less than an hour ago. It was transmitted from an operating location in the north-central United States to the Pentagon Operations Center. It's a very classified message."

"And what did this message have to say that sent you flying in here in the middle of dessert?" Eduardo prompted the man.

"Ahh, well, yes." The South African cleared his throat nervously. "It was a transmission from Charlie Squad. That's why it was brought to my attention right away. They were reporting…" He looked down at the top piece of paper clutched in his hand. "Let me read it to you: 'Charlie Squad commander regrets to inform ops that the primary target of Operation Moneybag has met with a most unfortunate accident and has died. Photographic confirmation to follow.'"

A sick feeling started at the bottom of Cari's stomach and began to worm its way upward as Eduardo growled, "What the hell is Operation Moneybag?"

The South African cringed a little as he answered, "It's not *what*. It's *who*. Operation Moneybag was your daughter, Julia. Charlie Squad has killed her."

Chapter 17

Cari leaped up out of her seat at about the same time as Eduardo did.

"What?" her father bellowed.

"That's not possible!" Cari cried out at the same moment.

"I'm afraid it is very possible," the South African replied regretfully. "I have the pictures right here if you'd like to see them, sir…." The guy advanced down the length of the table, holding out the bundle of photos in his hand like a talisman to ward off evil—or, in his case, a swift death to the messenger.

Eduardo snatched what turned out to be several eight-by-ten photographs, and Cari moved to peer over his shoulder at the grainy black-and-white images.

"Those were taken with a long-range camera, so the quality's not the best. But they're good enough to identify the, uh, victim and the men with her."

Cari stared down in horror. There was no doubt about it. That was Julia, all right, sprawled on the snow-covered ground with a huge black stain discoloring the snow around her. A blossom of black stained her coat, as well, directly over her heart. Her eyes were closed, her face a ghostly, ghastly white in the picture.

Two men crouched down beside her, both brandishing pistols in their hands. The legs of a third man were visible just entering the frame of the picture. But what riveted Cari's attention was the man at Julia's right, his face clearly visible. It was the driver who'd delivered her and Joe to Judge Cabot's house and then driven them here two nights ago. The man that Joe had called Tom. The man she'd believed to be Colonel Folly, the commander of Charlie Squad.

Eduardo stabbed a finger at the same face she was staring at. "That's Tom Folly!" he snarled. His voice rose in a roar. "That bastard killed my baby!"

Joe craned his neck to look at the pictures. Panic ripped through him. No way had Charlie Squad killed Julia! Hell, Dutch was planning to marry her. This message was a hoax.

Unable to see the incriminating photographs, he finally half stood and snatched one of them off the table.

Son of a bitch. That was Julia lying on the ground, all right. And that was the colonel beside her, and that was Julia's blood all over the ground. There wasn't a whole lot of background in the photograph, but he recognized that rise of rock behind Julia. Montana.

He remembered the night well. Julia had set up a meeting with her father, and Charlie Squad had staked out the site to catch the bastard. Except Eduardo had set an ambush of his own. Shooting had broken out and Eduardo had pulled a gun and aimed it at Dutch, the man Julia loved. She'd dived in front of Dutch and taken a bullet from her father's own gun.

That pair of legs just coming into the picture were his as he sprinted up to render first aid to Julia.

Where in the hell had this photo come from? He tried to

picture the scene that night at a rest stop along a lonely Montana highway. The angle this was taken from set it over in the large grassy area beside the picnic tables, where Eduardo's helicopter had been parked. There must have been some sort of surveillance camera mounted on the helicopter and this photo was lifted from the film footage of the meeting between Julia and her father.

The rat bastard! Eduardo had set this whole scene up tonight! Joe's mind raced. This was an elaborate trap....

Something exploded in Cari's brain. It was like a hundred isolated puzzle pieces of information had all suddenly flown into place and she could finally see the whole picture.

Charlie Squad had killed Julia. Joe was Charlie Squad! He was here to kill her father and had used her to get close to Eduardo. She stared down at the gruesome pictures of her sister's body—he'd kill her, too, if he had to!

Oh, God, Julia. Grief broke over her with the fury of a raging avalanche, turning her world upside down, burying her completely under its crushing weight.

And one of the men responsible for it was sitting across the table from her. He'd been making goo-goo eyes at her just moments before. She'd made love to him! God, she'd been such a fool!

"How could you?" she cried at him.

Joe looked startled. "How could I what?"

"How could you kill my sister? She was gentle and kind. She'd never hurt anyone. And you *murdered* her!" She heard the hysteria creeping into her voice. And she reveled in it. Embraced the madness. *Julia was gone.*

Joe looked up as Cari continued, screaming accusations at him. "What did she ever do to you? All we ever wanted was a normal life away from all of this!" She waved her arm, encompassing the room.

Damn. She was going to totally blow any chance of a cover he had left! "Honey," he said soothingly, "I didn't have anything to do with this. You know I'd never hurt an innocent."

Except he could see the memory of him stabbing Rico swimming afresh in her eyes. Rico wasn't an innocent, dammit!

"Will you kill me, too, Joe? Or whatever your name is?" Cari cried out. "Or are you only here to kill my father?"

At that, several of the men near him lurched. Dammit! She was going to get *him* killed if she didn't shut her mouth!

His heart bled for her. He ached to put his arms around her, to comfort her. To take away the grief that was eating her alive. To tell her there was *no way* Julia could be dead.

If it was only his life on the line, he wouldn't hesitate to tell her this was a hoax and take the consequences himself. But there were the other five members of his team to protect. He wasn't about to spout off that they couldn't have killed Julia last night because four of them were here in Gavarone, staked out around this building, and that Dutch was with Julia.

That would send all of Eduardo's men outside with guns blazing and land the squad in a firefight they couldn't hope to win. No matter how much it pained him to make Cari suffer like this, he couldn't offer her concrete proof that Julia had not been murdered. All he could give her was his word.

Cari collapsed against her father's shoulder, crying hysterically. Joe looked up at Eduardo, who was all but gloating over her head at him.

He stood up. "You low-down, selfish, twisted son of a bitch. How could you do this to your own daughter?"

Cari looked up, her eyes red and furious. "Don't you dare say anything to my father! He makes no excuses for who he is. But you…you're a liar!" she finished furiously.

Joe looked her square in the eye. "Cari," he said reasonably, desperately. "I've never lied to you. Ever. I swear. I've refused to answer certain questions, but I've never lied. I love you, and I'm telling you now, Julia isn't dead."

"If you truly loved me, you wouldn't have let Charlie Squad kill her, would you? So there's the biggest lie of all! You never cared for me one bit!" Cari pushed away from her father and advanced toward him. She stabbed a finger at the picture Joe held in his hand. "He—that man—drove us to get married! You're in Charlie Squad up to your neck! You could have stopped them from killing Julia."

She'd gone and put that final nail in Joe's coffin. The intensity of her shock and grief was such that she wasn't using her head. She couldn't see this lie by Eduardo for what it was.

"Grab him!" Eduardo ordered, a small smile playing around the corners of his mouth. "And take him downstairs."

About half the table charged Joe. Shit. He was going down. But he couldn't leave Cari like this. He couldn't die with her believing that her sister was dead. Hands shoved him and he fell back into his seat. He looked up and noticed that, oddly enough, Gunter hadn't moved. Eduardo's chief of security hadn't budged when it was revealed that one of his boss's archenemies was sitting at the dinner table.

As fists rained on his head and rough hands snatched at him, dragging him from his seat, Joe snatched the cell phone out of his pant pocket. Under the table, he flipped it across the floor in the direction of Gunter's feet.

"Cari," Joe shouted over the din of yelling men, "make the call! She's not dead!"

And then he went down, under a punishing barrage of fists and feet, and his frenzied thoughts turned to the immediate necessity of blocking the worst of the blows pummeling him from all sides.

"Take him downstairs!" Eduardo ordered again.

Joe was dragged to his feet, the beating suspended for the moment. Somebody had landed a vicious kick to his right kidney, and the shooting agony from that overrode most of the other contusions and injuries.

He vaguely heard Cari sobbing, and the sound tore at his

heart. He'd tried so damned hard to spare her more of this violence at her father's hands. And he'd failed. How much more pain had he set her up for in his clumsy efforts to protect her?

He registered Gunter's voice comforting Cari. Herding her out of the room. He had no idea whether or not Gunter understood his last shouted words to Cari. Furthermore, he didn't have the slightest idea whether or not the German would give her the phone. He could only hope the man thought enough of her to spare her the unnecessary misery of wrongly believing her sister was dead.

A phalanx of thugs dragged him into the kitchen and down the same stairs he'd explored last night. They shoved him into a darkened room and someone started punching him again before the lights were even turned on. Aww, hell. He was going to get to see the business end of that padded interrogation room, after all.

Cari was only dimly aware of Gunter's strong arm around her shoulders, guiding her upstairs and away from all the shouting and swearing downstairs. The quiet in her room was shocking, in contrast.

"Come in here, child." She was startled when Gunter led her not to her bed or to the sofa but rather into the bathroom. He closed the door behind her, propped her against the counter and turned on her shower's hot-water tap full blast.

"What are you doing?" she gathered herself enough to ask.

He smiled gently. "You didn't honestly think I didn't know about your safe room, did you?"

She stared at him in surprise. "Is it really safe? Or do you have something in here that I haven't found?"

He shook his head. "No, those little jamming devices you installed are top-notch. Even if I hadn't decided to let you have a certain amount of privacy, they would have been difficult to overcome. You designed them well, *querida*."

A fresh flow of tears gushed at the endearment that Julia

had used with her so often. Gunter handed her a tissue and said quietly, "You and I need to talk."

She blew her nose ungracefully and grabbed another tissue to swab at her eyes. "About what?" she mumbled.

"Joe gave you a message and gave me something just before he was taken out of the dining room. You and I need to figure out what to do with them both."

"I hope Daddy kills him for what he did," Cari spat out. "He could've told them not to kill her, but he didn't. He let them kill my sister!"

"Ah, Cari. You are so young. So naive."

She frowned. Joe had said the same thing to her in this very room not so long ago. "I wish you all would quit treating me like a child! I'm not, you know."

Gunter smiled. "No, you're not, are you? You've grown up. And now it's time to make a grown-up decision. Joe told you to make a call. And then he threw this to me." He reached into his pocket and pulled out Joe's cell phone. The same one she'd modified so he could call Charlie Squad. What did it mean?

"I assume you know what 'call' Joe was referring to? I'm guessing you know how to get in touch with Charlie Squad?"

She frowned. "Not really. Although I could probably figure it out. He called someone on that phone earlier today."

She stared at the small instrument lying in Gunter's callused hand. "It won't make any difference. They'll lie to me the same way Joe did. They'll tell me they didn't kill Julia. Except I've seen the pictures with my own two eyes." Her voice broke into a sob and she fell apart again, crying uncontrollably as her grief swamped her anew.

Gunter shrugged. "I don't know what they'll tell you. You won't know until you make the call. I do know this, though. It's possible to see what you expect to see when sometimes the truth is very different."

"You think I should talk to those bastards?" Cari asked incredulously.

"I think you should act as an adult. I think you should not take what just happened at face value and I think you should decide for yourself exactly who is telling the truth here."

She stared at the German long and hard. He'd worked for her father for as long as she could remember. He'd always been loyal to her father, steadfast in his duties as Eduardo's chief of security. Was he actually going behind her father's back here? If so, it was a monumental event.

She looked up at Gunter. "You think I should make the call, don't you?"

He looked her in the eye. Seemed to search for the right words. And then said, very slowly, as if each word weighed heavily on his conscience, "I've stood by over the years and watched your father do some terrible things. But this—" he swallowed thickly "—this is too much. If it were just Joe, I'd let Eduardo kill him. But I can't stand by and let your father take away a man who loves you like that boy loves you."

Cari stared at him long and hard. Finally, she whispered, "What are you saying?"

Gunter closed his eyes. His face looked pained. He opened his eyes and looked right at her. "I swore I would never betray your father. And I *won't*," he ground out. "But I'm telling you there's more to what you just saw downstairs than meets the eye. You need to decide whether you are always going to be your father's daughter and take him at face value or whether you're going to be your own person and think for yourself."

Had he and Joe compared scripts with each other? *Was* she nothing more than her father's daughter? Was she bought and paid for in blood, trained too well to do Daddy's bidding to ever stop jumping when he ordered her to? She didn't like the person who had accepted jewelry in payment for prostituting herself, who let men like the Slav paw at her to please Daddy. She didn't like being *used*. Not by her father and not by Joe.

She closed her eyes, the pain of his betrayal so raw she didn't know if she could stand it.

Gunter had taken a huge risk in picking up Joe's phone, and an even bigger one in giving it to her.

"Why?" she asked him.

"Why what?"

She half-laughed, half-sobbed. "Why couldn't you have been my father?"

The older man gathered her in the first hug he'd ever given her. "Aww, honey, I wish I was."

She buried her face against his shoulder and let out a shuddering breath.

Slowly, she opened her eyes. Reached out. And took the phone. She'd make the call. But not for Joe. Not because Gunter asked her to. But for herself. Because Gunter was right about one thing. It was time for her to stand on her own two feet. To make decisions for herself.

She stared at the phone for a few seconds, pondering how to find out the last number Joe had called. Could it be as easy as hitting the redial button? What the heck. She gave it a try.

The phone connected and began to ring at the other end. She started when a male voice barked in her ear, "Go ahead."

"Uh, hello. My name is Cari. I'm calling to…" Who *was* she calling to speak to?

"Miss Ferrare? Has something happened to Joe?"

"Uh, yes. But that's not why I'm calling…." God, this was hard. Was she supposed to just blurt out a demand to know if this guy had murdered Julia?

"What's happened?" the man asked urgently.

She took a deep breath. Quelled an urge to disconnect the phone and flush it down the toilet. "A man came to the house tonight. He had pictures."

"Pictures of what?" the man prompted with gentle urgency.

"Of my sister. Dead."

"What?" the man exclaimed. "How? When?"

"He said it happened last night. She was shot."

The man at the other end of the phone swore violently.

"Just a moment. Stay on the line. I'm going to make another phone call. Okay? Will you wait for me?"

"Uh, okay." She'd hung in there this long. What were a few more minutes?

Somebody knocked at her bathroom door. Her gaze snapped over to Gunter, who signaled with his hands for her to send away whoever was out there. Didn't he want anyone to know he was in here with her? The size of the risk he was taking by being here, by handing over Joe's cell phone, struck her forcefully.

"Go away," she called out. She didn't have to fake the wobble in her voice.

"Miss Cari. Your father told me to make sure you're all right."

It was Grace. Her longtime maid. "I'll be okay, Grace. I just want to be alone."

"You're sure, ma'am?"

"I'm sure," she called back firmly. "I'm going to take a shower and see if I can relax a little."

"All right. I'll be right outside your room. You just call for me if you need anything."

"Thank you," she replied in genuine gratitude.

"Still there?" the man said in her ear.

"Yes," she answered.

"Julia's fine. I just spoke with her on the phone."

Cari blinked. Her brain couldn't seem to wrap around the words. "You didn't kill her? Charlie Squad didn't murder her?"

"Good Lord, no!" the man exclaimed. "What the hell's going on over there?"

"A visitor showed my father a message from you—from Charlie Squad—to the Pentagon, saying that Julia died in an accident. The guy also had pictures of her. Lying on the ground. Shot in the heart. And the man standing beside her, holding a pistol, was the man who drove Joe and me to get married."

"Listen, Cari," the man said tensely. "I'm the man who drove you and Joe to Judge Cabot's house. My name is

Colonel Tom Folly, and I'm the commander of Charlie Squad. Julia is alive. Nobody shot her. At least, not last night. She was shot last month, though."

"Last month?" Cari exclaimed.

Folly added hastily, "She went to a meeting with her father and some of his men. Charlie Squad was there, too, and shooting broke out. Your father tried to kill one of my men and Julia dived in front of him to take the bullet. She was hit in the chest. But Joe was able to control the bleeding and we got her to a hospital in time. She's still recovering from the wound, but she's going to be fine. You must have seen photos of that incident."

"You could just be saying she's alive to save your man," Cari said.

"I'm going to give you a phone number. I want you to call it. Julia will be there. Talk to her. When you've assured yourself that she's all right, call me back." He rattled off a phone number and Cari repeated it aloud. Gunter nodded, took out a little notepad and jotted it down.

Cari's hands fumbled so badly she could barely dial the number. But in a few seconds, the phone started to ring.

A female voice cried out on the other end "Cari? Is that you?"

Cari's knees collapsed out from under her and she sank to the floor, sobbing in relief. "Julia?" she choked out.

"Oh, God, Cari, it's me. I'm alive. I'm fine. Colonel Folly told me what Daddy did to you. I swear to God, I wasn't shot last night. I took a bullet last month, but it was daddy dearest who shot me. He was aiming at Dutch, but… It's a long story. I'll tell you some other time. Are you okay, honey?"

"I am…now," Cari hiccuped.

"Colonel Folly asked me not to talk too long with you. He needs to speak to you again as soon as you know I'm okay. I can't wait to see you. I've got a ton of stuff to tell you."

Cari laughed through her tears. "I've got a ton of stuff to tell you, too. And, Julia?"

"Yes?"

"I love you."

"I love you, too, little sister."

She hung up, and Gunter lifted her gently to her feet. Cari couldn't help it. She flung her arms around the older man and sobbed her relief into his shoulder. "She's alive, Gunter. She's alive!"

"I'm glad to hear it, sweetheart. But I'm afraid your young man won't be alive for too much longer if you don't do something soon."

Joe. Oh, God. Joe. He was down in the basement, no doubt being beaten to a pulp. And it was her fault! No. Delete that. It was Eduardo's fault! He'd set the trap for Joe and used her—again!—to set up the man she loved. What an unmitigated son of a bitch!

She checked her mounting fury. She didn't have time to be angry at her father right now. First things first. She had to rescue Joe, and then she'd strangle her father.

She hit the Recent Calls button and redialed Colonel Folly. He answered on the first ring.

"You were right. Thank you so much. I'm sorry I believed the worst."

"It's all right. I'm glad we got it straightened out. But we've got more pressing matters to deal with. We've got to get you out of there. Now. Let me speak to Joe."

"Uh, my father has Joe. He knows he's in Charlie Squad. I...I let that slip when I thought Charlie Squad murdered Julia. I'm so sorry—"

Folly cut off her apology. "No time for that. You say Ferrare's got Joe?"

"Yes. He's probably in the basement." Gunter nodded beside her. "Yes, he's definitely in the basement. My father's got a—a torture chamber...down there. He'll do terrible things to Joe before he kills him."

"We don't have anywhere near enough firepower to storm

your father's house," Folly replied. "Is there anyone inside who can help you? We need to get you out. Now."

"Yes, there's someone who'll help me. But I'm not leaving without Joe!"

"This is no time for heroics, Miss Ferrare. My job will be easier if you're not running around in the line of fire. When we come in, I don't need to be worrying about pulling you out, too."

"I won't go," she said stubbornly. "Besides, I can help you. How close are you?"

"I'm looking at your father's house, as we speak."

"I can probably drop some of the perimeter security systems and let you in. I'll call you back when I've done it." She disconnected the line before Folly could argue with her anymore.

Gunter's brow furrowed. His betrayal of her father might extend to passing her Joe's cell phone, but it might not extend to letting the enemy in the front door.

"We've got to save him, Gunter," she said earnestly. "It's my fault that he's in trouble. We can't let him die. I *love* him!"

Chapter 18

Gunter sighed heavily. "I took a vow once that I would never betray or harm your father. He saved my life and, in turn, I swore I would never turn on him."

"I'm not asking you to kill Eduardo," Cari pleaded. "I'm begging you to help me save Joe. Please. If you've ever cared for me, do this now."

Gunter stared at her for a long time. Then he said heavily, "I'll do what I can."

They left the bathroom and headed for the hallway door. And stopped short when the knob wouldn't turn under Cari's hand. Gunter tried the door. Shook his head. It was locked.

She called through the panel, "Grace? Let me out."

"I'm sorry, Miss Ferrare," a male voice said outside. "I can't do that. I'm under orders to keep you in your room until further notice."

Gunter called out, "Guillermo, it's Gunter. Let me out."

"I'm sorry, sir. Eduardo was explicit. No one comes into or goes out of Miss Cari's room until he says otherwise."

Cari blinked. And stared at Gunter in dismay. Had Eduardo figured out what Gunter was up to? Had the German just thrown his own life away in the name of rescuing Cari from her grief?

The German shrugged, his face set in grim lines.

"I'm so sorry, Gunter," she choked out.

"I knew something like this might happen. It was my decision. I accept my fate."

Her eyes narrowed. One thing she'd learned from Joe was never to say never. She wasn't going to roll over and play dead yet. There had to be a way to get out of here and help Joe.

"The ladder," she whispered to Gunter, acutely aware of the bugs in her room.

A grin broke across his face. He nodded and the two of them sprinted across the room toward her balcony. Gunter grabbed her arm and stopped her from bursting outside. He stood to one side of the French doors and peered out from behind the curtains.

She whispered in his ear, "Joe says that the cameras all line up facing away from the balcony every few minutes. We can slip out then."

Gunter's eyebrows shot up. "Is that how you two got out for that skinny-dip?"

She smiled briefly and nodded.

"How long is the coverage gap?" he muttered.

"About fifteen seconds," she replied.

"We'll have to be fast, then." He glanced down at the high-heeled sandals on her feet. "Go put on tennis shoes while I watch for the cameras to line up."

She raced to her closet and threw on the black slacks and turtleneck from the night before, along with the tennis shoes. She was just tying the last shoe when Gunter gestured for her to come to the door.

"Next pass of that camera to the right," he murmured.

She nodded her understanding.

There. It was swinging away from them. They slipped outside silently and threw the ladder over the side railing.

Gunter looked twenty years younger as he disappeared over the edge of the balcony. But she didn't have time to stop and wonder why as she swung her legs over the edge and raced after him.

I'm coming for you, Joe. Hang on just a little longer.

They tag-teamed pounding on him. When one thug got tired, the next one would step in. Thankfully, the pain from his bruised kidney made Joe pass out quickly enough that he didn't suffer through much of it.

He came to when a bucket of cold water was thrown on him. Eduardo was standing in the corner, grinning like a damned shark. He didn't bother telling the bastard what he thought of him. Ferrare wasn't worth wasting his breath on.

"Now that we've got him tenderized a bit, what say we move on to something a little more interesting?" Eduardo gloated.

Several of the men left the room, no doubt to fetch some lovely toys like car batteries and filleting knives.

The door opened and another guard stuck his head into the room. "Excuse me for interrupting, sir, but there's something going on down in security that you need to take a look at. We're picking up a transmission out of the house."

Eduardo turned in irritation. "What *sort* of transmission?"

"We're not exactly sure. It's sort of like a phone signal. You need to come see it."

Eduardo cursed and headed for the door, followed by two more of his flunkies. That left Joe alone with just two guys. He felt like hamburger, but it was probably the best and only chance he'd get to try something. He spoke up derisively. "Can't you sissies do any better than this? It feels like I've had a nice massage, but that's about it."

On cue, both thugs advanced on him. His arms might be tied to the chair, but his legs weren't. He held his feet still until both men were well within his reach, then lashed out viciously, kicking the nearest man in the face. As the guy went down, shouting in pain, Joe flung the chair onto its side, rolled and came up, bent over but on his feet. He charged forward, ramming the top right corner of the chair into the second guy's groin. The thug went down, gasping like a dying fish.

Joe slammed himself into the table, praying the chair would give way before the table. It did. Damn, that hurt his kidney! The back partially tore free of the seat. Struggling to stay conscious as waves of pain poured over him, he worked the ropes binding his wrists free enough for him to turn around partway in the chair.

The first guy was back on his feet. Joe raised the chair overhead and smashed it down on the thug. The guy dropped like a rock, but even better, the chair busted the rest of the way. He shook his hands free of the wreckage, looped both ends of the rope around his hands and choked the first guy until he turned an ugly purple color and was well and truly unconscious.

He spun around and kicked as hard as he could, nailing the second guy, who was still down on the ground, in the groin again. The guy screamed. He wouldn't be standing—or fathering children—anytime soon. The guy appeared to pass out.

Thankfully, the padded walls had absorbed the sound of the fight, and nobody would think twice about screams coming out of this room right now. Joe cracked open the door. Two thugs were moving quickly away from him toward the stairs. He could hear Eduardo talking excitedly in the security office, barking orders, but Joe couldn't make out the words. Nor did he have the time to try.

He slipped outside into the hall and tried to run for the freezer. But the best he could manage was an old-lady limp. They'd busted him up good, all right. He hobbled down the hall, ducked inside the meat locker, closed the door and turned on the light. Got to keep moving. He grabbed a mop from the corner and wedged it into the big stainless-steel handle so the door couldn't be opened from the outside.

He headed for his stash of tools. He grabbed the crowbar and tore the lid off one of the crates marked C-4. He stuffed a couple dozen blocks of the heavy gray putty into plastic grocery bags he grabbed off the shelves. Into another bag he threw the pliers, wire cutters and wire he'd stashed earlier.

And now for a weapon. He hoped. He applied the crowbar to the large, coffinlike crate. One of the padlocks popped off and he pried open the lid, peering inside.

He recoiled and let the lid slam down. Those weren't guns in the box. They were an expensive pair of leather men's shoes. An *occupied* pair of shoes. Eduardo actually had a dead man stored down here beside his food! How twisted was that? Joe examined the other boxes quickly and found none marked as weapons. Quickly, he tore the lids off all the C-4 boxes and dumped their contents on the floor. When it blew, it should set off all the remaining ammunition in here, and hopefully it would take a good chunk of the house overhead with it.

He grabbed a coil of detonator cord out of one of the crates and tossed it over his shoulder. He jammed one end of it into a block of C-4 and fed the cord off his shoulder as he headed back toward the door.

He pressed his ear against the thick steel and faintly heard a ruckus outside. His escape must have been discovered. He heard shouting and what sounded like pounding feet. After a few seconds, the noise died down. Very slowly, he cracked open the door of the freezer. The hallway was empty. Laying the detonator cord on the floor along the wall, he fed it down the hall as fast as his broken body would go. He stepped into the interrogation room, which was now empty. He wrapped the cord around a block of C-4, set it on the floor by the door and, after a quick check of the hall, slipped outside once more.

Next, he ducked into the big storage room. Lots of good flammables in here. He wired another block of C-4 and took the detonator cord over to the big generator in the back. He pulled out the wire cutters and pliers and connected the cord to the timer he'd wired up the night before. Then he started a second strand of detonator cord, leading away from the timer.

He set the alarm clock on top of the generator for twenty minutes from now. That ought to be enough time to head upstairs, find Cari and get the hell out of Dodge. If it wasn't enough time, they were both screwed anyway and it wouldn't matter if they were still in the house when it blew. He wound the old-fashioned clock and it started to tick. He checked his watch. Nineteen minutes and fifty-five seconds to go.

And now to create a more ideal working environment for himself. He shouldered the detonator cord, picked up his bags of C-4 and grabbed a pair of wood-handled garden loppers. He put his pocket flashlight between his teeth and stepped out into the hall.

It hurt like hell to reach up over his head with the loppers. Must have a couple of busted ribs. He gritted his teeth and reached for the first electrical bundle. He snipped through it. He snipped through two more bundles of wire before it suddenly went pitch-black around him. Bingo. He'd just hit the house lighting system. He heard shouts erupt upstairs and a couple of guys inside the security office next door started yelling back and forth in the dark.

Joe flipped on the flashlight and put it back between his teeth. Two more bundles to go. He snipped through the last one and turned off his light, just as the first man came charging out of the security office, flashlight in hand. Joe melted back against the wall.

That flashlight was a mistake. It was a beacon saying, Here I am, come get me. Joe jumped the guy from behind. He grabbed the guard's head and gave it a vicious twist. He didn't like using the move because it killed the recipient as often as not. But he was unarmed and didn't have time to screw around with gentler tactics.

He patted the guy's ribs down. Thank God. The guy was packing. Joe lifted the guard's gun and identified it by feel. A

Glock pistol. He took the safety off and chambered a round, then stuck the pistol in the back of his belt. The second guy came out of the security office and was as easy to drop and disarm as the first one. Not used to operating in the dark, apparently. Too bad. That was Charlie Squad's native environment.

He grabbed the bags of C-4 and headed for the stairs, feeding out detonator cord as fast as he could. His joints seemed to be loosening up slightly, but he still felt like a dead man walking. He stepped out into the kitchen. Cari was up here somewhere. He ducked behind the center island as someone rushed past in the dark, shouting. While he was there, he laid down another block of C-4 wrapped with detonator cord, wedging it underneath the edge of the island.

He headed for the dining room, next. He planted another block of C-4 and moved on, this time into the TV room. He had to duck a couple of guys racing through.

The chaos was unbelievable. The guards had no plan whatsoever for dealing with a home invasion, which was dumb. No fortress was impenetrable. Joe planted several more blocks of C-4 as he made his way toward the stairs. He ran out of detonator cord before he got to the second floor. That was okay. He just dropped blocks of C-4 as he went. They'd make for an excellent secondary explosion once the first batch went up. He checked his watch. Twelve minutes to go. No sweat. In all this mayhem, he and Cari could stroll out the front door and nobody would notice them. He turned the corner into the hall leading to her room and was stunned to see an armed guard standing outside. Crap. Joe ducked back around the corner, thinking fast. He stood up and backed around the corner, arms out as if he held a guy, moving quickly and shouting in Spanish for the guard to get downstairs and help catch the American.

"Mr. Ferrare said not to move unless he personally told me to," the guard responded, obviously disoriented.

Whatever. Joe was close enough now to reach around and

grab the guy's gun, which he did. A quick twist, a jab with his fist to his gut to double him over and Joe smashed the gun down on the back of the guy's head.

He raced into Cari's room, slipping in low and spinning to the side. No movement. He didn't feel her presence, either. He cleared the room fast, spinning into her closet and bathroom, too. But there was no sign of her. Dammit! Where was she? He didn't have time to go roaming all over the house looking for her. The clock was ticking! Nine minutes to go.

He sprinted back into the hall and down the stairs. Adrenaline had suddenly done wonders for his mobility and his pain factor.

The balcony! Of course. Cari was already outside. Praise the Lord.

Joe ducked into the TV room as a couple of men charged by. He'd head for Eduardo's office and slip outside through the French doors there. He'd have to find Cari on the grounds of the estate and hook up with her out there.

It took him several precious minutes to make his way unseen to Eduardo's office. The men were starting to retrace their tracks, starting to slow down and apply their brains instead of running around like chickens with their heads cut off.

He stepped into the white room. And lurched violently as a shadow rose from one of the armchairs. He reached for his pistol, but the figure turned enough for him to make out the .45 revolver in the guy's hand. It was pointed straight at him. Joe heard a click. And froze.

Out of the thick shadows, a malc voice said, "I thought you might be passing through this way."

Damn. Eduardo.

Cari ducked under the oleanders beside Gunter. "What's going on in there?" she whispered. The house and grounds had just gone pitch-black, and men were shouting like crazy inside.

Gunter murmured back, "I'd say your boy has pulled a

miracle out of his hat. Obviously, he's done something to the power supply."

"Why hasn't the emergency generator kicked on?" she replied.

She felt Gunter's shrug. "He either disabled it or cut the power wires down line. He'll be heading outside fairly soon. I imagine he'll go upstairs looking for you, first. When he discovers you're gone, he'll come out here. We'll wait right here for him to emerge."

She nodded, grateful not to have to sneak around anymore. She was out of breath, and shadows were flitting back and forth inside the house. Gunter studied the house carefully beside her.

"Your husband could use a little help, I think. Why don't you call that phone number of yours and see if a little diversion could be staged at the edge of the grounds? Something loud that would pull a bunch of men outside."

"Uh, good idea." She fumbled with the cell phone and hit the Redial button. She winced as the electronic beeping sound sounded like a full-blown marching band.

"Go," a voice snapped in her ear.

She whispered frantically, "This is Cari. Joe could use a diversion. Uh, something loud to draw men out of the house. Like, over by one of the fence lines."

"What's going on? The lights just went out," Folly demanded, all business.

"We're not sure. We think Joe knocked out the power. He's still inside. I'm outside already."

"Hide, Miss Ferrare, on the beach side of the house and don't move. You've got your diversion."

"That's where I am. And, thank you," she whispered.

The line went dead.

In a matter of seconds, the sounds of gunfire erupted on the west side of the house. The effect was startling. There was utter silence inside the house for a couple of seconds and then all hell broke loose. Men streamed out of the house like angry fire ants, rushing toward the sounds of gunfire.

A movement inside the now-still house caught Cari's attention. "Gunter. Look!" She pointed at Eduardo's office.

The French doors burst open like something heavy had just slammed into them and a pair of men grappled in the doorway. Joe and Eduardo.

Gunter swore beside her and stood up. She jumped to her feet next to him. As the German took off running, she did, too. "We've got to help him!" she cried.

Gunter yelled back, "I swore I'd protect your father's life. I can't let Joe kill him!"

Stunned, she chased after the German, who accelerated away from her. No! She couldn't let Joe get this close to making it, only to have Gunter kill him now!

They sprinted past the swimming pool. Gunter had almost reached the two men. She had to do something, fast!

She gathered herself and took a flying leap. She lay out full length in midair, sailing toward Gunter. *Please, God, let me not be too late!* Gunter's hand reached inside his coat for his gun. And a split second later, she came crashing down on the back of his knees. She wrapped her arms around Gunter's ankles and held on with all her strength. The German went sprawling and his gun flew up into the air in a wide arc, landing somewhere in the bushes by the dining room.

Joe and Eduardo's arms were locked over their heads, their chests butting up against one another. She could see the rage in both of their eyes. Only one of them was walking away from this fight alive. Joe kneed Eduardo hard, and the bigger man grunted. He fell back from Joe but came up in a half crouch. A knife glittered in his hand.

"Knife!" she screamed.

Joe didn't acknowledge her by so much as a flicker of his eyelashes. But aloud, he grunted, "Get out of here, Cari. Run. Down toward the beach. Get away from the house!"

Eduardo attacked and she screamed again. She clambered to her feet and gathered herself to jump into the fight when something big and heavy slammed into her, flattening her against the ground. The air whooshed out of her, leaving her gasping. Gunter stared down at her. "Eduardo will kill you, too. Stay out of this."

"You're not going to stay out of it," she snarled, a tigress defending her mate. "*I'm* bloody well not going to, either."

Cari and Gunter struggled to their feet, each doing their best to hold the other back. Eduardo took a swing at Joe. He sucked in his gut and dodged the blow.

"Get her out of here, Gunter!" Joe grunted. "I wired the house. It'll blow any second."

Gunter's hands froze, Cari's wrists trapped in his unbreakable grip. She looked up at him and saw terrible indecision dancing on his face.

"Go, Gunter!" Joe roared as Eduardo swung at him again.

Joe stepped in and grabbed Eduardo's arm, twisting up and away. But Eduardo broke the grip.

Her father was a renowned street fighter. He'd fought his way to the top of the food chain in back-alley fights just like this. He took another vicious swipe at Joe, who yet again managed to elude the swing.

Gunter looked up at the house towering overhead. And then down at her. He glanced over at the two men locked in mortal combat and then seemed to reach a decision. He kept his hold on her wrist but began dragging her away from the two men.

"No!" she shouted at him. "Let me help him!"

"You'll help him most by getting out of here so he doesn't have to worry about you!" Gunter growled back. "He knows what he's doing."

She gave in reluctantly and ran beside Gunter all the way to the tall fence down by the beach. They paused while Gunter tried to open the lock. Nada. The power had been cut, and the electronic mechanism failed to a locked position.

She looked over her shoulder to see how Joe was faring when, without warning, a tremendous flash of light erupted from the west wing of the house. For a brief fraction of a second, Joe and her father were silhouetted in the doorway, locked together in combat, two unyielding foes matched to the death.

Gunter leaped at her, throwing her to the ground just as an earsplitting explosion let loose. The blast wave slammed into her like a freight train, driving sand against her face like shards of glass.

A second tremendous boom rocked the night, and debris flew all around them. It looked like a giant tornado had struck, flinging the house behind her in a million directions at once.

She shoved up to her elbows. Where the house had stood was nothing but a blazing inferno. The heat scalded her skin so intensely it felt as if her hair might spontaneously combust.

Joe! He was in there, somewhere! She had to find him. Get him out of there!

Gunter pulled at her, trying to drag her away from the fire as she struggled toward it. "Cari, you can't do anything for him now," Gunter yelled over the roar of the blaze. "Nobody could have survived that. He's gone."

She stumbled backward over the mangled remains of the iron fence. Fell to her knees in the sand. And knelt there, too horrified to stand, watching her entire life go up in smoke.

A man ran down the beach toward them. Gunter spun around and dropped to one knee in the sand, reaching for his ankle. Cari looked listlessly over her shoulder and roused herself enough to call out, "That's Colonel Folly from Charlie Squad."

At the last second, before the two men shot each other, Gunter yanked his weapon up out of the way and pointed it at the sky. Folly did the same. Gunter laid his weapon in the sand and knelt, clasping his hands behind his head.

"Are you all right?" the colonel asked her briefly as he slapped plastic handcuffs on the German.

She nodded miserably.

"I'm sorry," Folly muttered at her, his voice sounding nearly as choked up as she felt. "There's no way they made it out of that."

She closed her eyes as grief tore through her for the second time in one evening. She'd thought losing Julia was going to kill her, but that had been a pale shadow compared to this. Her heart had been ripped out this time. Her lungs, liver and stomach had been torn out of her as well. Her very *soul* had been destroyed.

Another man jogged down the beach and stopped in front of Colonel Folly. "The survivors have surrendered, sir. The Gavronese Army has them under armed guard."

Folly gave a short nod. And then the black-haired, blue-eyed man turned beside his boss to stare morosely into the inferno.

A few minutes later, a third man came running down the beach from the other direction. He, too, stopped in front of the colonel. They spoke briefly, but Cari didn't pay any attention to their short conversation.

Joe was gone. Everything she was and ever would be was gone with him.

A small explosion sent another round of flaming debris sailing up into the black night. How could a sky so beautiful look down on a scene of such utter devastation? Surely, the moon and stars should be hiding their faces and weeping in grief, as well.

And then something caught her attention over by the swimming pool. Something big and black had just floated up to the edge. It rolled out onto the concrete. Stood up. Dragged something large and heavy out of the pool.

She took a step forward.

Could it be?

She took several more steps toward the blazing heat. And then took off running. A man had just climbed out of the swimming pool. And he was tall. Lean. Built not like her father, but like…

Joe!

He stumbled toward her and she flung herself against him, nearly knocking him over in her frantic exultation.

"Easy, baby," he mumbled.

"I thought I'd lost you. Oh, God, Joe. I love you. I don't ever want to lose you. Please, just tell me you'll give our marriage a real shot," she babbled.

He laughed painfully. "Hello to you, too, princess."

The other men were running toward them and Joe tensed in her arms. "It's Charlie Squad," she told him. "Everything's under control. The rest of my father's men have surrendered."

Joe's body went slack, but his arms stayed wrapped fiercely tight around her. "I love you, too," he breathed. "I never want to lose you, either. Your sister's alive—" he started.

She cut him off. "I know. I've already spoken with her on the phone."

Joe's arms tightened around her. "About your father—"

She frowned up at him, belatedly remembering that he'd been in the doorway with Joe when the house blew.

"He was between me and the house. Took the brunt of the blast. Shielded me from the heat—"

"What are you saying?" She already knew, but she needed to hear the words aloud.

"Your father didn't make it, sweetheart. He was thrown into the pool with me by the blast, and I pulled him out. He's dead."

A huge hollow opened up in her gut. Whether it was relief or grief or both she couldn't tell. But then she looked up at Joe and let her love for him flow into her, filling the empty space.

"Are you all right?" she asked softly.

Joe nodded. After a moment he murmured, "About our marriage…"

She held her breath.

"I'm game if you are."

She laughed and squeezed him until he groaned. She

loosened her grip hastily. "Oh, I'm game, all right," she retorted. "You're never going to get rid of me."

He smiled down at her. "I wouldn't have it any other way, princess. I figure we've both earned happily ever after out of this."

And as the sparks and ashes of her past drifted up into the night sky, they kissed. A single thought consumed her. *Happily ever after, indeed.*

*****

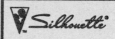

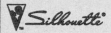

**Four sisters.
A family legacy.
And someone is out to destroy it.**

**A captivating new limited
continuity, launching June 2006**

The most beautiful hotel in New Orleans,
and someone is out to destroy it. But mystery,
danger and some surprising family revelations
and discoveries won't stop the Marchand sisters
from protecting their birthright…
and finding love along the way.

HOTEL MARCHAND

SPECIAL PRICE!

This riveting new saga begins with

by national bestselling author

JUDITH ARNOLD

The party at Hotel Marchand is in full swing when the lights suddenly go out. What does head of security Mac Jensen do first? He's torn between two jobs—protecting the guests at the hotel and keeping the woman he loves safe.

A woman to protect. A hotel to secure. And no idea who's determined to harm them.

On Sale June 2006

www.eHarlequin.com

HMITD